Sinful

A Bitter Creek Novel

Joan Johnston

D0057589

DELL · NEW YORK

Sinful is a work of fiction. Names, characters, places, and incidents either are the product of the author's imagination or are used fictitiously. Any resemblance to actual persons, living or dead, events, or locales is entirely coincidental.

A Dell Mass Market Original

Copyright © 2015 by Joan Mertens Johnston, Inc.
Excerpt from *Shameless* by Joan Johnston copyright © 2015 by Joan Mertens Johnston, Inc.

Published in the United States by Dell, an imprint of Random House, a division of Random House LLC, a Penguin Random House Company, New York.

DELL and the HOUSE colophon are registered trademarks of Random House LLC.

This book contains an excerpt from the forthcoming book *Shameless* by Joan Johnston. This excerpt has been set for this edition only and may not reflect the final content of the forthcoming edition.

ISBN 978-0-8041-7866-2
eBook ISBN 978-0-8041-7867-9

Cover design: Lynn Andreozzi
Cover illustration: Alan Ayers

Printed in the United States of America

www.bantamdell.com

9 8 7 6 5 4 3 2 1

Dell mass market edition: May 2015

Praise for Joan Johnston

"Joan Johnston does short contemporary Westerns to perfection."
—*Publishers Weekly*

"Like LaVyrle Spencer, Ms. Johnston writes of intense emotions and tender passions that seem so real that the readers will feel each one of them."
—*Rave Reviews*

"Johnston warms your heart and tickles your fancy."
—New York *Daily News*

"Joan Johnston continually gives us everything we want . . . fabulous details and atmosphere, memorable characters, a story that you wish would never end, and lots of tension and sensuality."
—*Romantic Times*

"Joan Johnston [creates] unforgettable subplots and characters who make every fine thread weave into a touching tapestry."
—*Affaire de Coeur*

BY JOAN JOHNSTON

King's Brats Series
Sinful

Mail-Order Brides Series
Texas Bride
Wyoming Bride
Montana Bride

Bitter Creek Series
The Cowboy
The Texan
The Loner
The Price
The Rivals
The Next Mrs. Blackthorne
A Stranger's Game
Shattered

Captive Hearts Series
Captive
After the Kiss
The Bodyguard
The Bridegroom

Sisters of the Lone Star Series
Frontier Woman
Comanche Woman
Texas Woman

Connected Books
The Barefoot Bride
Outlaw's Bride
The Inheritance
Maverick Heart

This book is dedicated to
Carmela Lucy Manfrey
In loving memory from her family.
July 12, 1930–October 24, 2013
You will be missed.

Sinful

Prologue

KING GRAYHAWK COULDN'T believe he'd found his long-lost son. When Matt was seventeen he'd walked away from King's ranch in Jackson Hole and disappeared. King had been searching for his missing son for twenty years, and at long last he'd found him. But nothing King had said so far had tempted Matt to return home.

King eyed the thirty-seven-year-old man standing before him and liked what he found. Matt was easily as tall as King, who stood a regal six foot four. The boy had grown broad in the shoulder but stayed lean at waist and hip. His thick black hair hung over his collar like some teenage hippie's but was already silver at the temples. Piercing blue eyes webbed with sun-etched crow's feet stared back at him defiantly.

"There's nothing you can say to change my mind," Matt said, his voice hard, his mouth flattened in anger. "Go back where you came from and leave me the hell alone."

King's temper flared. No one spoke to him like that. He was the richest man in Wyoming and former governor of the state. He wasn't about to lose the battle of wills because this barnyard pup had chosen to growl at him.

What was it about this prodigal son that made him so precious? King wondered. He only knew that he would do anything, give anything, say anything to bring this black sheep back into the fold.

He kept his voice even as he said, "Come home so we can get to know each other."

Matt snorted. "You wanted nothing to do with me as a kid. What's changed?"

"I have." King had recently survived a bout with cancer and realized that he was mortal after all. He wasn't exactly making amends, but he wanted his curiosity about this lost son satisfied before it was too late. Where had Matt been all these years? What had he done with his life? So far he'd gotten no answers, but he intended to have them.

"Come back—" King began.

"No."

"Don't interrupt!" he snapped. "I haven't finished."

King watched his son's jaw muscle flex before Matt said, "There's nothing you've got that I want."

"You haven't heard what I'm offering," King persisted.

"I don't give a damn what you're offering."

King gritted his teeth and held on to his temper. "If you come home, I'll give you the Big House, the cattle, the quarter horse operation, and the vast acres of land surrounding Kingdom Come. I'll even throw in the gas reserves under all that land. All you have to do is live at the ranch one year and it's all yours. A year from now you can sell it or give it away or abandon it and go back where you came from."

He watched as Matt's steely gaze slid to the sun setting on the glistening waters of the Timor Sea, off the coast of Darwin, Australia. The detective King had hired had discovered Matt rounding up a mob of brumbies—feral Australian horses—in a remote part of the Northern Territory. His son had agreed to meet him in Darwin only if King promised to leave him alone—forever—once they'd talked.

King was certain that if he couldn't convince his son to take this deal, Matt would disappear, and he might never see him again in this lifetime. He waited, forcing himself to be patient, for his son's answer.

"One year, and it's mine to do with as I please?" Matt confirmed.

King nodded.

"What about those three Brats you've got living there now?"

King raised a bushy black brow in surprise. How did Matt know that his three youngest daughters, women in their twenties, were still living at the ranch? And if he knew about them, why hadn't he mentioned Leah? "It's not just the Brats," he replied. "My stepdaughter, Leah, lives there, too."

"I want them out."

"It's the only home—"

"That's not negotiable."

King felt his heartbeat ratchet up a notch and took a deep breath to calm himself before speaking. "It's a big house."

"I don't like the idea of living with strangers."

King scowled. *Strangers?* Matt might not have

seen them since they were small, but the girls all shared his blood. Except for Leah. Leah was . . . a surprise. Leah had always been different, from the moment she'd come into his life as a five-year-old. His stepdaughter was the glue that had kept his relationship with his three youngest daughters from falling apart. He wasn't about to throw her out like an old boot.

"Once the ranch is yours, you can do as you like. Until then, the girls stay. And that's not negotiable."

Except for Leah, his daughters came and went from the ranch like shifting leaves in the wind. Chances were, they'd leave of their own accord soon enough. But he wasn't willing to shove them out without warning, not even for this prodigal son. King felt certain Matt wanted what he was offering more than he was willing to admit, or he wouldn't still be standing there.

"Tell you what," King began. "I'll speak to the girls and tell them—"

"I want sole use of the north wing of the house."

King kept his features even, but he was astonished by the request. Why would Matt need three complete bedroom suites? The detective hadn't said a thing about Matt having a wife and kids.

"You've got a family?" King blurted.

Matt's lips curled in disdain. "I'm no better at hanging on to a wife than you were."

King felt furious at his son's condemnation, even though he deserved it. He'd loved one woman in his life, Eve DeWitt, and she'd been stolen away by another man. King had managed to destroy every other woman he'd married, from his first wife, Matt's mother, to his last, the mother of his three youngest daughters, who'd brought Leah with her to the marriage.

When Matt's mother had died of an overdose of barbiturates, her younger brother, Angus Flynn, had become King's mortal enemy. Angus had done his best ever since to make King's life hell.

Abandoned by their mother, his three youngest girls had gotten into enough trouble with the Teton County sheriff over the years to become known as "King's Brats." His only consolation was that Angus's four sons, better known as "those wild Flynn boys," had an even worse reputation.

King knew he should have taken a firmer hand with the Brats when they were young, but he was wealthy enough, and politically powerful enough, to get them out of whatever trouble they'd gotten into. King was used to getting what he wanted when he wanted it, so he was finding his wayward son's resistance frustrating.

At least now Matt was talking terms. King wasn't sure he'd get an answer, but he asked the question anyway. "Why do you need so much space? Are you bringing someone along to put in those bedrooms?"

Matt nodded curtly. "I've got kids. A girl and a boy."

King hid his surprise and asked, "How old?"

"The girl's twenty. The boy's six."

King's brow furrowed. He couldn't fathom how his son could have a daughter born the same year he'd left home. There had been a fifteen-year-old girl Matt had gotten into trouble when he was sixteen. But that girl had died in childbirth, along with the child. So where had this daughter come from? Had there been a second girl? Another pregnancy? Was this unexplained child the reason Matt had gone so far away and stayed gone for so long?

King knew better than to ask those questions. Matt would either tell him, or he wouldn't. The important thing was to get his son back to Wyoming.

"Do we have a deal?" King asked, extending his hand.

Matt met his gaze with wary eyes, grasped his hand firmly, and said, "We have a deal."

Chapter 1

HER NAME WAS Eve. Not Evelyn or Eveline or Evette. Just Eve. The day she was born, her father, King Grayhawk, took one look at her large blue eyes, soft blond curls, and bowed upper lip and whispered, "Eve." Apparently, she reminded him of some woman he'd fallen in love with as a younger man. That Eve, he'd declared, was the only woman he had ever loved.

Those words, spoken as her mother lay recovering from labor, must have been the final insult, because Eve was still a babe in arms when her mom ran off with one of King's cowhands. Eve had grown up with the knowledge that her birth had caused a terrible rift between her parents. That marital fracture had left her and her fraternal twin sisters, Taylor and Victoria, and their older half sister, Leah, as motherless children.

Eve felt burdened by her name. It didn't help that she shared it with the woman who'd tempted Adam to sin in the Garden of Eden. In high school she was teased and taunted as she began to acquire seductive curves. She was sure one of those pain-in-the-butt Flynn brothers had started it, but the other boys had quickly followed his lead.

"Show me an apple, and I'll eat it," a boy would say, "so long as you come along with it, Eve." Or, "Too bad you ate that apple, Eve, or we'd all still be running around naked," followed by a lurid grin.

She'd gotten pretty good at sending back zingers like, "If God had seen you naked, Buck, He might have decided He made a real mistake only taking out a rib." But the constant innuendo made Eve's teenage life miserable.

That was the least of the trouble those four awful Flynn brothers—Aiden, Brian, Connor, and Devon—had caused her and her sisters over the years.

From her father's rants at supper, Eve had known he was feuding with Angus Flynn. It wasn't until she was eight years old that she understood why. Angus's older sister, Jane, had been King's first wife, and Angus blamed King for his unhappy sister's death from an overdose of barbiturates. Eve had no idea whether her father was innocent or not, but he was sorely tried by Angus's efforts to blight his life.

The animosity should have remained between their fathers, but it had bled onto their children. Angus Flynn's four sons were infamous around Jackson Hole for wreaking havoc and causing mischief. After their aunt Jane died, as though a switch had been flipped, the Flynn brothers began aiming all that tomfoolery toward Eve and her sisters. It didn't take long before King's Brats, who'd done their own share of troublemaking around Jackson Hole, were giving as good as they got from those wild Flynn boys.

Eve could remember vividly the year fourteen-year-old Leah's blueberry pie had been mysteriously doused with salt at the Four-H competition. Her sister had retaliated by shaving the flank of fourteen-year-old Aiden's Four-H calf so it looked like it had the mange.

Some of the mischief she and her sisters perpetrated was merely a nuisance. Like putting an ad in the paper for a cattle auction at the Flynn ranch, the Lucky 7, beginning at 6:00 A.M. on a Saturday morning, offering their prize bull for sale, when no such auction existed.

Eve had helped Taylor and Victoria punch a tiny hole in the gas tank of Brian's truck, so that when he and Devon headed off to hunt deer in the mountains, where there was no cell phone reception, they'd ended up making a long, bitterly cold walk back to civilization.

The Flynns had retaliated by placing slices of bologna in a vulgar design on the hood of Taylor and Victoria's cherry-red Jeep Laredo. The next morning, when her sisters pulled the deli meat off the hood, the preservatives in the bologna caused the top layer of paint to come off as well, leaving the distinct imprint of male genitalia.

It wouldn't have been so bad if the pranks had remained physically harmless. They hadn't. When Eve was a freshman in high school, the cinch of her saddle had been cut before a barrel race at a local rodeo, and she'd broken her arm when the saddle broke free. Eve could remember how enraged Leah was in the moments before the ambulance carted her away. The Flynn boys were competing at the same rodeo in calf roping. They should have known to check their cinches, but Eve supposed they hadn't expected Leah to retaliate so

quickly. When Aiden roped a calf his cinch broke—
along with his leg.

The mischief escalated into attacks involving other
people. Taylor's and Victoria's prom dates were kidnapped by a couple of boys wearing hoods, who tied
them to a tree so they never showed up. The twins
were devastated. The fallout afterward was even worse.
The kidnapped boys made it clear that it wasn't worth
the trouble to date a Grayhawk when it meant putting up with all the horseshit being shoveled by those
crazy Flynn boys.

Since Eve had lived in the same small town her
whole life, the "harmless" high school prank involving her name had been a continuing source of irrita-
tion. Most of the kids who'd gone to high school with
her still lived in Jackson, and there was always some
jerk who couldn't resist prodding her, hoping to get
under her skin.

Like now.

Eve wasn't looking to hook up or make waves.
All she wanted to do was sit at the Million Dollar
Cowboy Bar on the square in Jackson, along with the
tourists who'd come to enjoy the last of the black-
diamond ski season on the Grand Tetons, review the
digital photographs she'd taken that day of the herd
of wild mustangs she'd rescued, and enjoy her martini.

"Is that an *apple* martini, Eve?" a man called
from behind her.

Eve turned to find Buck Madison, the former Jackson Broncs quarterback, grinning like an idiot at one
of the pool tables in the center of the bar. Two of his
former teammates stood shoulder to shoulder with

him, giggling like teenage girls. All three were obviously drunk. She purposefully turned her attention back to the digital shot of the only colt in her herd. With any luck, Buck would give up and shut up.

Eve smiled as she studied the image of Midnight frolicking with his mother, his black mane and tail flying, his back arched, and all four hooves off the ground.

"You look good enough to tempt a man to sin, *Eve.*"

Buck's voice was loud in a bar that had suddenly become quiet. Eve shut off her camera and laid it on the bar as she dismounted the Western saddle on a stand—complete with stirrups—that served as a bar stool. She glanced at Buck in the mirror over the bar as she gathered her North Face fleece from where it hung off the saddle horn. She wasn't going to get into a war of words with a drunk. It was a lose-lose proposition. She had one arm through her fleece when Buck stripped it back off, dangling it from his forefinger.

"Uh, uh, uh," he said, wagging the finger holding the fleece. "I'm not done looking yet."

She turned to confront Buck, her chin upthrust, her blue eyes shooting daggers of disdain. "I'm done being ogled. Give me my coat."

She held out her hand and waited.

She felt a wave of resentment toward the Flynns, who'd started that whole Garden of Eden business in the first place. She couldn't help the fact that she'd developed a lush female figure in high school. At twenty-six, she'd made peace with her body. There was no easy way to conceal her curves, so she didn't try. But she did nothing to emphasize them, either.

She was dressed in a plaid western shirt that was belted into a pair of worn western jeans. She had on scuffed cowboy boots, but instead of a Stetson, she usually wore a faded navy-blue-and-orange Denver Broncos ball cap. She'd left the cap in her pickup, but her chin-length, straw-blond hair was tucked behind her ears to keep it out of her way.

"My coat?" she said.

As she reached for it, Buck pulled it away. "How about a kiss first?"

Eve had opened her mouth to retort when a brusque male voice said, "Give the lady her coat."

Eve hadn't heard anyone coming up behind her, which surprised her. She photographed wild animals in their natural habitat and prided herself on her awareness of her surroundings. In the wilderness, missing the slightest sound could result in being bitten by a rattler or attacked by a bear or mountain lion. She glanced over her shoulder and felt her heart skip a beat when she recognized her unlikely savior.

Connor Flynn.

Connor was third in line of the Flynn brothers, but he'd been at the top of the teenage troublemaking list. He was thirty now but, if anything, his reputation was worse. He'd done three tours as a Delta sergeant in Afghanistan before leaving the military with several medals to prove his heroism in battle.

He'd paid a high price for his long absences from home serving his country. A year ago his wife, Molly, who'd been Eve's best friend, had died in a car accident while Connor was overseas. After the funeral, he'd agreed to let Molly's parents take his kids into their home while he served the nine months left on his final tour of duty.

Now they were threatening to keep them.

Connor had ended up in a court battle to get his two-year-old son and four-year-old daughter back. So far he hadn't been able to wrench them away from his late wife's parents. They'd argued to a judge that Connor was a battle-weary soldier, a victim of post-traumatic stress, and therefore a threat to his children. According to all the psychological tests he'd been forced to endure to prove them wrong, he was fine. But seeing him now, Eve wondered for the very first time if Molly's parents might not be completely off the mark.

Connor looked dangerous, his sapphire-blue eyes hooded, his cheeks and chin covered with at least a two-day-old beard, and a hank of his rough-cut, crow-wing-black hair resting on his scarred forehead. His lips had thinned to an ominous line.

If she'd been Buck, she would have handed over the coat in a heartbeat. But Buck wasn't known for his smarts.

"Butt out!" Buck said. "This is between me and Eve."

Without warning, Connor's hand shot out and gripped Buck's throat. Buck dropped the coat to protect his neck, but Connor didn't let go. His inexorable grasp was slowly choking the big man to death. Even using both hands, Buck couldn't get free.

Eve looked around the bar, expecting someone, anyone, to intervene. No one did. She wouldn't have interfered except she knew that Connor might be turning the lock and throwing away the key where custody of his kids was concerned. She didn't step in for Connor's sake. Ordinarily she wouldn't have thrown a glass of water to douse a Flynn on fire. But she cared very much about the future well-being of her dead friend's children, who needed their father alive and well and out of jail.

Despite Connor's long absences, Molly had been convinced that he would take good care of their children if anything ever happened to her. Eve owed it to her best friend to make sure Connor didn't ruin his chance of becoming the wonderful father Molly had always believed he could be.

As carefully as if she were approaching a feral wolf, Eve laid her fingertips on Connor's bare forearm, the one that led to the hand grasping Buck's throat. She turned so she was looking into his narrowed eyes. "Connor," she said in a quiet voice. "This won't help. Let go."

She watched his upper lip curl as though he was snarling while his gaze remained focused on the helpless man in his grasp.

"Think of the kids!" she said more urgently. "For their sake, let go. Please."

He turned to look at her when she said "kids" and then seemed to hear the rest of her sentence. He looked at his hand and seemed surprised to discover that he was still choking Buck. Suddenly, he let go and took a step back.

Buck gasped a breath of air, and with the next breath croaked, "Molly's parents are right. You should be in a cage!" Now that Buck was free, his two football buddies, each brandishing a pool cue, moved up to flank him.

Connor stood as though in a daze, rubbing his forehead where the scar from a war wound loomed white against his tanned skin. Eve realized that if Connor didn't leave in a hurry, there was likely to be a free-for-all. She grabbed her fleece from the floor and her camera from the bar, gripped Connor's hand, and pulled him out the door after her.

She headed away from the bar in case the three drunks decided to follow them outside into the frosty March evening. She hadn't realized where she was going until she reached her Dodge Ram pickup, which was parked under the colorful neon cowboy on a bucking bronc that lit up the bar. She let go of Connor's hand in order to hang her camera by its strap around her neck, then pulled on her fleece. She shook her head in disgust at his behavior in the bar as he frowned back at her.

"What were you thinking?" she said. "Were you trying to get arrested? Don't you want to be a father to Brooke and Sawyer?"

"I was thinking that son of a bitch was being a pain in the ass, all because of something I started in high school."

Eve stared at him in shock. *Connor* was responsible for all those cruel taunts about her name?

He shoved a hand through his hair, but a hank of it fell back onto his forehead. "Thanks for getting me out of there."

"I wish I hadn't bothered, now that I know you started that 'Eve' business. Do you have any idea how much aggravation you caused me in high school?"

He shot her a mutinous, unapologetic look. "No more than you caused me by telling Molly I'd take her to that Sadie Hawkins dance her freshman year. No thanks to you it turned out all right."

Eve felt a stab of shame. Molly had been crazy about Connor Flynn in high school. So had Eve. But she might as well have aspired to date the man in the moon. Not just because Connor was a senior and she was a freshman, but because Connor was a Flynn. A broken arm. A broken leg. Ruined dreams. Too many years of hurt and harm stood between them.

Molly had desperately wanted to ask Connor to the Sadie Hawkins dance, but she'd been too shy to do it. Eve had told her friend that she would ask for her but then chickened out. Besides, she didn't want her best friend dating the boy she had a crush on herself. She'd lied and told Molly that she'd asked Connor and he'd said yes, figuring that Connor would blow Molly off when she came running up to him, excited that he'd accepted her invitation, and Molly would be humiliated and never speak to him again.

Admittedly, it was not her finest moment.

Instead, Connor had met Eve's gaze as she stood by her locker across the hall while Molly smiled up at him, delighted that he'd accepted her invitation to the dance. His eyes had narrowed at Eve, as though he knew she was the one responsible for this further bit of Grayhawk-Flynn monkey business. Then he'd smiled down at Molly as though he was glad to be going to the dance with Eve's best friend.

To Eve's dismay, Molly and Connor were going steady by the time Connor graduated at the end of the year. He'd told Molly not to wait for him when he enlisted in the military, and Eve had felt a flare of hope that they might break up. But Molly called or texted or emailed or wrote Connor every day while he was away learning all the skills he'd need to fight a war.

When Connor was home on leave, he and Molly picked up where they'd left off. He took classes in warfare for two years, and not once was there a break in Molly's devotion, or in Connor's, for that matter. With a sinking heart, Eve had realized that once Molly graduated from high school, they were probably going to get married.

Eve had no one to blame but herself. She should have spoken up. She should have said something to Molly about her feelings for Connor, no matter how unrealistic they were. After that freshman Sadie Hawkins dance, it was too late.

Eve stared at the man for whom she'd felt a hopeless love most of her adult life.

Both Connor's jaw and his fists were clenched. He was trouble looking for a place to happen. But despite all the damage he and his family had caused her and her family in the past, she couldn't leave him here. She didn't want her efforts in the bar undone. She made a face. "Get in. I'll drive you to your truck. Where is it?"

"I left it at the Snow King Resort. Aiden dropped me off in town before he headed back to the ranch. I planned to spend the night with—"

He cut himself off, and Eve realized he'd planned to pick up some girl in one of the many Jackson Hole bars and spend the night with her. He was good-looking enough and rich enough to attract locals, but it was more likely one of the ski bunnies would have carted him back to her hotel room.

"I have to be in town for court early tomorrow morning," he explained, "so I figured there was no sense making the drive back out to the Lucky 7 tonight."

Eve gave him a once-over from head to foot. He stood more than six feet tall and looked rock solid, his broad shoulders braced like a soldier ready for battle. Unfortunately, his impressive fighting skills were hardly likely to impress a judge deciding his children's fate. He needed to look like good *father* material. "Is that what you're planning to wear?"

He glanced down at the white oxford-cloth shirt, sleeves rolled up to expose sinewy forearms, comfortablable jeans, western belt, and cowboy boots he had on. "What's wrong with what I'm wearing?"

"It's not a suit, for starters."

"My navy sport coat is on the back of my chair at one of the bar tables. There's a regimental tie in the pocket."

Eve stared at the door to the bar, wondering if there would be a scene if they returned for his sport coat. Of course there would be a scene. He was a Flynn, wasn't he? She sighed. "I'll take you home, and you can get another one."

"Don't bother. I'll call one of my brothers to come get me."

"And wait in a bar, I suppose," she said, pulling her fleece more tightly around her to ward off the chill. *Getting into more trouble.* "Let me take you home. You don't want the police finding you on the street in this condition."

"This condition? Meaning what?"

"You're drunk. And if Buck makes an issue of what just happened, disorderly. You don't want to give Molly's parents any more ammunition than they already have to shoot you down."

"Perfect metaphor," he retorted. "Because that's exactly what it feels like they're doing. Killing me with supposed kindness. I gave them my kids because I thought they'd be the best caretakers while I was gone. Now I have to fight to get my own kids back! And I'm not drunk."

She shot him a skeptical look.

"It was lime and Coke. No rum."

"Then why would you do something so stupid as to assault Buck?"

He palmed his eyes and made a guttural sound of frustration. "It's this custody hearing. I want it over. I want my kids back."

Eve heard the anguish in his voice and felt her heart wrench. But it was the kids she felt bad for, not their father. While he'd grieved the loss of his wife, Connor had shut himself off from Brooke and Sawyer. When he'd returned from overseas after an absence of nine months—an eternity to children only three and one when he'd left—Brooke and Sawyer had barely recognized him.

Eve knew how hard it was for vets to reinsert themselves into their former lives. Over the past couple of months since he'd returned home, Connor had more than once exhibited questionable behavior, like the attack tonight, which might have ended badly if she hadn't been there. She could understand why Molly's parents were concerned.

But she could also see Connor's side of the issue. He hadn't been able to take his kids with him while he was serving his country. Now that he was home, and had proved to the doctors that he was of sound mind and body, he had the right to raise his children.

During the months-long custody battle, Connor had only been allowed supervised time with his kids, who weren't quite sure where he fit into their lives. Their grandparents were the only stable thing in their world right now.

Except for me.

Eve had spent a lot of time with Molly and the kids while Connor was deployed. Being essentially a single parent of two kids had been a crushing responsibility for her friend, and Eve had more than once taken Brooke and Sawyer for a walk in the forest or on a picnic to give Molly a break. After Molly's death, she'd done the same for the children's grandparents. She understood why Mr. and Mrs. Robertson were so worried about Connor wanting to raise two young children, who were just getting to know him again, all by himself.

It might have been different if there was a woman in the Flynn household, where Connor had been staying since he'd returned to Jackson Hole. But it was all men, from Angus on down. After the stand Molly's parents had taken, if Connor got his kids back, he was unlikely to ask the Robertsons for help.

Molly would have hated the tug-of-war over her children, but she'd left no will stating her wishes, and her parents had argued to the judge that not only was Connor an unfit parent, but that their daughter had wanted them to care for her children if anything ever happened to her. Eve knew better.

Which was why, despite the hard feelings between their two families, Eve planned to testify on Connor's behalf in court tomorrow. When her sisters had demanded to know why she was helping a Flynn after all the nasty things they'd done, she'd made it plain that she was only speaking in court to ensure that her best friend's final wishes were carried out.

Eve sympathized with Connor's suffering over the loss of both his wife and his children, but his conduct tonight had been worrisome. Was she making a mistake helping him to get custody of Brooke and Sawyer, even if it was what Molly had wanted? She knew he must be terrified that the court would take his children away tomorrow. Surely that explained, even if it didn't excuse, his overwrought behavior.

"I'd appreciate a ride up the hill to the Snow King Resort," Connor said. "I'm staying in the suite my dad keeps available for out-of-town business associates."

"Sure," she said. "Let's go."

The cab of the truck was frigid, and Eve let the engine heat up before she put the vehicle in gear. Their breaths fogged the cabin, and Connor shivered with the cold.

"The heater should have you warm in a minute," she said.

He rubbed his hands together. "Feels like Afghanistan in here."

"I thought it was mostly desert there."

"Deserts are plenty cold at night, but I spent most of my time in the mountains."

"Did they remind you of home?"

"Nothing compares to the beauty of the Tetons. Besides, I wasn't there to admire them. They were filled with places for hostiles to hide, which made them an unfriendly place to be."

It was the first conversation of more than a few words she'd had with Connor Flynn since he'd "accidentally" run into her on the fairgrounds at Old West Days at the end of her junior year of high school, knocking her ice cream cone out of her hand. The news had been all over town that he had orders to go to Afghanistan. He was still dating her best friend, who didn't happen to be with him.

Eve had figured the jarring collision was one more example of Flynn harassment, until Connor apologized and insisted on buying her another cone. He met her suspicious gaze with laughter in his eyes and said, "Molly would never forgive me if I didn't."

She felt warm everywhere his eyes touched her. She trembled when he slid an arm around her waist to move her out of the way of a bunch of rowdy cowboys. And a shiver ran down her spine when he gently thumbed a bit of ice cream from the side of her mouth after she'd taken a bite of her new strawberry cone.

His infectious grin. His surprising kindness. His incredible blue eyes. His muscular shoulders and lean hips. The knowledge that he was forbidden to her because he was a Flynn—and her best friend's boyfriend. All of those things had conspired to make her fall even more deeply and completely and irrevocably in love with him.

Eve believed she'd seen something in Connor's eyes—an equal yearning for what might have been?—

but realized that was probably a combination of her imagination and wishful thinking. Still, she came away from the encounter feeling that something irreplaceable had been lost.

Eve's only solace was the knowledge that any relationship between them would have caused terrible trouble at home. Her father would have howled like twenty tomcats if he discovered she'd fallen in love with one of those damn-fool Flynn boys, and her sisters would have joined the chorus.

Connor had gone to war, and that was the last she or Molly had seen of him for another year.

The day he arrived in Jackson for Molly's graduation Eve had realized that if she was ever going to say something about her feelings, it was now or never. In the end, she'd opted for *never*. It was impossible to ignore the glow on Molly's face as she looked into Connor's eyes when they met after their long separation. Or the tender look in Connor's eyes as he gazed back at her best friend.

There was simply no possible future in which Eve could be happy at her best friend's expense. She bitterly regretted the choice she'd made in high school to keep her feelings secret from Connor—and Molly—and she'd never stopped wishing things were different. Unfortunately, and despite the fact that Connor had married her best friend, Eve had never fallen out of love with him. Not that anyone knew her deep, dark secret. As far as her best friend or her sisters or anyone else was concerned, she had the same aversion to those wild Flynn boys as the rest of her family. No one knew that she'd coveted her best friend's husband.

Even now she found Connor attractive. Her heart leapt when she imagined him holding her and kissing her. But there was no way she was going to act on those feelings. She'd seen the tears on Connor's cheeks at Molly's grave. She'd heard his muffled sobs. She knew how much he'd loved her friend. He was never going to love another woman like that. And she wouldn't settle for less.

Eve felt guilty and sad sitting next to Connor and wishing for what might have been. She was a terrible person for wanting his love during the years he'd been married to her best friend. She was a terrible person for wanting him now, knowing that he was grieving the loss of his wife, knowing that he could never love her the way he'd loved her best friend.

Eve saw that Connor was still blowing on his hands to warm them. "Do you want to go back and get your jacket?"

"I'll have the bartender put it in a cab and drop it at the hotel. You're welcome to join me for a drink while I wait."

Eve knew she should turn down the invitation. Having anything to do with Connor Flynn was bound to turn out badly. She opened her mouth to say, "I have to head home." What came out was, "Sure. Why not?"

There were a thousand good reasons why not, but she refused to listen to any of them. What was the harm? She would share a drink and perhaps some memories of Molly. They'd discuss Connor's chances of getting his kids back from their grandparents. She'd do her best to cheer him up—and calm him down—and then she'd go home to Kingdom Come. Alone.

"I didn't think you'd say yes," he said, eyeing her askance.

"Why not?"

"Because you're a Grayhawk. And I'm a Flynn."

"You're Brooke and Sawyer's father, and I'm their godmother. And we both loved Molly."

He said nothing the rest of the way to the hotel. She spent the short drive reminding herself of the calamity that had resulted when the very first Eve had given in to temptation. Reminding herself that she should keep her distance. Reminding herself that she was going to get burned if she got too close to the fire.

None of it did any good. When they reached the hotel and he invited her up to his room, she went.

Chapter 2

EVE COULDN'T HELP wondering why Connor had invited her to his suite instead of waiting for his coat downstairs in the bar. Was it really the noise from the live band that he'd wanted to avoid? Or did he have some other reason for getting the two of them alone?

Eve eyed Connor sideways, wondering if she was the only one who'd felt the electricity arcing between them in the elevator. The possibility of being kissed by a man she'd loved since she was fourteen had her whole body tingling in expectation. That excitement was matched with equal feelings of dread over betraying her best friend.

Molly's dead. She's never coming back. You can't hurt her anymore by loving Connor.

It was no longer a sin to love Connor, but that didn't keep Eve from feeling guilty for all the years she'd coveted her best friend's husband. That didn't keep her from feeling that she didn't deserve a future with Connor because it had come at the cost of Molly's life.

"Maybe this isn't such a good idea," she said when she felt Connor's hand at her back, ushering her off the elevator and into the suite.

"It's just a drink, Eve. I'd like to talk to you about the kids, if that's all right."

"Oh." So he didn't have designs on her body. That was all wishful thinking on her part. "Of course."

"I'll take your fleece."

She slipped it off and felt exposed, which was silly, because Connor didn't seem aware of her as a female of the species.

He tossed her coat over the back of the studded brown leather couch and said, "Make yourself comfortable," then flipped the switch to turn on the gas fireplace as he crossed to a bar set up near the kitchen. "What can I get you to drink?"

"How about hot tea?"

He raised a surprised brow. "All right. I'm sure there's tea here somewhere."

"You don't have to wait on me." She joined him in the kitchen. "Let me help you look."

Together, they rummaged through cupboards until she found some Stash lemon-and-ginger tea. A hot water dispenser at the sink provided boiling water at the tip of a finger. Within a very few minutes they were settled on opposite ends of the couch holding pottery mugs of aromatic tea, the fire flickering before them.

"Are you still going to testify on my behalf tomorrow after what happened tonight?" he asked.

"Why wouldn't I?"

He made a face. "Despite my good intentions I ended up choking that idiot."

Her lips tilted in a wry smile. "Buck can do that to you. I've often wished I could throttle him to shut him up."

"Was he right?"

Eve didn't have to ask about what. "No. I don't believe you belong in a cage. I think you're a man who's been pushed to his limit. I'm sure that once you have your kids back and you settle down to life together as a family you'll be fine."

His eyes looked stark. "Am I going to get them back?"

"You will if my testimony means anything. Molly never intended for her parents to raise Brooke and Sawyer. She was always worried that something would happen to you, and that the kids would never get to know what a wonderful husband and father you were."

"Some husband. Some father. I was gone most of our marriage. My kids barely know me!"

It was hard to argue with the facts, but she gave Connor what encouragement she could. "Your kids have the rest of their lives to get to know you."

"Presuming I get custody tomorrow."

She took a sip of her tea. There was no sense guessing what would happen, because there was no way to know how the judge would rule.

She was expecting another question about the kids when Connor said, "I hear your long-lost brother is back in town. Where's he been all this time?"

Eve's face immediately felt flushed with heat. Every time she thought of Matt's arrival at Kingdom Come three weeks ago, and the ultimatum her father had given her and her sisters the day before he showed up, she got angry all over again. "He was living in Australia." She didn't trust herself to say more.

"How long is he staying?"

"Who knows?" But if he stayed for three hundred and sixty-five days every bit of Kingdom Come was his, and she and her sisters were out.

"Doesn't sound like you're happy he's home."

"I'm not." She still couldn't believe her father had given the prodigal son everything, instead of rewarding the dutiful daughters who'd stayed home and helped run the ranch all the years Matt had been gone.

"What's your brother ever done to you?" Connor asked.

"For one thing, he's made it clear that he wants me and my sisters gone from Kingdom Come."

Connor sat forward and set his mug on the glass-topped, antler-based coffee table in front of them. "What?"

"You heard me. We're being thrown out, bag and baggage."

"That's crazy!"

"In order to get Matt to come home, my father made this stupid agreement with him that if he stays for a year, the ranch is his. I don't care about living at the Big House. I can find somewhere else to hang my hat. But if I'm forced off the ranch I won't have a place to run the wild mustangs I've rescued. There's no place in Teton County—ninety-seven percent of which, as you very well know, is devoted to national parks—where I can afford to keep them."

"Surely Matt will—"

She laughed bitterly. "Matt won't."

Eve's chest physically ached every time she thought about her father's betrayal. She felt anew all the pain of being cast off by the father she'd loved and obeyed her whole life, for the sake of a son who'd run off and stayed gone for twenty years.

"Any chance Matt won't hang in for the whole year?" Connor asked.

"He brought his twenty-year-old daughter and six-year-old son with him from Australia. That sounds pretty permanent to me."

"It's hard to believe King would screw you over like that."

"Not if you know my father," she said, unable to keep the resentment from her voice. "He isn't much of a family man. Turns out that kowtowing to him all my life didn't do me a lick of good. Come March 1 of next year, my mustangs and I will be out in the cold."

"Are things really that bad for you financially?"

"My dad's rich. I'm not."

"I've seen your photographs of wild mustangs in every gallery in town. They're amazing. I figured you must be raking in the dough."

"I make a living from my work, but I'm still not nationally recognized, so it's not as much as you might think. And I recently spent every spare penny I had to rescue a bunch of wild mustangs from the slaughter-house."

"The slaughterhouse? Who eats horse meat?"

"You'd be surprised."

"How does that end up happening?"

"When the Bureau of Land Management thinks the mustang population has gotten too big in an area, they round them up, take them off the land, and put them in pens, where they're fed and watered. They get three chances to get adopted. If they aren't claimed by someone who wants a saddle horse, they usually end up getting bought by 'kill buyers' who take them across the border to Canada or Mexico to be slaughtered. Those beautiful, wild creatures end up as dog food—or as a delicacy on a European dinner plate."

"And your herd was on its way to slaughter?" Connor asked.

Eve nodded. "Which is why I'm so mad at Daddy for this deal he made with Matt. I have no idea what I'm going to do with twenty-two wild horses when I have to move."

"Any chance you can change King's mind?"

"My dad's every bit as stubborn as yours. Otherwise, the two of them wouldn't still be feuding over something that happened a lifetime ago. Apparently, Daddy had to bribe Matt with the ranch to get him to come here."

"Pretty big bribe."

"I'll say. And a pretty nasty joke on me and my sisters." Eve sighed. "Sorry to lay all this on you. I miss having Molly around to share my troubles with. She was a good sounding board, smart and sensible."

"She was good at a lot of things." Connor lowered his head and rubbed at the newly healed scar on his forehead.

"Are you all right?"

"My head aches. It'll go away. It always does."

She set down her tea and scooted across the couch to his side. "Maybe I can help."

Eve kept her eyes on the two-inch scar that slanted upward from his right eyebrow as she set her thumbs on his temples. She held her breath as her fingers slid into his hair, which was surprisingly soft. She didn't know where she'd gotten the courage to reach out and touch. But since the opportunity wasn't likely to come again anytime soon, she took full advantage of it, softly massaging her way across Connor's forehead until her thumbs met at the jagged scar, then working her way back to his temples.

When she finally dropped her gaze to his, she discovered Connor's eyes were closed. When he opened them, she dropped her hands self-consciously to her lap. Could he tell from the mere touch of her hands how much she wanted to be held by him? To be loved by him? Their faces were only inches apart, and she saw his eyes focus on her mouth, which was open to draw breath to lungs that suddenly seemed stripped of air.

"Eve."

Her name had never sounded so sensual. She shivered as a frisson of awareness skittered up her spine.

His hands were warm and gentle, not at all what she'd expected a warrior's touch to be, as he unknotted her hands and took them in his own.

"Eve. Look at me."

With a giant effort of will, she raised her gaze to meet his. Connor's heavy-lidded blue eyes were focused intently on her face. His nostrils were flared for the scent of her, as though he were a predator seeking prey. She felt his hands tighten on hers as though to prevent her escape.

"I've always liked you, Eve. Molly loved you like a sister. She—" He cut himself off and lowered his gaze to their joined hands.

"Connor, I'm so sorry she's gone. I wish more than anything that Molly could be the one here with you tonight."

She tugged on her hands, and he let her go.

Eve wasn't sure why she'd wanted her hands free until she reached up and cupped his stubbled cheek with one of them. It was a gesture of comfort, but her pulse leapt when he leaned into her hand, then angled his face to kiss her wrist. Her other hand brushed the errant lock of hair off his forehead, so she could kiss the scar that proved how close she'd come to losing him forever.

She felt Connor's hands at her waist, lifting her into his lap, and slid her arms around his shoulders. They sat quietly together, offering solace to one another for the loss of his wife and her best friend.

She imagined he was missing Molly. She was regretting past choices, wishing things could have been different. Wishing that they were a couple and had their whole lives ahead of them.

She shivered at the touch of Connor's lips beneath her ear. His warm breath made her quiver in anticipation. She felt his fingertips on her chin, angling her head toward him.

Eve felt her heart skittering as their lips touched. She felt Connor's tongue tease the seam of her lips and after a brief hesitation she opened to him. She made a sound of satisfaction as his tongue intruded and she tasted him. She broke the kiss to look into his eyes, seeking confirmation of the wonder she felt at this first moment of coming together. What she saw caused a furrow between her brows.

Not desire. Despair.

Eve shoved herself out of Connor's embrace and stumbled to her feet. A second later he was on his feet as well, his hands bunched into fists, his eyes glittering in the light from the fire.

"I have the feeling that you're not ready for this," she said tentatively. "That you're still grieving."

Eve wanted him to tell her it was fine, that he was ready to move on. He said nothing, just stared at her, looking sad.

"Why did you start this," she demanded, "if you're still—" She cut herself off, unwilling to bring Molly's name into the conversation.

"I'm sorry."

It didn't help to have him confirm the fact that he was still in love with Molly. Of course he was. That was the way it should be. She was the one who wanted more than he was ready to give.

She grabbed her fleece, but he caught her by the shoulders before she could take two steps.

"Don't leave. I don't have many friends, Eve. I can't afford to lose one."

A *friend*? Was that how he saw her? Eve felt mortified. She should have kept her distance. She should have kept her feelings hidden. She shouldn't have let him see even a little of what she felt for him. That must have been what he'd responded to. That must have been why he'd kissed her.

"I don't want things to become awkward between us," he said. "You're my children's godmother. I promise nothing like that will happen again."

Eve felt like wailing. It would be torture spending time with Connor knowing that she felt something for him when he felt nothing for her.

He dropped his hands from her shoulders, and she was free. The choice was hers. She could go or stay. She looked into Connor's eyes and responded to the sorrow she found there. She owed it to Molly to watch out for him.

And to herself to keep her distance.

"All right." She crossed back, dropping her fleece on the back of the couch as she settled onto the leather cushions, tucking one leg beneath her. "Let's talk."

He shoved both hands through his hair, leaving it awry, huffed out a breath, and settled on the other end of the couch. He shot her a chagrined smile. "I have no idea where to go from here."

Eve forced herself to return his smile in an effort to get things back on an even keel. "How about sharing your plans for when you get Brooke and Sawyer back?"

"I've bought a ranch. I'm planning to take them there and work on being a better father."

"You're moving away?" Eve wondered if her face looked as stricken as her voice sounded to her. "I thought you'd be staying with your father and brothers, so they'd be around to help."

"I take it you think I'm going to need help. I've managed a Delta team. I think I can manage two little kids."

"Soldiers don't cry because they're scared of the dark," she said quietly.

"You might be surprised. The dark can be a very scary place."

"Are you telling me you were scared of the dark in Afghanistan?"

"Lots of times."

"But you've got a bunch of medals!"

"Medals don't mean you weren't scared. They just

mean you didn't run away, that you stayed around to fight."

"Oh." Looking at Connor, it was hard to imagine him sitting frightened in the dark waiting to do battle. "Do you ever have nightmares?"

"Sometimes. Not as bad as some guys, though. I feel bad for the ones who can't leave it all behind."

"And you have?"

He shrugged. "Mostly. That's why I bought my ranch, so vets can come for R&R—that's rest and recuperation—if they find they need a break."

"When did you buy this place? Why didn't I hear about it?" Eve asked.

"The deal didn't go through until after Molly died."

That explained why she hadn't heard more about his plans from her friend. But pretty much everything the Flynns did got discussed over the Grayhawk supper table, so why hadn't she heard about Connor's purchase of a large tract of land in Teton County? He answered her question before she asked.

"I made the purchase through a corporation I created. I didn't want either of our fathers interfering," he said with a wry smile. "So the Flynn name isn't anywhere on the documents."

"Oh." That explained a lot. "How big is this ranch of yours?"

"A thousand acres, which includes the main house where I plan to live with the kids, a lodge for dining and recreation, a bunkhouse, and several cabins. It used to be a dude ranch, so it's already set up for a lot of people to live there comfortably. I'm calling it Safe Haven."

"Where is this place, exactly?"

"A little east of my dad's ranch. My land actually borders the Lucky 7 in a couple of places."

"I wonder what Molly would have thought about what you're doing," Eve murmured.

"Frankly, she wasn't in favor of the idea. But it doesn't really matter now, does it?"

Eve wondered why Molly hadn't discussed this plan of Connor's with her. More likely she'd kept it to herself because she'd known Eve would be on Connor's side. Molly had talked endlessly about moving away from Jackson Hole—a tiny town that swelled up like a bloodthirsty tick with tourists on their way to or from Yellowstone National Park in the summer—to some metropolitan area like Denver, once Connor left the army.

Eve thought the ranch was a fantastic idea. But she could see where it wouldn't have appealed to Molly, who was sick and tired of Jackson Hole, where the peace and quiet was often far too peaceful and quiet. Molly didn't ski, so she'd itched for something more exciting to do through the long winter months than watch the feathery snow fall or listen to bull elks bugle during mating season.

"You're not even a little worried about being alone with Brooke and Sawyer?" Eve asked. "About them fearing the dark, or missing Molly, or not wanting to leave their grandparents?"

"Just give me my kids," Connor said fiercely. "I'll worry about the small stuff later."

Chapter 3

"THEREFORE, I'M AWARDING full custody of the children, Brooke and Sawyer Flynn, to their father, Connor Flynn."

Dead silence reigned in the courtroom at the judge's pronouncement. Connor was stunned. He'd won. He rose and found his three brothers, Aiden, Brian, and Devon, jostling to their feet behind him, smiling from ear to ear. Aiden reached out first to hug him across the courtroom rail. Connor held on, afraid that if he let go, the tears that were threatening would fall. His chin began to quiver, and he gritted his teeth to still it.

He felt Brian slap him on the back and saw Devon's reassuring thumbs-up through eyes blurred with tears of joy. One escaped, and he let go of Aiden to roughly brush it away. He turned to shake hands with his father, who put a comforting hand on his shoulder as he shot a nasty look in the direction of King Grayhawk, who was sitting directly behind Molly's parents.

"A hundred to one that son of a bitch had something to do with the Robertsons trying to steal my grandkids away," Angus said.

Connor wasn't so sure, especially since it was Eve Grayhawk's testimony about Molly's wishes that seemed to swing the judge in his favor. Surely King's daughter wouldn't have defied her father's wishes when he was sitting right there in the courtroom.

Then he remembered what Eve had told him last night. How she and her sisters had been given one year to find somewhere else to live. How she would soon have no land on which she could graze the wild mustangs she'd saved from slaughter. Most likely he had King Grayhawk's bad behavior to thank for Eve being so determined to testify on his behalf.

Connor couldn't believe he'd kissed her. Or how much he'd enjoyed it. He'd wanted to hold her in his arms and keep on kissing her, but he'd been stabbed with thorns of guilt. He'd loved his wife, but he'd been attracted to Eve Grayhawk ever since he'd seen her standing by her locker, which happened to be directly across from his locker, the year she started high school.

Connor had been stunned by the change in Eve's appearance over the summer. The gangly girl was gone. In her place was a voluptuous siren. His body had reacted so quickly and strongly to the sight of her gamine smile, sparkling blue eyes, and spectacular curves that he'd been late for his first class while he waited for his arousal to subside. It had taken a while for his heart to catch up to his little head, but before long he'd been besotted.

After all the things she and her sisters had done to him and his brothers, however justified, it would have been blasphemy to admit that he liked her. But he shot longing looks at her whenever he was sure nobody was looking. That whole "Eve" business had started when his younger brother, Devon, had caught him watching her, and he'd needed to come up with something to deflect attention from the fact that he was ogling one of King's Brats.

His eyes had locked with hers once as they passed each other on the way to class, with the result that his heart had pounded and his palms had been sweaty and his throat had been dry for five minutes after she turned away. A couple of times he thought she was going to cross the hall to speak to him. But she never did.

Instead, Molly Robertson, whose locker was right next to Eve's, had come running up to tell him how glad she was that he'd agreed to go to the Sadie Hawkins dance with her. He'd lifted his gaze and seen the guilty look on Eve's face as she stood by her locker. He'd put a sneer on his face that only she could see, then turned his most winsome smile on the petite, pretty girl standing in front of him. "I'm looking forward to it," he told her.

His chest ached for an hour afterward.

The date with Molly had turned out to be a surprise. He'd been determined to have a good time, just to show Eve she hadn't gotten the better of him. He'd also had visions of making her jealous. But Molly wasn't just cute as a button—an expression he never would have applied to Eve, who held herself far too regally ever to be called "cute"—she was also a lot of fun. She was a good dancer, quick-witted, and had hazel eyes that shone all night with joy and excitement. It was impossible not to like her.

He'd shot one long glance at Eve during the Sadie

Hawkins dance, and she'd ignored him a little too pointedly. He'd figured maybe he was onto something with that jealousy idea, especially since it turned out Molly and Eve were best friends. So he and Molly had gone out again, along with a couple of friends. And had a wonderful time again.

There was a lot of satisfaction in the disgruntled look on Eve's face the whole next week when she showed up at her locker. Enough to send him out on a date with Molly for a third time.

That was when he'd made his mistake. Molly had turned to him before getting out of his pickup at the end of their date and looked into his eyes. He'd known what she wanted. It would have seemed odd if he didn't end their third encounter with some show of affection. In fact, she'd looked at him strangely at the end of their second outing when he'd walked her to her door, then ruffled her hair and patted her butt before sending her inside.

So he'd kissed her.

He hadn't expected to like kissing Molly. He hadn't expected to become aroused by it. He'd thought his heart was too firmly fixed on Eve for any other girl to grab hold of it. Boy, had he been wrong. Molly was an irresistible force. And pretty soon he'd no longer wanted to resist her.

They'd gone steady the rest of the year. He'd stopped looking at Eve, although he couldn't avoid seeing her every day, since their lockers were so close. He'd told himself he'd been lucky to escape one of those fanatical Grayhawk girls.

He'd known all along that he would be joining the army and leaving Jackson at the end of the school year, and that there was at least a chance that he was never coming back. When he headed off to boot camp, Molly was just starting her sophomore year. He'd told her not to wait for him, but he might as well have saved his breath.

Molly never stopped writing. Never stopped caring.

When he was home on leave a year later he'd seen Eve at Old West Days and felt anew that sense of loss—and a pang of regret for what might have been. Her eyes were suspicious when he'd purposely "by accident" bumped into her, knocking her ice cream cone from her hand. Replacing the cone had given him a chance to speak to her. His heart had raced as he reached out to thumb away a bit of ice cream on the edge of her mouth.

He'd known then that he wasn't really over her. That he would probably never be over her. But if anything, the animosity between their families had gotten worse. It was that stupid bet Brian had made with Aiden that he couldn't get Leah to fall in love with him.

She'd fallen. And then found out about the bet.

After all the heartache, Grayhawks were never going to get along with Flynns. And Flynns were always going to resent Grayhawks for what had happened to Aunt Jane.

He loved being with Molly, loved who she was as a person. She always believed in the good in people. And she could always make him laugh. By the time he'd spent a year in Afghanistan, he'd needed someone like her in his life. He'd known the hell he would be making for himself if he married Molly, because

Molly and Eve were inseparable friends. But he didn't want to take the chance of some other guy stealing Molly away while he was overseas, as had happened to so many of his buddies. So he'd proposed.

He wondered later if he'd done it because he was headed for another tour in Afghanistan and feared his luck might be running out, and if he wanted to leave a part of himself—a son or daughter—behind after he was gone from this world, this might be his last chance. Whatever had impelled him to commit, he'd ended up marrying Molly.

He and Molly had gotten along well throughout their marriage, and they had two amazing kids. He just hadn't counted on how often he'd end up having to spend time in Eve's company. His kids adored Eve as much as his wife did, so she was always around. Connor believed in fidelity in marriage, so he'd been careful never to be alone with her. He'd always figured better safe than sorry. He didn't have to resist temptation if it was never in his path.

He'd felt guilty whenever he found himself listening to Eve a little too attentively or laughing with her a little too eagerly or—God help him—wanting her a little too much. He'd had dreams in Afghanistan from which he awoke breathing erratically, his body hard and ready. Far too many of them did not feature his wife.

No wonder he'd felt ashamed and upset last night when he'd gotten hard as a rock holding the woman who'd haunted those dreams. He was finally free to pursue a woman he'd secretly loved the whole time he was married, but the cost had come too high. Molly had been precious to him, and it was hard to imagine his life without her.

When he'd kissed Eve last night, shame and regret had swelled in his chest. Desire had died a quick and certain death, and grief and guilt had taken its place.

It was painful to admit that he hadn't been a very good husband. He'd left his wife alone too often. She'd raised their kids by herself during the long months he'd been deployed. He could have used injuries he'd suffered to avoid that third deployment, but he'd wanted to be there to watch out for his buddies. He should have been home watching out for his wife. He should have taken better care of her. If he had, she might still be alive.

He was glad Eve had stayed to talk after he'd made that stupid move to kiss her. Glad that they were going to continue the truce—an unspoken agreement to forgo Grayhawk-Flynn hostilities—that they'd managed to maintain throughout his marriage.

Connor's musing was interrupted by Mrs. Robertson, who was sobbing loudly into a lacy handkerchief. He couldn't help feeling sorry for his late wife's parents. He hadn't wanted to take their grandchildren away from them, but they'd given him no choice. Maybe someday they could mend fences. Right now, he didn't trust them. No one was stealing his children away again.

"What time should we expect you and the kids at the house?" his father asked.

Connor hesitated. After the purchase was complete, he'd told his family that he'd bought Safe Haven, but he'd represented his purchase of the former dude ranch to them as a charitable project, a much-needed refuge for returning vets. He hadn't been at all sure he'd win in court, so he'd said nothing to them about his plans to move there himself if he got custody of his kids.

Connor was anxious to take Brooke and Sawyer to their new home. Anxious to start his new life as a single father. "I won't be bringing the kids back to the Lucky 7 tonight," he said at last.

"Is there some problem picking them up?" his father asked.

"No, Dad." In fact, they were being taken care of in another room at the courthouse by a social worker, who had instructions to deliver them and their belongings to whichever party arrived with the appropriate court documents.

Connor glanced from face to sobered face as he announced to his brothers, "I'm going to spend my first night with my kids at Safe Haven."

He expected outbursts of protest, but his brothers had apparently been stunned into silence.

"Just you and the kids?" Devon said. "Isn't that a little risky?"

"What do you mean?" Connor asked.

"I mean, what if they miss their grandparents? What if they start crying? What are you going to do?"

Connor gave Devon the same answer he'd given Eve. "I managed a Delta team. I think I can handle two little kids."

"It's not the same thing," Devon warned.

"I agree. It should be a lot easier handling the kids," Connor said with a wry grin.

"Safe Haven is a long way off if you need to call for help," Aiden pointed out.

What he said was true. Jackson Hole was bordered by the Teton, Gros Ventre, and Wind River mountain ranges, each reaching more than ten thousand feet in elevation, which made the first half hour of the drive to his ranch, through Grand Teton National Park, absolutely spectacular. The second half of the drive, on mostly dirt roads, ran smack through the Bridger Teton National Forest. Even in the best of conditions—and conditions weren't always good—the trip took an hour.

"I'm not going to need help," Connor said stubbornly.

"You're out of your mind," his father said. "You can't possibly take care of two babies—because they're just babies at two and four—on your own."

Connor felt the flush begin at his throat and rise to his cheeks. He'd never been able to control the blush that rose on his fair Irish skin when he was angry or excited. Right now he was both. "Say it a little louder, why don't you, Dad, so the judge can hear you?"

Aiden, ever the peacemaker, stepped into Connor's line of vision and asked, "When are you supposed to pick up Brooke and Sawyer?"

"As soon as I have the documents from the court clerk."

"Are you sure you don't want to spend at least the first night at home?" Devon asked. "I mean, just in case?"

Connor smiled confidently, a look he'd given to soldiers under his command which hid the terror he felt before a firefight. "I appreciate your offers of help. Really, I do. But I've got this."

"Since Molly . . ." Aiden's voice trailed off. "We've missed the kids. Will you at least bring them to visit sometime soon?"

"Sure," Connor promised as he fought to speak past the sudden knot in his throat.

Connor realized he had to get away from his family or he was liable to break down in tears again. He was feeling joyful all right, but also angry. About the time he'd lost with Brooke and Sawyer. About having to live his life without Molly. About wanting a woman with the wrong last name. About losing buddies who shouldn't have had their lives cut short.

He fought back the anger, which a very good army therapist had told him he needed to deal with sooner rather than later.

It was the unpredictability of war that had finally gotten to him, the sheer arbitrariness of who lived and who died in battle. Even when a good man survived the war, he wasn't home free. There were inner demons to be battled, the consequences of killing other humans or holding some buddy in your arms as he died an agonizing death, torn apart by bullets or a bomb. Worst of all was the guilt you felt for being fiercely glad that you were still alive when your buddy was dead.

It was a friend's death that had given Connor the idea to buy a ranch and run it as a sanctuary for returning vets. Any soldier who needed a quiet place of peace where he could let go of the horrors he'd witnessed in war was welcome.

Connor had several friends still in the army who'd

been willing to refer vets to him. Over the past two months, three dozen returning soldiers had come and gone from Safe Haven. Some of them only stayed for a weekend, some for a week, and some were still there two months later.

Connor hadn't decided yet on a time limit for how long a man could stay, but he'd realized he was going to need some support, so he'd hired a couple of the visiting vets, one of whom had been a therapist in the army. Each soldier worked for his supper doing chores on the ranch, everything from feeding chickens and milking cows to mending the barbed wire fence that defined his property. But there was no other charge.

Connor was pretty sure this wasn't the way his father had expected him to use his trust fund, but so long as the money held out, he was determined to help as many vets as he could. Eventually he was going to have to come up with a way to fund his sanctuary, but his trust fund would keep the ranch in operation for a long time.

Connor had built an addition to the small ranch house to make sure there was plenty of space for the children and a room for the nanny he was planning to hire. For the short term he planned to do all of the child care himself. He wanted to reestablish his relationship with his children, and that meant spending time with them.

Connor retrieved the papers he needed from the court clerk and turned to get a few last hugs from his brothers.

"Call if you need us," Aiden said.

"Aw, Aiden," Devon complained, "you shouldn't

have said that. Now he won't call because he'd be admitting he needs our help."

Connor grinned. "You are so right!" Now that he had custody of his children, it felt like a tremendous weight had been lifted off his shoulders. The future felt bright and full of possibilities. "I'll be fine. Now, if you'll excuse me, I'm going to go get my kids."

He didn't want his brothers around when he picked up Brooke and Sawyer, because he was afraid he might end up teary-eyed again. Before he left, he searched the courtroom looking for Eve, to thank her for speaking on his behalf, but she'd already gone. Maybe he'd see her in town sometime and thank her. He wasn't going to call her. He wasn't going anywhere near Eve Grayhawk if he could help it.

He'd just finished that thought when he opened the door to the room where his children were being held and found himself face-to-face with her.

Eve was down on one knee and had both children in her arms. Her eyes were brimmed with tears and her chin was wobbling as she tried to smile at them. She rose, the children still clinging to her, and swiped at a tear that spilled over. She shot a woeful look at him and said, "I'll get out of your way. I was just leaving."

She'd only taken one step before Brooke gripped her at the waist on one side and Sawyer wrapped his arms around her hip on the other. Both children were crying. She shut her eyes and caught her lower lip in her teeth as she put a loving hand on each child's head.

"Please don't leave us, Aunt Eve," Brooke begged. "Please!"

Sawyer looked up at her, tears streaming, his nose running, and cried, "Don't go! Don't go! Don't go!"

Eve shot Connor an imploring look. "I know I shouldn't be here. But I wanted to say goodbye to the children before you take them away."

He suddenly realized that Eve must be afraid that she was no more likely to see the children on a regular basis in the future than Mr. and Mrs. Robertson were. He shifted his gaze to his children, who were clearly anxious. This would be the first time they'd been alone with him in the nine months since Molly's death. He'd spent a few hours of court-ordered time with them each week over the past two months since he'd been home, but it had been at a neutral location, supervised by a social worker, and they'd known their grandparents would be coming to get them again. Now he was scooping them up and taking them somewhere strange, without any of the people who'd been their anchors since Molly's death.

He could feel his heart racing as adrenaline flowed into his system, much as it always had before combat. He recognized it as a response to the sudden fear he felt. Could he raise two happy, healthy children all by himself? He was about to face the biggest challenge of his life—and the most important one. He took a deep, calming breath and said, "Brooke, Sawyer, it's time for us to go home."

As he stepped toward them, they clung more tightly to Eve.

"Where's Nana and Bampa?" Brooke asked.

Connor didn't want to lie and tell his daughter she'd be seeing her grandparents soon. But he recognized the stark fear in her eyes at the thought of losing someone else from her life. "They're still in the courtroom. Right now you and Sawyer need to come with me."

"Can you come, too, Aunt Eve?" Brooke asked.

"No, I—"

"Of course she can." Connor met Eve's gaze over the kids' heads and added, "She can help you get into your car seats."

Connor's heart was in his throat until Eve nodded. She favored each child with a sweet smile. "You're going to have a wonderful time with your daddy."

Connor handed the paperwork to the social worker, then collected the kids' bags and carried them out the door. Eve followed behind him, a child's hand in each of hers. What would he have done if she hadn't been there? Connor had visions of a scene that would have had everyone in the courthouse running to see what all the commotion was about and the judge changing his mind and giving the kids back to Molly's parents.

He shot a grateful look at Eve over his shoulder as he headed for his truck. He could see she was talking to the kids but he couldn't hear what she was saying. He threw the bags into the back of the pickup and opened the backseat door. He reached to pick up Sawyer, worried that the boy might shrink from him. To his surprise, Sawyer reached up both hands and gripped him around the neck.

Connor resisted the urge to hug the boy tighter. Instead, he enjoyed the few moments of holding his son's slight weight in his arms, of smelling his little boy's hair and brushing it back from his forehead.

Then he settled him in the car seat he'd put in that morning and attached the belts.

By the time he was done, he saw that Eve had coaxed Brooke into her car seat and was attaching the belts that would keep her safe. She whispered something in his daughter's ear as Brooke looked at him with wide eyes. Then Eve stepped back and closed the door.

Connor came running around the truck to catch her before she could leave. "Thank you. I don't think that would have gone nearly as well if you hadn't been here." That was the understatement of the century.

"I'm glad I could help."

"What did you say to get them to come with me?"

She looked into his eyes and said, "I told them you were their mother's most favorite person in the whole world and that Molly would want them to go with you and be as good as good can be to show what wonderful children she'd raised."

Connor didn't speak, because a lump the size of a grenade was clogging his throat. He merely nodded, glanced at the two children calmly looking back at him, then got inside and started the truck.

Chapter 4

EVE HAD MANAGED to avoid her father at the court-house, but when she arrived in the dining room at Kingdom Come for supper, he was already seated at the head of the table. Taylor and Victoria were out of town, but Matt's family was there, along with Leah. Eve had barely settled the cloth napkin in her lap when King said, "What bee got into your bonnet this morning at the courthouse? Why did you tell the judge that Molly wanted the kids to go to that Flynn boy?"

"Did you want me to lie?" Eve retorted.

Leah leaned across Eve to set a bowl of mashed potatoes in the center of the table, where she'd already set a platter of fried chicken and a bowl of string beans. "You know Eve and Molly were best friends. She had to tell what she knew."

"Phil and Helen Robertson are devastated," King said, glaring at Eve.

"How do you think Connor felt when he came home from the war and Molly's parents wouldn't give him back his children?" Eve countered.

"I told you the friendship between those two girls was a bad idea," he said to Leah.

"Molly was a nice girl from a good family. There was no reason to keep Eve away from her."

"The Robertsons and Flynns were always thick as fleas on a barn cat," King muttered.

"That didn't happen until after Molly married Connor," Leah reminded him.

Eve had been almost grown before it dawned on her just how much responsibility her father had placed on his stepdaughter's shoulders. She'd resented and defied Leah's admonitions to behave. Eve had been the odd sister out, since her twin sisters did everything together, but she hadn't bonded with Leah, either. It was Molly who'd held the role of beloved sister. Leah had been an authority figure to be obeyed. Or, more often, disobeyed.

With the benefit of hindsight, Eve was glad and grateful that Leah had been there all the years she was growing up. Leah was a bulwark against which her father could not stand, probably because Leah never asked for anything for herself. Her eldest sister thought of everyone else first and herself a long way after. If anyone deserved to stay at Kingdom Come, it was Leah, but she was being thrown out right along with the rest of them.

Eve shot an aggrieved look toward the other end of the pine trestle table, where Matt sat flanked by his daughter, Pippa, and his son, Nathan. Pippa had gray eyes and flyaway, sun-streaked chestnut hair. She was undeniably beautiful, nearly six feet tall with a willowy figure. Nathan was a miniature of his father, with sapphire-blue eyes and black hair. The boy was small for his age and had a limp, but Eve had heard no explanation of how he'd gotten it.

There were secrets to be discovered, she was sure, about Matt's beautiful daughter and his limping son, starting with the reason for the fourteen-year gap between their ages. Eve wondered what had happened to Matt's wife. Or was it *wives*? Like father, like son? Matt hadn't volunteered any information, and both he and his children had remained tight-lipped about their existence before they'd shown up in Wyoming.

Not that anyone was asking. She and her sisters had treated Matt and his family like the interlopers they were, doing their best to make them feel unwelcome.

That hadn't been as easy as it sounded. Victoria had come up with the idea of eating breakfast when it was still dark out and leaving cold eggs and bacon on the table for their half brother and his family to eat when they got up at a reasonable hour. Unfortunately, by the time the girls made their bleary-eyed, crack-of-dawn appearance in the kitchen, Matt had already eaten his breakfast and taken off for parts unknown. Pippa never showed up for breakfast at all. And Nathan announced he *liked* cold eggs and bacon.

Leah quickly nipped that sort of petty behavior in the bud. She suggested that Eve and her sisters confront Matt directly to get the concessions she was sure he'd be willing to make, considering the fact that they were related. But that wasn't as easy as it sounded, either.

The first Saturday after Matt arrived, Eve showed up at the stable with her twin sisters to take a morning ride and caught Matt saddling Taylor's favorite mount for himself.

"That's my horse," Taylor said.

Matt lowered the stirrup that he'd apparently adjusted for his longer leg. He stroked the Appaloosa's neck and said, "He's a good-looking animal."

"You'll need to find yourself another mount," Taylor continued as she grabbed the reins, which were knotted and slung over the western saddle horn, near the bit. "Steeldust is mine."

Eve watched several emotions flicker across Matt's face as he made the decision whether to concede the issue or contest it. There were plenty of saddle horses in the barn. While Steeldust was Taylor's favorite mount, the gelding was by no means the only horse she rode.

"You'll have to get yourself another horse," Matt said at last. "I've got somewhere I need to be." Rather than stay on the ground where they were on equal footing, so to speak, he threw himself into the saddle without using the stirrups, a graceful move that spoke of how many times he must have done it.

Before he could kick his mount into action, Taylor applied pressure on the bit, holding Steeldust in place.

"You're not going anywhere on my horse."

Instead of spurring the horse so the reins would be jerked from Taylor's hands, Matt relaxed in the saddle, crossing his wrists over the horn. "We need to get a few things straight."

Eve bristled at Matt's tone, while Victoria's mouth thinned to a furious line. Taylor's whole body snapped upright, as though Matt had slapped her.

"No, *you* need to get a few things straight," Taylor said through gritted teeth. "You left. You walked away. You can't come back now and play cock of the walk."

"I agreed to come back to the ranch on one condition."

Eve waited for Matt to name that condition. He waited for one of them to ask.

"What condition?" Victoria said at last.

"I'm the boss."

"You're not the boss of me!" Taylor snapped.

Eve cringed at Taylor's use of an expression they'd tossed back and forth when they were little, however much it fit the situation.

"Take it up with Dad," Matt said.

Taylor's face bleached white at the reminder that Matt was as much one of King's kids as they were. He seemed sure King would tell them that he had, in fact, put Matt in charge.

But they hadn't been named King's Brats for nothing. Taylor let go of the reins and took a step back. She glared at Matt and said, "This isn't over."

Matt's eyes narrowed as he nodded at each of them in turn, daring them to do their worst. Then he kicked Steeldust into a lope and rode away.

Matt hadn't conceded a thing. Not only that, he'd refused to be drawn into an argument. He'd never raised his voice, and he hadn't given an inch. It was infuriating behavior for Eve and her sisters, who were used to raging arguments with their father. It was impossible to win a battle, let alone the war, when the damned man refused to fight!

"I'm going to make you sorry you ever left Australia," Taylor muttered at Matt's back.

They spent every minute of their ride seeking a way to oust Matt from Kingdom Come, but it was hard to know how to get rid of him when they didn't know why he'd shown up in the first place.

Now, three weeks after his arrival, Matt was as

much an enigma as he'd been on the day he'd arrived. But every day he was at Kingdom Come, he insinuated himself and his family more deeply into the fabric of life on the ranch.

Eve noticed that Matt's six-year-old son was gnawing on a chicken leg with relish, while his twenty-year-old daughter pushed her mashed potatoes around the plate without taking a bite. Pippa didn't look happy to be here, which Eve could understand. It would be difficult for any young woman to leave her friends behind and move to a strange place, and Matt had taken his kids halfway around the world.

Apparently Pippa hadn't been in college, or if she had, she'd agreed to leave in midterm to come here with her father. Eve would have dearly loved to be a fly on the wall during that conversation. She wondered why the nearly grown girl had agreed to come, if she was so unhappy to be here.

At least Matt wanted his kids with him, which was more than she could say for her father. King had found plenty of reasons to be somewhere other than at home for most of her life, leaving her and her sisters behind to be supervised by Leah, a housekeeper, and a couple of hired hands.

Eve had never considered just how much Leah must have given up to be their surrogate mother until she overheard her sister arguing with King in his study the same night he announced his deal with Matt. Who could not, when both were shouting at the top of their lungs?

"It's not fair!" Leah cried. "You can't do this to the girls, King. This is their home."

Likely because Leah had come into the family as a

five-year-old, she'd always called her stepfather "King," but Eve knew her father respected Leah and loved her like a daughter, which was to say, as much as he was capable of loving anyone.

"I had to offer Matt something to get him home," her father replied.

Eve heard a scornful laugh before Leah said, "It was a lot more than something. You gave him everything!"

"I wanted him back here."

"Why?"

The word hung in the air for a long time before King said, "I made some mistakes. I'm trying to atone for them."

As their voices quieted, Eve moved closer to the door to hear better.

To her astonishment, noble, selfless Leah said, "Where am I supposed to go, Daddy? What am I supposed to do?"

Eve's stomach knotted at the plaintive note in her always-so-confident sister's voice.

The silence that ensued was evidence of how seldom Leah asked for anything for herself. Or maybe it was the shock King experienced at being called "Daddy."

Finally he said, "I'm working on something that might solve the problem. It's taking longer than I thought."

"I don't want to leave Kingdom Come," Leah said. "This is my home. I thought—"

Leah cut herself off, but it was obvious to Eve that her eldest sister had planned to live and work on the ranch the rest of her life.

Eve heard a choked-back sob before her father cleared his throat and said, "Here. Take my handkerchief."

"One handkerchief won't do the job," Leah said bitterly. "I have a lot more tears to cry if you can't fix this."

Eve heard Leah's boots crossing the hardwood floor of her father's study and slipped away before she could get caught. The next day, when Matt took over operations on the ranch, it was clear that even Leah's rarer-than-rubies tears had not convinced King to change his mind.

Since Matt's arrival Leah had continued her role as surrogate mother, devoted sister, and ranch manager as though her world had not been turned upside down. She treated Matt and his children with courtesy, if not warmth, and made them comfortable in a home that would soon no longer be her own. But her attitude toward their father wasn't just frosty, it was glacial.

For his part, King seemed to revel in his role as patriarch, presiding over a supper table that now included his long-lost son. "What are Taylor and Victoria up to?" he asked Leah.

"You mean since you told them you're throwing them out of house and home?" Leah said. "I wouldn't know."

Eve wondered what Matt and his kids thought when they heard the suppressed rage in Leah's voice. She glanced toward their end of the table and realized that none of them were paying any attention to King and Leah. Pippa was shooting dark glances at her father over the head of Nathan, who seemed oblivious to the sparks flying between father and daughter.

What had surprised Eve about her sister's response to King regarding the whereabouts of Taylor and Victoria was not the resentment in her voice but the blatant lie. Whether they were traveling or home in Jackson, Leah always stayed in touch with her siblings. That hadn't changed since Matt's arrival. Eve wondered what Taylor and Victoria were up to that Leah wanted to conceal from King.

Eve realized that she had no idea where her sisters had gone. With any luck they were off figuring out a way to make Matt's life in Wyoming hellish enough that he'd be on the next plane back to Australia.

"I found a herd of what appear to be wild mustangs in the north pasture," Matt said. "Who do I call to have them moved off the ranch?"

Eve was out of her seat before Matt had finished speaking. "Those are my horses! They're staying right where they are."

Matt's eyes narrowed. "What are you doing with a herd of mustangs?"

"Saving them from becoming dog food."

"I need that land for quarter horse breeding stock I've bought. You'll have to move your animals."

Eve felt a surge of panic. "Move them where?"

"I don't care. I just want them gone."

She looked to her father for support. "Daddy? Are you going to let him do that?"

"Matt can't very well run the ranch if he can't make decisions about how to use the land."

"You said the ranch wasn't his for a year. He's acting like he already owns it!"

King blustered, "I had to make a choice—"

"And you chose him." Eve's face was hot and her hands were shaking. She felt like throwing something. Screaming. Raging. She felt helpless and hopeless and angrier than she could ever remember being.

Her horses. Her beautiful mustangs. What would happen to them now?

Leah held out her hands in supplication. "Please, sit down, Eve. I'm sure we can work out something with Matt."

"I wouldn't count on that." Matt focused his gaze on King. "Do you want me here? Or not?"

King fisted his hand around his napkin. "Of course I want you here! But I expected—"

"You expected me to coddle those three Brats the way you always have," Matt said. "I won't. You've given them plenty. I'm sure they've got trust funds overflowing with cash," he said with a sneer. "It's time they make their own way in the world."

Eve felt like she was going to vomit. "Is that what you think? That because King Grayhawk is wealthy his daughters must be rich?"

"Yeah. That's what I think," Matt said.

Eve gave a harsh, raucous laugh that became a sob. She turned to King, her face crumpling in defeat as she dropped back into her chair. "Oh, Daddy, what lies have you been telling him?"

For the first time, Matt looked uncertain. "I know you set up trust funds for Libby and North," he said to King, mentioning his sister and brother, Jane Flynn's other two children. "You never put money away for the Brats?"

King shrugged. "It was never necessary. They've

pretty much taken care of themselves. I bought them whatever they needed and gave them a place to stay."

"Which you've promised to this *prodigal son*," Eve said, making the expression an epithet.

"Now that you know the truth, Matt," Leah interjected, "surely you can rearrange your plans."

Matt shook his head. "My quarter horses are already on the way. They'll be here by the end of the week." He focused his gaze on Eve. "You've got that much time to move your mustangs out."

Eve turned to King. "What do you suggest I do, Daddy? Send them to the slaughterhouse?"

"Find another piece of land, of course."

"In Teton County? How am I supposed to pay for it?" Eve left the words hanging, expecting her father to at least offer to help her with the cost of relocating her mustangs in a county with some of the most expensive real estate in the country. When King didn't speak, she said in disgust, "Don't worry, Daddy. I'll figure something out." She turned to Matt and demanded, "Why did you come here? Why are you doing this? How can you be so cruel?"

To her astonishment, it was Pippa who answered her. "My dad doesn't want anything to do with you Grayhawks. We had a great life in Australia until *he* showed up." She jerked her chin toward King. She lurched to her feet and snarled, "I can't wait till this year is up! Maybe then you'll leave us alone and stop making my dad so sad."

Eve's gaze shot to Matt, whose eyes had lowered to the plate in front of him. Nathan had dropped his drumstick and was staring at his sister, his jaw slack.

"Sit down, Pippa," Matt said quietly, "and finish your supper."

"I'm not hungry." She threw her napkin halfway across the table and marched out of the dining room.

Eve waited to see if Matt would call her back, but he said nothing.

Tears welled in Nathan's eyes. He looked at his father and asked, "Is Pippa gonna run away again?"

Again? Had she run away in Australia? Was that why Matt had come here? To be sure his daughter couldn't run to wherever she'd gone before?

Matt stood and gathered his son in his arms. Nathan clung to his father as Matt turned to face the rest of the Grayhawks at the table. "This isn't easy for us, either. But you made the deal," he said to King, "and I'm holding you to it." He shoved Nathan's chair out of his way with a loud scrape as he left the room.

Eve glanced at King to see what he thought of everything that had just been said.

It was Leah who asked the question that had crossed Eve's mind. "What's going on, Daddy? Why didn't you offer to buy a piece of land where Eve can keep her mustangs?"

King hesitated so long, Eve wasn't sure he was going to answer. At last he said, "Everything's tied up somewhere else."

"What do you mean by *everything*?" Leah asked.

"Just what I said," King replied. "Don't ask me where I've put it, because that's none of your damn business."

The hurt look on Leah's face came and went so fast Eve wouldn't have seen it if she hadn't been staring right at her.

"Fine. Keep your secrets." Leah folded her napkin and set it neatly beside her plate. "Excuse me, please. I've lost my appetite." A moment later she was gone through the swinging door that led to the kitchen.

Eve searched her father's features, looking for some hint of what he was thinking. But King Grayhawk had been a politician too long. His thoughts and feelings were hidden behind the impenetrable facade he'd perfected during years of purposeful deception.

"I hope the price of having Matt here was worth it," Eve said as she tossed her balled-up napkin onto her plate.

"It's worth anything and everything I have."

King's answer made her throat ache. "Why, Daddy? What is it about Matt that makes him more precious than the rest of us? Can you just tell me that?"

Before he could answer, Leah came rushing back through the swinging door. "It's for you," she said, handing a portable phone to Eve. "It sounds urgent."

Eve took the phone and held it to her ear. Her blood ran cold as she listened to the frantic voice on the other end of the line. She answered, "Yes, I can. Hold on. I'll be there soon." She handed the phone back to an anxious Leah and rose from the table.

"Who was that?" King asked.

Eve looked him square in the eye and said, "None of your damn business."

Chapter 5

EVEN COMPARED WITH his bloodiest battle in Afghanistan, the hour between his frantic phone call to Eve and the moment she arrived on his doorstep was the most harrowing of Connor's life. His kids were crying, and he couldn't get them to stop.

"Thank God you're here," he said as he ushered Eve inside along with a blast of frigid air. "They've been bawling nonstop since I put them to bed. It started with Sawyer. He said he wanted his Nana. Once Brooke heard him sobbing she joined in. Nothing I've said, nothing I've done, has been able to comfort them."

"Take me to them," Eve said as she dropped her coat on a rocking chair in the living room.

"I had rooms set up for each of them, but right now they're huddled together in Brooke's bed," he said as he led her along the creaking hardwood floor toward the rooms at the back of the seventy-year-old ranch house. "After I turned out the light in Sawyer's room and left, he must have run in there. A few minutes later I heard them howling like a pack of coyotes. When I turned on the light to see what was wrong, I found them holding on to each other as though a tornado was threatening to rip them apart. When I asked what was wrong, they hid their faces and cried louder."

Connor knew he was rambling, but he couldn't stop. He was scared. What if he couldn't do this? What if the kids wouldn't stop crying? What was he going to do? He couldn't lose his kids. He loved them. And they needed him, whether they knew it or not.

"I tried picking them up and holding them in my lap to comfort them, but I could feel them quivering like scared rabbits. I wasn't sure whether they were scared of being alone with me or just scared of being in a strange place," he said, continuing to babble like an idiot. "I put them down and called you. Thank God you were home. Thank God you were willing to come."

If she hadn't answered, his next call would have been to the Robertsons. He was glad that hadn't been necessary, but he would have done it. He couldn't stand to see his children weeping. He couldn't stand to see them so unhappy. It made his heart hurt.

Connor had figured the kids would take one look at Eve and quiet down. He couldn't have been more wrong.

The moment Brooke saw Eve in the bedroom doorway, she reached out her arms to her. But when Eve sat down on the bed and embraced her, she cried even louder. Sawyer grabbed Eve around the neck and wouldn't let go, his sobs escalating as well.

Connor stood by his daughter's bed feeling helpless and hopeless. Eve looked him in the eye and gestured with her chin for him to sit down beside Sawyer, but he couldn't move. His feet felt rooted to the floor.

The sound of his children weeping so horribly made his stomach clench. He balled his hands into fists so Eve wouldn't see how badly they were shaking.

"It's all right, Brooke," he heard her murmur. "Your daddy's here and I'm here and everything's going to be all right."

At the word "daddy" Brooke shot an anxious glance in his direction. Then she hid her face against Eve's throat and slid her arms tighter around Eve's neck, nearly choking her. At his wit's end, he responded the way he would have in the army. He started barking orders.

"That's enough, both of you! I brought Aunt Eve here to visit, and you're dripping tears and snot all over her. Stop that wailing this instant!"

Maybe it was the shock of hearing an adult shout at them, when they were used to kinder treatment. Maybe they were just cried out. Maybe it was Eve's reassuring presence. But suddenly, as though he'd shut off a dripping faucet, the crying stopped.

Connor stood where he was, his useless hands hanging at his sides, feeling totally enervated, while Eve calmly snatched a couple of Kleenex from the box next to the bed. She handed one to Brooke and said, "Blow your nose, sweetie," then used the other to wipe Sawyer's runny nose.

Connor knew he should be doing something, but he was afraid to move in their direction, afraid he would incite another bout of crying.

Eve patted the bed and said, "Come join us."

Connor managed to unroot his feet and sat beside Sawyer, who was perched on the bed to Eve's left. Brooke was still sitting on Eve's lap.

"Now tell me," Eve said as she grabbed another Kleenex and dabbed at Brooke's swollen eyes. "What was all that crying about?"

"We were scared," Brooke said, darting a glance at Connor from beneath tear-drenched, spiky eyelashes.

"Of what, little one?" Eve said, patting the tip of Brooke's nose with her forefinger.

"We were all alone," Sawyer blurted.

"You slept in separate bedrooms at Nana and Bampa's house," Eve reminded them.

"This isn't Nana and Bampa's house," Brooke pointed out.

"No, it isn't," Eve said with a laugh of agreement. "It's your father's house. It's where you'll be living from now on."

"Do we have to stay here?" Brooke asked plaintively.

"I want to go home," Sawyer said.

Connor said nothing. His throat was swollen too tight to speak. His children felt *alone* even with him—their father—in the house. It was his own fault for not staying in closer touch with them during the nine months after Molly's death, while he finished his tour of duty. Brooke was too young to remember much of the life they'd led as a family before Molly died, and it was likely Sawyer had no memory of him before Molly's death at all. He'd known this period of adjustment wasn't going to be easy, but he hadn't thought it would be this hard, either.

"It's too late to go anywhere tonight," Eve said, suggesting by the way she'd phrased her statement that the children might be allowed to go home in the morning.

He opened his mouth to make it clear they were here to stay, then shut it again. A day at a time. That was how he was going to become their father again. Tomorrow he could come up with another reason to delay their departure, and another reason on the day after that. Soon, he prayed, they would stop asking to leave.

"Can I sleep in Brooke's bed tonight?" Sawyer asked.

Eve shot an inquiring look in Connor's direction.

He saw Eve's slight nod suggesting that he agree. "I suppose that would be all right." He'd put a queen-size canopy bed in Brooke's room, because he'd liked the girly way it looked on the showroom floor. He'd put bunk beds in Sawyer's room, thinking of the fun his son would have climbing up and sleeping on the top bunk when he was older.

"Let's get you both under the covers," Eve said, standing and sliding Brooke upright until her bare feet hit the floor.

Connor had put both kids in long john pajamas to be sure they'd be warm enough. He hesitated, then reached over to lift Sawyer into his arms as he stood. While Eve helped Brooke get settled under the covers, Connor walked around to the opposite side of the bed. Sawyer kept his arms tucked in front of him, separating their bodies, until Connor gently eased him onto the bed and reluctantly let him go.

His son scooted toward his sister, so the two of them ended up lying next to each other in the center of the bed. Connor sat down beside his son, tucking the covers under Sawyer's arms as Eve did the same for Brooke. Then Eve leaned over and kissed each child on the forehead. To his surprise, Brooke caught Eve's face with both hands and pulled her close to brush her eyelashes against Eve's cheek in a butterfly kiss.

Connor knew what it was because, once upon a time, he'd been the beneficiary of those kisses, which Molly had taught to his daughter. He felt Sawyer's hand wrap around his thumb and pull and turned his attention back to his son. Sawyer kept tugging and Connor leaned in until Sawyer caught him by the ears and pulled him close.

He felt Sawyer's cheek against his own as the two-year-old tried to mimic his sister. His son's lashes weren't long enough to administer a butterfly kiss, but Connor's chest ached with the joy of having his son close, longing for the day that his children would love and trust him again.

"Sleep tight. Don't let the bedbugs bite," he said to his son.

"Mommy used to say that," Brooke said accusingly, as though he wasn't allowed to use phrases that Molly had used.

Connor turned to find his daughter's bright eyes on him. "I know."

"Mommy's dead," Sawyer said.

He met his son's sober gaze with one of his own. "I know."

"I miss Mommy," Brooke said.

"Me, too," Sawyer said.

"I do, too," Connor choked out. He brushed a lock of hair off Sawyer's forehead. He remembered Molly saying it was the lock of dark hair that fell on his own forehead that had caused her to fall in love with him. "I could never marry a man without flaws, because I could never measure up to such a God," she'd said with a laugh. "You'd be absolutely perfect," she'd said as she looked into his eyes after making love with him, "except for that ornery lock of hair."

"Will you read us a story?" Sawyer asked.

"It's late. You need to get to sleep."

"Mommy always read us a story," Brooke said, a wistful tone in her voice as though he should know these things. He did. He simply hadn't realized how important such familiar routine was to his children. He wouldn't make that mistake again.

"I will tomorrow night," Connor promised. "Time now to sleep. We've got a big day tomorrow."

"Doing what?" Brooke asked.

"Lots of fun things," Eve said when Connor couldn't think of what to reply.

"Will you be coming with us?" Brooke asked.

"I don't think—" Eve began.

That was as far as she got before Connor interrupted. "I'll do my best to try and talk Aunt Eve into joining us."

He could see that the idea pleased both children.

Eve got to her feet and headed for the bedroom door, and Connor jumped up to follow her.

He stopped at the door and said, "All right if I turn out the light?" He suddenly realized that he hadn't asked either child earlier, he'd simply tucked them in and darkened their rooms.

Both kids snuggled down under the covers.

"Okay," Brooke said.

"Okay," Sawyer echoed.

Connor breathed a silent sigh of relief and turned out the light. He left the door open a crack so he could hear if either child called to him during the night. Then he hurried after Eve, hoping she wouldn't rush off before he had a chance to speak to her.

She already had her coat on by the time he got to the living room.

"What's your hurry?" he said, feeling panic at the thought of being alone with his kids again. "Take your coat off and stay awhile." Brooke and Sawyer were calm now, but he wanted Eve there until he was sure they were asleep. "Can I offer you something to drink? It's the least I can do to thank you for coming to my rescue."

He saw her hesitation and said, "Please, Eve. I owe you one. I was a dead man walking until you showed up."

"They would have settled down eventually," she said as she slipped her coat off and dropped it back onto the rocker. "They were pretty much cried out by the time I arrived."

"If you say so." He wasn't so sure. "What would you like? A glass of wine? A beer? Something stronger?"

She smiled. "Hot tea?"

He smiled back at her and felt all the tension leave his body for the first time since he'd gotten his children back. "Sure."

He was grateful there was no hot water dispenser at the ranch house. She'd have to stick around long enough for him to boil some water, which gave him a few minutes to get her to drive all the way back out here tomorrow.

"You've really fixed this old house up nice," Eve said as she perched on one of the stools at the granite breakfast bar.

"I added a modern bathroom for the kids and upgraded the kitchen, but I kept the old clawfoot tub, the log walls, and the hardwood floors."

She surveyed his simple western décor, which was done in warm browns and reds. A large cowhide covered the area in front of the floor-to-ceiling stone fireplace, where a wood fire popped and crackled. "It feels like a home."

"If only Brooke and Sawyer agreed with you, I'd be a happy man."

"You'll be surprised how quickly they settle in."

"Tonight was rough. I was hoping you might be able to join us tomorrow for whatever it is we end up doing."

"I can't."

No explanation, just a refusal. Connor wasn't used to taking no for an answer. There had to be a way to convince her to come back tomorrow. He set a cup of hot tea in front of her, then sat down on the stool next to Eve with his own cup of tea. He tried the simplest method first.

"I need your help."

A pained expression crossed her face.

"What's wrong?"

"I have my own problems, Connor. I have a lot to do this week."

"Like what?"

She chewed on her lower lip for a moment, then blew on her tea to cool it and took a sip.

He sipped his tea as well, waiting for her to share whatever was troubling her.

"It doesn't really matter," she said at last. "I just can't come."

"Would it help if I told you I'm desperate?"

"Brooke and Sawyer are wonderful kids. They'll adjust."

He sighed heavily. "How long is that going to take?"

"Honestly, they're going to be fine. You'll all be fine."

"So you say. Won't you join us tomorrow?"

"I can't!"

She sounded agitated, but he wasn't ready to give up. "If something had happened to me, you would have helped Molly."

To his dismay, she burst into tears.

He stood and reached out to wrap his arms around her to comfort her, but she lurched from the stool and took several steps away from him. He stuck his hands in the back pockets of his jeans to make it clear he wasn't going to touch her.

Connor regretted bringing Molly into the conversation. His dead wife was a constant specter that disturbed his waking days and haunted his dreaming nights, but he hadn't realized how upset it would make Eve to bring up her name. His heart still ached whenever he thought of his wife. "I miss her, too."

Eve swiped at the tears on her cheeks with the backs of her hands. "I'm so sorry, Connor."

"For what?" He'd been too far out of it to hear most of what was said to him around the time of

Molly's funeral, but as far as he knew, Eve hadn't been involved in Molly's accident.

"I wasn't in the mood to sit through a horror movie that night, so I offered to babysit instead. If only I'd gone with her, we would have been in my truck, which had better traction than her car."

"It wasn't your fault." It wasn't anybody's fault, really. It was simply a freak accident. Molly had hit some black ice on the way home and slammed into a tree. She must have turned her head the wrong way, or maybe it was her short stature. In any event, the air bag broke her neck.

If anyone was to blame, it was him. He should have been home with his wife. He would have been happy to see a horror movie with Molly. She loved being scared when he was there to cling to both during the movie and afterward.

Connor missed his wife. He missed their life together, which had been cut so disastrously short. He regretted the choice he'd made to leave his family for a third time, but there was no way to take it back.

"I just wish . . ." Eve left the sentence hanging, and he wondered what she'd been about to say.

"Wishing can't change the past," he said. "Molly is gone and I'm alone with my kids, who have no memory of the times we spent laughing and playing together when they were babies. They don't understand why their mother had to go to heaven or what role their father is supposed to play in their lives."

"I can't help you, Connor," she said firmly. "I have things I have to do."

He gave her a smile intended to charm and then felt guilty for trying to charm his dead wife's best friend into playing mother to his kids. That thought lasted until he remembered his crying children, at which point he said, "The kids would feel a lot better with you around."

"That's not fair!" she snapped. "I told you, I've got problems of my own. I can't be babysitting your kids."

He could tell she was angry, but he didn't know what he'd said, exactly, to make her so mad. "Fine. You've got problems. Have a seat. Let's talk. Maybe I can help."

She eyed the stool she'd vacated. "I doubt it."

"It can't hurt. Besides, you haven't finished your tea."

She sat again, but he could feel her putting up a wall between them. He wondered if she could tell that he still felt the same mesmerizing attraction to her now that had struck him the first day he'd seen her standing by her high school locker. Maybe she could. Maybe that was why she wanted to keep her distance.

She perched on the edge of the stool with her back to the kitchen and stared into the fire, her mug in both hands.

Connor sat down beside her and waited for her to speak.

She chewed on her lower lip. And said nothing.

At last he said, "Does your problem have anything to do with a certain missing black sheep returned to the fold?"

She made a disgusted sound. "Of course it does."

"What's Matt done this time?"

"I have a week to get my herd of wild mustangs off the ranch."

"A week? I thought you said you had a year to find a place to graze them."

She turned to him, her blue eyes fierce. "Matt might not own Kingdom Come yet, but my father gave him the power to decide how the land is used from day one. Matt intends to run quarter horses on the pasture where I've been keeping my mustangs. He's demanded I move them by the end of the week."

"Can't King help you out?"

"That isn't an option."

Eve didn't explain, and he saw from the way her jaw was clamped tight that she didn't want to talk about it.

Connor realized he must have been thinking about a solution to her problem even before the situation turned into a crisis. He took a deep breath and said, "I might know a way to fix things."

"I'm desperate," she admitted. "What have you got in mind?"

"Bring your mustangs here."

She looked surprised but intrigued.

"There's plenty of land for them to roam. If you like, we could even plant some hay for winter feed."

She stared at him with wide, hopeful eyes. "You'd do that for me?"

"I'd want something in return."

She frowned. "Like what?"

The idea had been forming in his mind ever since his kids starting crying. He made the request without thinking twice about the problems it might create between his father and hers, between their siblings, or between the two of them, for that matter. "What would you think about coming to live at Safe Haven?"

"Not much."

He put a hand on her arm to keep her from sliding off her stool. "Hear me out. You need a place for your mustangs. I need someone to help me ease Brooke and Sawyer through this difficult period of adjustment. You get what you need. I get what I need."

She looked a lot more anxious than excited about the idea, which meant she knew as well as he did the ramifications of such a decision. "You mentioned keeping my horses over the winter. How long are you suggesting I hang out here?"

"Just a month or two, until Brooke and Sawyer get to know me again. The kids know you and trust you. Hell, they love you. As sad as it makes me to say it, my kids don't remember what it was like to have me as a father. Tonight was a pretty big wake-up call. I'm drowning here, Eve. I need help. And where my kids are concerned, I'm not too proud to ask for it."

"I'd be glad to come here whenever you call."

He was already shaking his head before she was halfway through her sentence. "That won't work."

"Give me one reason why not?"

"It takes you an hour to get here."

Eve made a face, conceding the difficulty of driving back and forth to Connor's ranch every day or even every two or three days.

"Besides," he continued, "the kids have to know that the adults in their life will be there for them. That means morning, noon, and night. They need you—I need you—here."

"They've got you."

"I'm not enough. Not yet."

"And you think in a month or two you will be?"

He grinned, showing a confident face, hiding his fear that she would leave him high and dry. "I do."

Her blue eyes looked bleak. "I feel trapped. If I had anywhere else to turn, I wouldn't consider it."

"I guess it's lucky for me you don't."

"You realize this is blackmail."

"It isn't blackmail if both of us get something out of it."

He held his breath as she pursed her lips and shook her head. She was going to refuse.

"You'd have your own room," he blurted.

She laughed. "That's a comfort. I'm glad I won't have to share a bed with the kids. Or with you."

The instant she said it, the smile froze on her face.

Connor spoke quickly to defuse the sudden sexual tension. The last thing he wanted her to do was refuse because she thought he would hit on her. "I told you before, Eve. What happened between us at the hotel won't happen again. Our relationship will remain purely platonic."

He hoped his kids appreciated the sacrifice he was making. For their sake, he was going to keep his hands off Eve Grayhawk the whole time she was living under his roof. It wasn't going to be easy, but sacrifices had to be made.

Eve looked like she needed a shoulder to cry on, but he made no effort to take her in his arms to comfort her. He'd already flirted with disaster once tonight. She'd made it plain she didn't welcome his attentions. Right now, he needed her help with his children more desperately than he needed her long legs wrapped around him in bed.

"All right," Eve said as she rose. "I'll do it. But

only until the kids are comfortable with you. Once they've adjusted, I'm gone." She reached out a hand for him to shake. "Agreed?"

Connor pulled her into his arms—purely platonically—and gave her a hug. "Thank you, Eve." She was taller than Molly and fit him in all the important places. He felt his body responding to the rightness of holding her close and let her go. He tucked his hands in his front jeans pockets to hide the evidence of his rock-hard body and said, "When can you move in?"

Chapter 6

EVE HAD FELT cherished in Connor's embrace. She'd kept her eyes lowered so he wouldn't see the desire she felt, the longing to have him kiss her and touch her and put himself inside her. She fought back the feelings of guilt. Wanting him was no longer sinful. But it wasn't prudent, either. The chances were good that she would get her heart broken if she hoped for more than friendship.

At the exact moment she realized that Connor had become aroused, he'd stepped away from her, leaving her feeling bereft. His actions made it abundantly clear that, even if he was attracted to her, he intended to do nothing about it.

"Why don't you go home, pack whatever you need, and spend the night here?" Connor suggested. "I'm sure the kids would feel better if they found you here in the morning when they wake up."

The worry in his eyes prompted her to say, "All right."

"I really appreciate this. You'll never know how much."

Remembering how relieved and happy Connor had looked when she'd agreed to return kept Eve from changing her mind about the whole thing on the long drive home, even though there were a lot of reasons why what she was about to do wasn't a good idea. Why, oh, why had she agreed to live in Connor's house? How was she going to keep her feelings secret when they were sleeping under the same roof?

By the time Eve pulled up to the back porch at Kingdom Come, her mind was racing with all the things that could go wrong. The situation she'd put herself in was a disaster waiting to happen. She reached for her cell phone to call Connor and tell him she couldn't do it. Then she remembered Brooke's and Sawyer's woeful faces, and Connor's fearful eyes, and realized that she couldn't abandon any of them.

Connor wasn't a bad father. He was simply inexperienced and overwhelmed. If she spent time at Safe Haven she could help him discover what he needed to know and give the kids time to learn to love him again. She'd hidden her love for Connor a very long time. She could hide it a little while longer.

Besides, Connor had offered Safe Haven as a sanctuary for her mustangs, and she saw no other way of saving them. She wasn't entirely sure that offer would remain open if she backed out of helping him with his kids. She was over a barrel. Out of options. Up the creek without a paddle. Stuck.

When Eve stepped into the kitchen she could feel the tension arcing as dangerously as a live wire among her three sisters. Leah was leaning back against the sink, arms crossed. Taylor stood at the end of the breakfast bar, fisted hands at her sides. Victoria sat perched on the edge of a bar stool, her back stiff.

"What's going on?" Eve asked as she moved toward an empty seat at the bar.

"Just a small difference of opinion," Leah said through tight jaws.

"About what?" Eve asked, looking from face to tight-lipped face. "Let me guess. It has something to do with Matt."

"Bingo!" Victoria said.

"I flew Daddy's jet to Texas with Vick," Taylor said. "We were hoping at least one of Matt's siblings could tell us why he left home twenty years ago." Taylor had gotten her pilot's license as early as the law allowed. She worked as a pilot for whoever would hire her, everything from crop-dusting to dumping fire retardant on forest fires to corporate flights around the world. She often flew King's jet for him when his regular pilot was on vacation.

"What did Libby and North have to say?" Eve asked.

"Nothing! Not a damned thing," Victoria said. "That mangy dingo is still a complete mystery."

"So what's the problem here?" Eve asked, her gaze skipping from Taylor's balled fists to Victoria's tensed shoulders to Leah's crossed arms.

Taylor's eyes narrowed. "Leah wants us to leave Matt alone. She says Daddy's working on a way to fix things so we have a place to go, and we should wait and see how that works out before we turn our guns on Matt."

Eve slid onto the bar stool next to Victoria. "You should listen to her." She pursed her lips wryly. "Daddy might not be able to get you off if you actually end up shooting him."

"This is no time for jokes!" Taylor snapped, turning to confront Eve. "I want that bossy, high-handed, disgustingly self-satisfied intruder gone. I was hoping we could discover what made Matt take off in the first place and use that information to force him to leave again. Libby said she was gone from Kingdom Come a couple of years before Matt disappeared, and she has no idea what happened. North told us to go home and mind our own business."

"Maybe because he doesn't know anything," Eve surmised.

"Taylor thinks he's hiding something," Victoria said.

"I just wish we had a clue *why* he left," Taylor said, frustration rife in her voice.

"King did something to him," Leah said in a quiet voice. "Something terrible."

All eyes turned to Leah for an explanation of her pronouncement.

"How do you know that?" Taylor asked.

"You know how close King came to dying last year," Leah replied. "He's lucky to be alive. Every other word out of his mouth lately has something to do with making amends. I think that's what bringing this wayward son back is all about. Making peace with Matt while he still has the chance to do it."

"Is the cancer back?" Victoria asked, her eyes bleak.

"As far as I know, he's still cancer-free."

Victoria's question made Eve realize that, however much they all might condemn their father for what he was doing, they still loved him. Maybe too much. Certainly more than he deserved, after the way he'd abandoned them most of their lives. This latest betrayal shouldn't have surprised them as much as it had. Maybe it was the enormity of it, the sheer unexpectedness of it. Whatever his reasons, Eve was as aggrieved as her sisters over their father's treatment of them.

"I'm asking you to be patient," Leah said. "King says he has some big deal in the works, but it isn't progressing as fast as he'd hoped."

"When is this magic bean supposed to grow into a beanstalk?" Taylor demanded.

Leah shrugged. "I don't know."

"What kind of investment are we talking about?" Victoria asked. It wasn't a casual question. Victoria was a day trader online and followed the stock and foreign markets closely. Apparently she was good enough at it to make a comfortable living, because during the summer she volunteered as a smoke jumper and was off fighting forest fires all over the country.

"I don't know," Leah admitted. "He wouldn't tell me that."

"We're just supposed to trust that everything will turn out all right?" Taylor said.

"It always has in the past," Leah said.

"Vick and I don't intend to leave things to chance," Taylor retorted.

"Meaning what?" Leah asked.

"We're going to do whatever it takes to get Matt to go back where he came from."

"I think that's a mistake," Leah argued.

"Not the way we see it," Taylor shot back.

"What, exactly, do you have planned?" Eve asked her sisters.

Before either of them could answer, Leah said, "They won't tell me." She met Taylor's and Victoria's gazes in turn and added, "But I'm sure it's something they'll regret once it's done."

"He deserves whatever he gets," Victoria said sullenly.

"What about his kids?" Leah asked. "Do they deserve to be hurt, too?"

Victoria lowered her gaze to her hands. Taylor stared defiantly at Leah, then surprised Eve by turning to her and demanding, "Are you with us? Or not?"

"I'm moving out tonight."

Eve hadn't meant to blurt it out like that, but she didn't want her sisters thinking she didn't support them, even though she wasn't sure she would have.

Leah unfolded her arms and stood bolt upright. "What?"

"It's not that I wouldn't like to help you," she said to Taylor. "But Matt gave me a week to get my mustangs off the ranch." She turned to Leah and said, "I don't have time to wait for Daddy's deal to go through, so I've made other plans."

"What plans?" Victoria asked, coming off her bar stool.

Eve realized she should have kept her mouth shut. She should have said she'd go along and let her sisters figure out later that she wasn't going to be there to help them in whatever perfidy they intended. Now she was left with no choice except to admit what she'd done.

"I made a deal with Connor Flynn. I'm moving in with him to help him take care of his kids in exchange for him keeping my mustangs at his ranch."

Leah's face bleached white. "You're moving in with Angus Flynn at the Lucky 7?"

"God, no! I'm moving to Connor's ranch, Safe Haven. It's an old dude ranch he's converted into a refuge for veterans. I'll have—"

"Are you out of your mind?" Taylor interrupted. "What on earth were you thinking to agree to such a thing?"

"I was thinking I need to save my mustangs," Eve said. "And I was thinking Brooke and Sawyer Flynn need someone to reassure them that everything will be all right while Connor learns to be their father again."

"Do you have to *live* there?" Victoria asked, apparently aghast at the thought.

"It's an hour back and forth to town. Staying there makes the most sense."

"What does King think about this arrangement?" Leah asked.

"He put me in this predicament," Eve replied. "He has no right to say what I can or can't do to get myself out of it."

"How about Angus? What does he think of this plan?" Taylor asked.

"I have no idea, and I don't care. Connor and I are adults. We can do as we like."

"Except you're a Grayhawk, and Connor's a Flynn," Leah reminded her.

"So what?"

Taylor and Victoria both laughed, but with scorn and derision rather than amusement.

"You really think you can just move in with Connor Flynn and none of his brothers is going to say a word about it?" Taylor asked.

"Why not?"

"How naïve can you be, Eve?" Leah said. "This is a terrible idea. It could end very badly."

"Nothing could be as bad as watching my herd of mustangs go to slaughter." Eve met the concerned and confused gazes of her sisters. "Besides, I can't abandon Molly's children."

"Do you hear yourself?" Victoria asked. "They're *Molly's* children, Eve. Not yours. They'll manage fine without you."

"*Fine* isn't good enough," Eve shot back. "I love Brooke and Sawyer. I can't stand for them to be unhappy. Right now they need me. I'm going to be there for them, even if it means spending the next two months living under the same roof as Connor Flynn."

Eve didn't wait for one of her sisters to come up with another argument against going to Safe Haven. She marched out of the kitchen with her head held high.

She heard Taylor calling after her, "You'll be sorry!"

Eve's throat felt thick and it hurt to swallow. Once she was out of sight she ran down the long hall toward the stairs, fighting tears all the way. She hadn't realized until it wasn't there how much she'd hoped for her sisters' support.

Eve heard raised voices—Pippa and her father arguing—as she approached the grand staircase and stopped abruptly in the shadows so they wouldn't see her tears.

"Lower your voice," Matt hissed. "Do you want the whole house to hear?"

Pippa's lowered voice was still so intense that Eve had no trouble making out her next words.

"I hate it here. I want to go home!"

"You know why you can't do that."

"It's not as though I've committed some heinous crime. I'm just pregnant!"

"With a married man's child," Matt snarled back.

"I loved him," she said in an achingly sad voice. "When I ran away with him, I didn't know he was married. He lied to me."

"The gossip would never have died in that back-water town. You'd have been a pariah the rest of your life. You know I'm right. It's why you came with me to America, even if you came kicking and screaming the whole way."

Pippa's silence confirmed the truth of Matt's words.

"You can start over here," Matt continued.

"And do what?"

"Whatever you want. You can give up the baby for adoption and—"

"Stop right there. Is that what you thought? That I'd give up the baby so no one would ever know what a sinner I am? Think again! I'm having this baby. And I'm keeping it!"

"Pippa, you don't know what you're—"

Eve heard pounding footsteps and realized Matt's daughter hadn't stayed to argue. She'd run from the Great Room toward the north wing of the house. Eve remained in the shadows, hoping that Matt would follow his daughter rather than head down the hall toward the kitchen. Otherwise, she was liable to get caught. When he headed the opposite direction, she breathed a sigh of relief.

Eve's tears had dried. Now she knew why a twenty-year-old woman had followed her father halfway across the world. Pippa had problems as great as—or maybe greater than—her own. She felt an unwilling spurt of sympathy for the girl.

Eve glanced toward the kitchen, where her sisters were busy plotting against Matt, wondering if she should reveal at least one of his reasons for coming to Wyoming, and realized she couldn't do that to Pippa. The girl was entitled to keep her secret, at least until it became impossible to hide.

When Eve was sure Matt was gone, she ran up the stairs to her bedroom and threw herself onto her bed, hugging her pillow to her chest. Pippa's problem had put her own situation in perspective. No life was perfect. There were always bumps in the road. The challenge was whether—and how—you decided to get past them.

She wasn't doing this for Connor. She was doing it for Molly's kids. And no one and nothing was going to stop her. Eve swiped at her teary eyes, got out of bed, and began packing. She was halfway done when she heard a knock on her bedroom door.

"Who is it?"

"It's me."

"Go away, Leah."

"We need to talk."

Eve surveyed the open suitcase on her bed and the clothes strewn around the room, which testified to her intention to leave, then called back, "You're not going to change my mind."

"May I come in?"

Leah had always been there when Eve was in trouble. Not that she was in trouble, exactly. But she was about to embark on what could only be considered a fool's errand. Nothing Leah said was going to change her mind so she might as well let her sister dispense her sage advice. She picked up a pair of jeans she intended to pack and said, "Come in."

Leah glanced at Eve as she took a few steps toward Eve's cluttered bed. "You seem to be packing quite a bit of stuff."

"I want to make sure I have everything I need."

"Give me a day to talk to Matt," Leah began. "Maybe I can get him to change his mind about keeping your mustangs here at Kingdom Come."

"Don't waste your breath asking for favors. Matt's every bit as ruthless as Daddy."

Leah threaded her fingers together, something Eve knew she did to keep from fidgeting when she was anxious. She met Eve's gaze with troubled eyes and said, "You can't move in with Connor Flynn."

"Who's going to stop me?" Eve waited for the scalding diatribe she knew was coming. If King was rabid on the subject of Flynns, Leah was worse. Eve wasn't sure what the Flynns had done to Leah, personally, to make her hate them. But someone had done something sometime, because Leah was militant about keeping her sisters away from them.

But Leah didn't go after the Flynns. She took a completely different tack. She set her balled hands on her hips and said, "King is going to have ten fits when he finds out about this."

"Daddy's made it clear he can't help me. Connor Flynn can."

"You know King would if he could."

"I know no such thing," Eve retorted. "Now, if Matt were the one in trouble, I have no doubt Daddy would figure out a way to loan him whatever he needed."

"King doesn't have the money!" As soon as the words were out of Leah's mouth, she clapped her hands over it.

Eve sank onto the bed. "You just got through telling Taylor and Vick that Daddy's got something financial in the works. Are you saying now that he doesn't?"

"What King told me wasn't meant to be shared. Just know, a great deal is at risk. For all of us. And for heaven's sake, don't say anything about this to King."

Eve's mouth twisted wryly. "I won't be around to say anything to him. I'm moving in with Connor Flynn tonight."

"Does it have to be tonight?"

"The light of day isn't going to change my mind." Eve rose and began packing again.

"Is there something romantic going on between you two?" Leah asked, a furrow of worry between her brows.

"What in the world gave you that idea?" Eve snapped.

"I have eyes, don't I? I watched you yearn for somebody else's husband all the years Connor and Molly were married."

Well. That was plain speaking. Eve flushed. "There's no great romance in the offing. Whatever I feel—or felt—doesn't matter. Connor doesn't think of me like that." To her great regret. "I'm staying there strictly to help him with his kids."

"Where will you sleep?"

"He's got an extra bedroom in the house."

"Watch yourself, Eve. You can't trust a Flynn. Give him a chance and Connor will steal your heart, then lie to you and let you down."

"Connor wouldn't do that."

"He was raised a Flynn. They're rotten, root to branch."

"Just for the record, I think you're wrong. At least about Connor. I've known him a long time, and he's not like that."

"They're all like that," Leah said flatly.

"Which one of them hurt you?"

Leah's face blanched.

"Aiden? Brian? Devon?" Eve watched for some reaction, but she didn't get it. Leah's features remained as frozen as chiseled stone. "Surely not Connor," she said, horrified.

"No, not Connor. Just believe me when I say that the Flynn brothers are trouble. Keep your distance. Protect your heart. Don't give one a chance to disappoint you, and you won't end up disappointed."

Eve stared at her eldest sister. She'd had no idea Leah had been hurt so badly by one of Angus Flynn's sons. Leah had always seemed so strong and indomitable. When had she given one of them her heart? And why had he broken it? Eve wanted to offer comfort, but Leah had erected an emotional barricade around herself that she'd never known how to breach. She settled for saying, "I'm sorry you got hurt, Leah."

Leah stiffened.

Eve wasn't sure whether her older sister appreciated the sympathy or was appalled at having revealed so much of her very private life. Eve closed her suitcase and zipped it up, then set the roller bag on the floor. "I'm out of here. I don't envy you having to deal with Matt every day. Where do you think you'll go when you have to leave?"

"I'm not leaving."

That statement, made with such certainty, flummoxed Eve. "How are you going to manage that?"

A look Eve had seen many times appeared on her sister's face. "I don't know yet. But this is my home. By hook or by crook, I'm staying right here."

Eve grinned. "I do believe Matt Grayhawk has met his match."

Leah shuddered. "Heaven forbid."

Eve laughed. "I didn't mean it that way. I just meant—"

"I know what you meant."

When Leah opened her arms, Eve stepped close enough to receive the hug that had meant love and comfort and safety all her life.

Leah was always there. Always reliable. Always available. It was good to know there would always be one person who would stand by her through thick and thin.

"I'll miss you," Leah said as she let Eve go. "Call if you need anything. I'll be right here." Her chin lifted as she added, "I'm not going anywhere."

A bubble of laughter escaped Eve at the image of Leah digging in her claws like a cat caught in the curtains and refusing to leave. "I shouldn't laugh. It isn't funny. But it is. I guess Daddy didn't figure on you when he gave Matt the ranch."

"Be careful," Leah whispered as Eve headed out the door, trailing her suitcase behind her.

"You, too," Eve shot back over her shoulder.

Chapter 7

EVE AWOKE WITH a start when she turned over and encountered a warm body in bed with her. She'd been dreaming of Connor kissing and caressing her and half expected to find him there. She sat up, her eyes full of sleep, her hair a mass of rats' nests, and smiled ruefully as she surveyed the two small forms on either side of her. Not Connor, but Connor's children. Sometime during the night Brooke and Sawyer had found their way into her bedroom at Safe Haven and into her bed.

Eve slowly pulled her knees up, looped her arms around them, then settled her chin on her knees to watch the two sleeping children with wonder. Brooke was lying on her back, her hair a spray of chestnut on the pillow, her arms splayed above her on either side of her head. Sawyer was tucked into a ball on his stomach, his arms curled under him. She'd always loved Molly and Connor's children, always been fascinated by their enthusiasm for life, always been amazed by their curiosity, and always been humbled by their willingness to love without limits. Surely it wouldn't take long for Connor to win their trust again. Which meant she wouldn't be here long enough to lose the battle with her good sense, which warned her to keep her distance from the children's father.

Eve's gaze was focused on Brooke and Sawyer, so she wasn't sure how she knew she was no longer alone. When she looked up she found Connor standing in the open doorway. His gaze wasn't directed toward his children. It was aimed at her.

"Good morning," he said in a husky voice.

He was bare-chested, exposing every ridge in a six-pack belly and the powerful curve of his impressive biceps. She saw several long, ridged scars running through the dark hair on his chest, which she presumed were injuries from the same improvised explosive device that had caused the wound on his forehead. The first two buttons of his jeans were undone so they hung low, exposing his hipbones and a line of down that began at his navel and disappeared into the worn denim. Her gaze traveled all the way down his long legs to his bare feet and then back up again.

She had to clear her throat to reply, "Good morning."

Eve hugged her knees tighter to her chest, aware that the white T-shirt she'd worn to bed was thin enough to see through and that all she had on beneath it was a pair of pink bikini underwear.

"I was worried when I didn't find the kids in Brooke's bed," he said quietly. "I thought you might be able to help me find them."

Eve felt her heart jump when Connor's eyes remained locked on hers. She realized now that being in Connor's home was fraught with a great many unexpected pitfalls, like being caught half dressed in bed by a half-dressed man you secretly loved. She felt her nipples peak as her body responded to the avid look in Connor's eyes. She tore her gaze away and concentrated it on the children. They were the reason she was here. The *only* reason she was here.

"They look like sleeping angels," she said.

Brooke suddenly opened her eyes and spotted her father. At first she didn't move. Then she subtly but surely inched herself closer to Eve, wrapping one of her tiny hands around Eve's ankle.

"Good morning, sweet pea," Connor said to his daughter, his voice gruff with emotion.

Eve watched him stuff his hands in the back pockets of his Levi's and figured he'd done it to keep himself from reaching for his daughter. Unfortunately for Eve, the move also outlined the hardened shaft behind his zipper. Eve was amazed at how little it had taken for him to become aroused. On the other hand, it hadn't taken more than a look from him for the same thing to happen to her. Except she *loved* him. He only *liked* her. His reaction was merely a physiological male response to a half-naked female. It could have been any female. It just happened to be her.

She heard Leah's admonition in her head. *Be careful.*

What if the children hadn't been here? Would he have acted on his attraction? Would she have acted on hers?

Connor had already admitted he wasn't heart-whole, that he was still mourning Molly. Was she willing to accept the little bit of himself that he had to offer?

Yes. I want him. I love him.

She had the awful feeling that a single look would

have been all he needed to have her flat on her back the instant they were alone. Pride kept her from giving Connor any encouragement.

As Brooke sat up, Eve brushed the little girl's bangs away from her face and said, "I was surprised to find you here this morning."

"Me and Sawyer woke up and wanted to go home. We were looking for a phone to call Nana and Bampa when we found you."

Eve saw Connor wince at his daughter's explanation.

"I'm glad you found me," Eve said.

"Are you gonna stay with us forever?" Brooke asked.

Eve glanced at Connor. "I'm here for as long as you need me." *And not one second longer.*

Sawyer rolled over onto his back, his feet flopping. He scrubbed at his eyes, then sat up and asked his father, "Can I have pancakes for breakfast?"

The matter-of-fact statement made it clear Sawyer's hunger came a long way ahead of anything else. Eve and Connor smiled at each other before he answered, "Sure."

"How about you, Brooke?" Eve said. "Pancakes?"

"With blueberries?" Brooke asked.

"We don't have any blueberries," Connor said. He hurried to add, "But I'll get some for next time."

Brooke scrambled toward the edge of the bed. "Come on, Sawyer. Let's go get dressed."

Sawyer scuttled after her on all fours.

"I'll come help," Connor said.

Brooke stopped short. "I want Aunt Eve to help."

If she'd been dressed in decent pajamas, Eve would

have gotten out of bed and followed the little girl to her room. But she wasn't about to stick so much as a naked toe out from under the covers while Connor was standing there watching. "I need to get dressed first."

She should have known better than to try reasoning with a four-year-old.

Brooke stomped her foot. "No. Come now."

Sawyer tried stomping his foot but stumbled sideways instead. He ended up clapping his hands. "Come now!"

Eve realized her modesty was going to have to suffer. She shoved the sheet aside and heard Connor's soft gasp as she threw her bare legs out from under the covers. She had a warm robe, but she hadn't unpacked it last night. She hadn't unpacked much of anything, which was why she'd gone to bed in a T-shirt. She reached for her jeans, which she'd left in a pile on the floor, stepped into them, and pulled them on, aware that Connor was standing frozen on the other side of the room.

When she stood upright, she saw his gaze fall to her chest, where her areolas were clearly visible through the thin cotton. Eve felt a hot flush working its way up her throat. She didn't bother trying to find her socks and boots, just ran to the doorway, grabbed one hand of each child, and hurried them across the hall toward their bedrooms.

Over her shoulder she said, "Why don't you get those pancakes started?"

Eve sent the two washed and dressed children to the kitchen ahead of her, telling them to help their father set the table while she got dressed. When she arrived in the kitchen ten minutes later, she found Connor dressed, the stove cold, the table not set, and both children sitting on stools at the breakfast bar with half-filled glasses of orange juice in front of them.

She stopped short. "What happened to breakfast?"

"I don't have any food in the house," Connor admitted sheepishly. "I didn't count on having to cook. I figured the kids and I could eat at the Main Lodge with everyone else."

Eve realized that was the sort of decision a man without a wife might make. But she was here now. There was nothing she could do this morning, but she was going to have a talk with Connor about how a family sat down to breakfast.

They put on jackets and took the short walk along a stone sidewalk to the Main Lodge, a log building where breakfast was being served to guests at the ranch. Connor held the door open as the two children skipped inside. Eve felt the heat of his hand when he laid it on the small of her back as they entered and walked more quickly to separate herself from his touch.

Distance, she told herself. *Keep your distance.*

She was amazed at the bustle in the dining room. At least two dozen men, some dressed like cowhands, some wearing military desert camouflage, sat on benches on either side of long tables.

A Native American with dark, lively eyes and black braids, wearing a cook's apron over a Pink concert T-shirt and a pair of jeans, was setting a large bowl of scrambled eggs on a table where a half dozen men sat with plates full of every imaginable breakfast food. No wonder Connor had wanted to come here to eat.

A huge log burned in the river-rock fireplace, which stood as tall as a man's shoulder, the chimney climbing all the way to the top of the cathedral ceiling. An enormous buffalo head, scruffy enough to have been there for seventy years, had been mounted above the fireplace, and a newer-looking buffalo hide lay on the stone floor in front of the flickering fire.

An exquisite Navajo rug hung from one log wall, while a Sioux war shirt made of buckskin and beads hung on another. The chandelier above them was made of moose antlers. A window the width of one wall revealed a breathtaking view of a vast evergreen forest that began in the valley and spread across a faraway ridge.

Eve supposed that what had been a place for tourists who wanted to experience a taste of the American West must seem like glamorous fare for a bunch of soldiers used to dining in a mess hall. She observed the smiles and easy camaraderie of the men eating breakfast—and then became aware of the prosthetic arms and legs and the burn scars. One of the vets smiled and held out his arms to Sawyer, who ran right up to him. The soldier lifted Sawyer far above his head, where the little boy gurgled with excitement.

"Good morning, Pete," Connor said. "I see you've met my son, Sawyer."

"Looks just like you," Pete said as he handed the boy to Connor.

Eve heard the pride in Connor's voice as he replied, "My wife always said so."

Brooke hung back by Eve's side, apparently shy

of so many strangers. Eve led her to a table where she saw two booster chairs, obviously intended for Connor's kids, clamped to one of the benches. Two men were sitting on the opposite side of the table.

"Hello," Eve said, smiling at the men to show Brooke there was nothing to be afraid of. "I'm Eve." She lifted Brooke into one of the booster chairs as she added, "This is Connor's daughter, Brooke." She sat herself to the right of Brooke, leaving the space between the kids' chairs for Connor.

One of the soldiers smiled back, the other kept his gaze on his food. "I'm Frank," the smiling man said. He pointed with his fork at the other man. "This is Jeff. He doesn't talk much."

Jeff's face had been ravaged by fire. Before Eve could reply, Connor arrived at the table with Sawyer in his arms. He put Sawyer in the empty booster chair and slid into the space between the two kids.

The woman who'd been doing the serving arrived at the table with silverware and plates. "I'm Maria Two Horses," she said to Eve with a smile of welcome. "Connor's probably already told you, it's every man for himself." She set down a stack of plates and a handful of silverware, then added, "Napkins and condiments are on the table." Then she was gone again as someone at another table called for more eggs.

The same large variety of food that Eve had seen on the men's plates sat in serving bowls and platters in the center of their table, including pancakes.

"Do you still want pancakes, Brooke?" she asked.

"Uh-huh," Brooke said. "With lots and lots of syrup."

Frank winked at Eve and said, "You're a sight for sore eyes."

Eve shot a glance in Connor's direction, but he was busy cutting Sawyer's pancakes into bite-size pieces.

"Thank you," she said, feeling an unwanted blush rise on her cheeks.

"Leave her alone," Jeff said. "She's Connor's girl."

"I'm not—"

"I was just paying the lady a compliment," Frank said.

"And I said shut your mouth."

Eve had grown up in a houseful of women, so she wasn't sure whether those were "fighting words" or just a case of "guys being guys." She glanced at Connor and saw he was calmly eating a forkful of eggs.

He swallowed his eggs and said, "She isn't my girl, Jeff. She's just a friend who's here for a while to help me take care of my kids. Frank wasn't trying to steal her away."

Jeff rose, taking his plate and silverware with him. He nodded in Eve's direction. "Sorry, ma'am."

"You don't have to leave," she said as he headed away.

"Let him go," Connor said. "He came home and found out his girl had left him for another guy. And that was before she saw his face."

"Oh," Eve said. So there were wounds, and there were *emotional* wounds. Maybe the rosy picture she'd seen when she'd entered the lodge wasn't the whole story. She supposed there must be some reason that each of these men had decided to escape from the world for a little while.

Frank got up a moment later, touched the brim of his Stetson in acknowledgment, then picked up his plate and silverware. "Sorry for the ruckus, ma'am."

"Eve," she said.

He grinned with a great deal of charm. "Okay, Eve." Before he left, he asked Connor, "Where do you want me today?"

"We'll be moving a bunch of wild mustangs onto the south pasture later this afternoon. Why don't you check the fence and make sure it's not down anywhere?"

"Where did you come up with a herd of mustangs?" Frank asked.

"They're mine," Eve said.

Frank lifted a brow. "Are any broken to saddle?"

Eve shook her head. "Not yet."

Frank turned to Connor. "Working with those mustangs might be a good project for the men."

"That's up to Eve. They're her horses."

Eve would have loved having the mustangs broken to saddle so they could be adopted out to good homes, but she was one person and there were twenty-two horses, some of which were still too young to be ridden. She'd never imagined having a bunch of veterans working with them, but it seemed like a good idea. Especially if they knew what they were doing, or at least were supervised by someone who knew what he was doing.

She studied Frank, who was dressed in jeans and western boots. "Do you have any experience breaking horses?"

"Yes, ma'am. I mean, Eve. I grew up on a ranch

in Montana. I'm not any kind of horse whisperer, but I know my way around a horse."

Eve liked the look of the man, and the fact that he'd sounded confident without bragging, but she also wanted to make sure her animals were safe. "Would you mind if I work with you at first?"

Frank grinned. "I'd like that just fine."

Eve turned back in time to see a funny look cross Connor's face. Her gaze shifted to a middle-aged woman headed straight toward them. She looked out of place dressed in a tailored gray pantsuit with a feminine bow hanging down the front of her powder-blue blouse. When the woman stopped behind Connor, Eve smiled at her and said, "I'm Eve. I don't think we've met."

"No, I don't believe we have," the matronly woman said.

The moment she spoke, Connor whipped around, lifting his feet over the bench and nearly bumping into the woman, who took a quick step to the side. He rose and steadied her as he gathered Sawyer up like a sack of clothes under his arm. "Mrs. Stack. I wasn't expecting you."

"Obviously. Otherwise, you would have made it clear to me where you were going to be. I had to find out from your father that you're not living either in the home you shared with your wife nor at the ranch with your father, that you've taken your children to live somewhere else entirely. Somewhere I've never seen. Somewhere I haven't vetted."

The visitor was obviously trying to control her temper, but not doing a very good job of it. It only took Eve a moment to figure out who she was. The social worker. One of the conditions of Connor's custody of his children was that he would be subject to visits from a social worker who would monitor the children's welfare, at least for a while. It seemed Connor had gotten off on the wrong foot with Mrs. Stack.

"I didn't think it would matter where the children and I lived, so long as it was similar to the other two locations," Connor said, keeping his voice even.

"Are you going to continue to hold that child upside down?" she asked.

Connor shifted the two-year-old so he was upright. From the smile on Sawyer's face, he hadn't minded being held like a football under his father's arm. "My home here has everything the other two homes have," Connor argued.

"And something else they do not," Mrs. Stack said, eyeing the collection of men sitting at tables in the lodge. "Why are your children eating breakfast here instead of in the house? Who are these men?"

"Veterans," Connor said. "Mostly soldiers who've fought in Afghanistan."

Eve saw the alarm on Mrs. Stack's face as she asked, "What are they doing here?"

"Resting and relaxing. And working," he added, when the look on Mrs. Stack's face turned vinegary.

"Working at what?" she asked suspiciously.

"They're going to be taming a band of wild mustangs for me," Eve volunteered.

That answer seemed to satisfy Mrs. Stack. But she didn't let Connor completely off the hook. "I'll want to monitor this situation closely," she said, nodding her chin in the direction of the vets. "And I want to see the children's bedrooms and the rest of the house, immediately."

"Of course," Connor said.

Eve rose. "I'll take care of busing the dishes while you show Mrs. Stack around. Then I'll bring Brooke to the house."

They'd only taken two steps when Mrs. Stack turned back to Eve and asked, "Who are you, exactly?"

"My name is Eve Grayhawk. I'm here to help take care of the children."

"Where are you staying?"

"I have a bedroom in the house."

"Are you married, Ms. Grayhawk?"

Eve couldn't imagine why Mrs. Stack would need that information, but she answered, "No, I'm not."

Mrs. Stack turned to confront Connor. "You have a single, young, *unrelated* woman living in the house with you and your children?"

Connor blurted, "Eve's my fiancée."

Chapter 8

CONNOR HAD NO idea why he'd lied to the social worker. Lots of folks hired a live-in nanny and many of them were young, single women. Mrs. Stack had just seemed so outraged that he'd panicked. He couldn't lose his children, not when he'd just gotten them back. A millisecond after he told the lie, Connor realized he should have said Eve was helping out because she was the children's godmother. Too late now.

"I didn't realize you were engaged," Mrs. Stack said as she looked from Connor to Eve.

Connor glanced sideways at Eve. Would she let the lie stand? If not, would he be in even worse trouble if he had to backtrack and tell Mrs. Stack the truth?

"Connor just proposed," Eve said, embellishing his lie. "I haven't even had time to tell my family yet."

Mrs. Stack raised a brow. "A Grayhawk marrying a Flynn? My, oh, my. Never thought I'd see the day."

Connor felt his heart sink as they put on their jackets and headed back to the house with Mrs. Stack. He should have thought of a better lie. Or just told the truth. The shit was going to hit the fan when their respective families heard the news.

As Mrs. Stack stepped inside the house she took

an appraising look around the open living room and kitchen. Then she walked straight to the refrigerator and opened it.

Connor knew what she would find and rushed to say, "I haven't stocked the refrigerator because I planned to have the children eat at the Main Lodge."

"That will not do, Mr. Flynn. The children need a *home*, where they will eat and sleep. Speaking of which, where are the children's bedrooms?"

"Why don't you show Mrs. Stack where you sleep?" Connor said to his daughter.

"Okay." Brooke ran down the hall toward Eve's bedroom and disappeared inside.

Connor exchanged a look of dismay with Eve as he tried to intercept the social worker. "That's actually Eve's room," he said as he gestured Mrs. Stack in another direction. "These rooms across the hall belong to the children."

"Then why did Brooke go into Ms. Grayhawk's room?"

Connor wasn't sure what to say. What answer did the social worker want to hear? What answer would make her believe he was doing the best he could?

"Brooke and Sawyer ended up in my bed during the night," Eve said with a smile that made it seem the most natural thing in the world for his children to abandon their beds for hers.

"Besides being Connor's fiancée, I'm also the children's godmother. Connor's wife and I were best friends. Brooke and Sawyer know me well and came to my room when they woke up in an unfamiliar house."

Mrs. Stack turned to Eve and asked, "Why haven't I met you before now?"

"I'm a wildlife photographer, and I've been away fulfilling an assignment for *National Geographic*."

Mrs. Stack's narrow-eyed gaze shifted from Eve to Connor and back again. "And yet, a year after your best friend's death you're engaged to her husband?"

Eve ignored the inference of wrongdoing in Mrs. Stack's question. "I love the children, and they need a mother."

Connor realized there was nothing in Eve's statement about loving *him*. Nevertheless, Mrs. Stack seemed satisfied with her answer. Which made no sense to Connor. Wouldn't a marriage based on love be more stable? Then he thought of his brother Brian, who'd been desperately in love with his wife when they'd married. She'd cheated on him and then divorced him to be with her lover. Apparently, romantic love was no guarantee of forever after.

Connor shot a considering look in Eve's direction. He wondered if she would seriously consider the sort of practical marital arrangement she'd described to the social worker. With his myriad responsibilities at Safe Haven, he wasn't going to have many opportunities to meet a potential wife. A make-believe marriage, something to appease the social worker, might not be a bad idea.

He was in no hurry to fall in love again. He missed the closeness he'd had with his wife, but he knew that finding someone as special as Molly wouldn't be easy. Brian's marriage was proof of that, if he needed it. He was also aware that if Molly had lived they might have ended up at odds. He believed his sanctuary for veterans needed the isolation of a place like Safe Haven. Molly had yearned to live in a more metropolitan area. He had no idea how they would have resolved such a potentially devastating conflict. Better to find someone, like Eve, who knew going in what he planned.

Connor wouldn't have gambled a dime on his chances of convincing Eve to agree to a marriage of convenience before Matt Grayhawk had shown up. But she was about to be thrown out of her home, not to mention needing a place to keep her mustangs. Luckily for him, he had an ace in the hole: She loved his children and wanted to be a part of their lives.

Eve had taken Sawyer's hand and the two of them had joined Brooke in Eve's bedroom, with Connor and Mrs. Stack right behind them. Brooke was sitting cross-legged on the bed, and Eve sat down beside her settling Sawyer in her lap.

Connor had a sudden image of Eve's long legs appearing from beneath the covers that morning and his brief glimpse of a pair of pink panties under her T-shirt. Eve's breasts had looked pert beneath the thin cotton, the nipples erect. At the time, he'd wondered what it would feel like to hold the soft weight of them in his hands, to take one of the nipples in his mouth.

Connor swore as his body responded to the vivid images in his head. He hid his arousal behind the doorway and willed himself to think of worms and fish guts.

"I'm sure the children will adjust quickly to their new surroundings," Eve said as she brushed an errant lock of dark hair off Sawyer's forehead. She pulled

Brooke close for a hug, and his daughter leaned close and laid her cheek against Eve's arm.

"I can see the children are comfortable with you," Mrs. Stack said. She turned to Connor and said briskly, "I want to see their bedrooms, and then I want to speak to the children alone."

He ushered the social worker across the hall, showing her the rooms he'd prepared with such love and care for his children, awaiting her judgment. Mrs. Stack was thorough and she took her time. Eve and the children came to join him in the hall. Eventually he picked up Sawyer, who was rolling around on the hallway runner, impatient to be doing more than just standing around.

"The children's rooms seem adequate," Mrs. Stack announced after she'd examined them both. "I'd like to speak to the children now."

Connor set Sawyer down as Eve gave both children a nudge and said, "Go with Mrs. Stack."

The children disappeared into Brooke's bedroom with the social worker while Connor paced the hall. He stopped in front of Eve and said, "What do you think she's asking?"

"She wants to make sure the children are all right, Connor. And they are. There's nothing for you to worry about."

"Easy for you to say," he muttered.

A few minutes later the children reappeared, followed by Mrs. Stack.

"I see no problems here at the moment," she announced. "But I will expect to see a better selection of healthy foods in the refrigerator the next time I come."

Connor had picked up Sawyer and was congratulating himself on his clever ruse regarding Eve's presence when Mrs. Stack asked, "By the way, when is the wedding?"

Connor turned to stare at Eve with his mouth half open.

"We haven't set a date," Eve said, smiling at Mrs. Stack again. She took a step closer to Connor, slid her arm around his waist, and then pressed her body next to his from breast to hip as though she'd been doing it forever. Every part of him lit up as though she'd applied an electric charge. He slid his free arm around her waist and realized for the first time just how small it was. Brooke glued herself to Eve's side so they presented a united family picture to Mrs. Stack.

Connor forced a smile onto his face as broad as Eve's and said, "You'll be the first to know."

Mrs. Stack headed for the front door again, and Connor thought he might be home free, when she suddenly turned back. Fortunately, he hadn't let go of Eve, and she was still pressed down his very-alive right side.

"I have one more question," the social worker said. "What do your families think about this union?"

"Our families?" Connor repeated to give himself time to think of how to reply. If it happened, his father was going to blow a gasket. His brothers were going to think he was crazy, and he wasn't so sure they'd be wrong. "The only two people whose opinions matter are Brooke and Sawyer," he said. "I believe you've seen how they adore Eve."

"Very good answer, Mr. Flynn," Mrs. Stack said. "But it avoids the issue I raised, which is whether your families will support you. I suggest you pursue the matter diligently between now and the next time I visit. I wouldn't want the children to end up in a vise between two powerful men like King Grayhawk and Angus Flynn."

"Are you saying their reaction to our wedding could influence whether I retain custody of my children?" Connor asked with alarm.

"In a word, yes."

"That's not fair!" Eve said. "Connor can't control his father any more than I can control mine."

"Precisely," Mrs. Stack said. "So I suggest you both do your best to convince your fathers to forgo their animosity toward one another when it comes to your marriage." Mrs. Stack opened the front door and said, "Till next time."

"When will that be?" Connor asked.

Mrs. Stack smiled. "My visits are unannounced for a reason, Mr. Flynn."

It aggravated him to be watched like a hawk when other parents could raise their children without someone looking over their shoulders. But if that was the price he had to pay, he was willing to pay it.

The instant the door closed behind Mrs. Stack, Eve said to Brooke, "Why don't you take Sawyer to your room? I remember seeing a brand-new box of Legos in there. I'll be in soon to see what you've made."

Brooke took Sawyer's hand and said, "Come on, Sawyer. Let's go play."

Eve waited until they disappeared into Brooke's room, then planted her hands on her hips. "Are you out of your mind? Why did you lie to Mrs. Stack? Why would you tell her we're engaged?"

"She caught me off guard. It was the first thing that came to mind."

Eve stomped across the living room and thumped herself down on the arm of the couch. "How are you going to fix this?"

"Actually, I wanted to talk to you about that." He took the few steps necessary to stand in front of her. "How would you like to marry me?"

Chapter 9

EVE FELT LIKE she'd been sucker punched. "Never in a million years would I marry you!" She held up a finger for every reason why a marriage between them was impossible. "In the first place, I don't love you." Eve barely hesitated over the lie. "In the second place, you don't love me. In the third place, our fathers hate each other's guts." Their siblings weren't too keen on each other, either. "If that weren't enough, you were widowed barely a year ago." She paused and added, "And your wife was my best friend."

When she had all five fingers extended she closed her hand into a fist. "Why on earth did you ask?" *And in such an unfeeling way?*

Through eyes blurred by tears, she saw that Connor had his hands outstretched in supplication. "Granted that wasn't the most romantic proposal a woman ever heard."

"You think?" she said sarcastically.

"I wasn't intending to be romantic."

"Now you're adding insult to injury."

"Stop and think for a moment, will you?" he said, his voice suddenly sharp. "This could work out very well for both of us."

Eve crossed her arms so he wouldn't see how her hands were trembling and stuck her chin in the air to make the point that she wouldn't be bullied. "I'm not going to marry a man I don't love." It seemed important to make the point that she didn't love Connor. She'd been hiding her feelings without a hitch for years. She didn't want to make a mistake now and accidentally reveal the truth.

"Fine," he said. "We'll keep pretending we're engaged."

"What's the point in that?"

"You're right. That's not as good a solution as marriage."

He tugged her hands free and held them in his. His fingers were warm and strong. She was staring at their joined hands when he said, "Look at me, Eve."

She lifted her gaze and realized that he'd let down the stone wall that normally kept her from seeing what he was thinking. His gaze remained locked on hers. "My children need a mother. You and your mustangs need a home. I think we could build a good life together."

She'd wanted to hear words like those last few from Connor Flynn for as long as she could remember. But this wasn't the way she'd ever dreamed of hearing them. She yanked herself free and snapped, "You don't know the first thing about me."

"I know my children love you. I know my wife thought the world of you. I've enjoyed your company every time we've been in the same room together."

"You've never seen me mad, which I'm about to get right now if you don't change the subject." She slipped past him and crossed into the kitchen to put the width of the breakfast bar between them.

Eve's stomach was roiling. The practical marriage Connor had suggested made perfect sense, but it still broke her heart to imagine a marriage based on logic, rather than love. The problem was that in less than a year she was going to be without a home for herself and twenty-two wild horses. Despite having a wealthy father, she wasn't rich. She'd been able to work as a wildlife photographer because she'd been living at Kingdom Come. Rents were sky-high in Jackson Hole, because it was a place where the wealthy had second homes.

She had a week to find somewhere temporary to graze her horses, and less than a year to move herself and her mustangs somewhere less costly. Even a small apartment was an expense she couldn't afford. She could ask her sisters for help, but she didn't want to do that if she could avoid it. Their lives had also been turned upside down, and they were going to need every spare penny to start over themselves.

Connor stood patiently waiting for her to work it all out for herself, like a hunter certain his quarry will be forced from its bolt-hole.

The real problem was that she wanted to be Connor's wife. She'd wanted it all the years he was married to Molly. But not like this. She didn't want to become his wife in a cold, calculated business arrangement. Twice she'd said *I don't want to marry a man I don't love,* when what she'd really meant was *I don't want to marry a man who doesn't love me.*

"Before you reject the idea of marriage entirely, hear me out."

"I've already rejected it."

He cocked his head, stuck his hands on his hips, and waited. And waited.

"For heaven's sake! Say what you have to say."

"I need a partner, a mother for my children. You need a place to keep your mustangs, and if I'm not mistaken, within the next year, a home. Plain and simple, it's a marriage of convenience."

"It's a marriage without love."

"Romantic love doesn't guarantee a happy marriage," Connor said. "My brother Brian was in love when he married and it ended in bitterness and betrayal. I like you and respect you, Eve, and I think you feel the same way about me. Am I wrong?"

She hesitated, then shook her head. "No, you're not wrong."

"My kids adore you, and I know you love them."

The one truly good thing about his suggestion was that she would get to be a mother to Brooke and Sawyer. She already loved them, and she would love to be their mother. Then she thought of what he hadn't mentioned. How did *sex* fit into a marriage of convenience? She took a deep breath and asked, "Are you intending this to be a marriage in every way?"

"Will we have sex? I hope so. When you feel comfortable with that kind of intimacy."

He was putting the ball in her court? She wanted desperately to make love with Connor, but she wanted it to be *making love*. She didn't want it to be just *sex*.

"If we do this," Connor continued, "I want to try and make it work for the long haul. My kids need stability in their lives. I don't want them losing another mother."

Eve's brow furrowed. "What you're suggesting sounds a lot more like the real thing than a 'make-believe' marriage."

"I guess it is," Connor conceded.

"I still don't see why we have to be married," she said stubbornly. "What if you fall in love with someone else? What if I do?"

"I was faithful to Molly, and I'd be faithful to you."

She wished he hadn't mentioned Molly. She wished he hadn't made fidelity sound like some military duty. It seemed clear that, even though she'd once coveted Molly's husband, he hadn't been the least bit interested in her. And apparently still wasn't.

"You heard Mrs. Stack," he continued. "She has reservations about an unmarried woman living with me. If we're not getting married, I have to find someone more appropriate to help me with my kids."

"You'd kick me out?"

"You'll always be the children's godmother. I'd never keep you from spending time with them. But I have to do what's best for my children."

Eve noticed he hadn't brought up the issue of whether her horses could stay, but the truth was, they were her responsibility. She needed to be wherever they were to take care of them. If she didn't agree to marry Connor and stay at Safe Haven, she had one week to move them somewhere else.

Eve was trapped as surely as a treed wildcat. She could snarl and hiss and bare her teeth all she wanted. The baying hounds weren't going anywhere.

Which meant she had to consider Connor's proposal seriously.

"Even if you get me to agree to this lunatic idea, what about our fathers? They're going to go after each other with both guns blazing and make our lives unbearable."

"We'll talk them around to the idea."

She laughed, but the sound was more hysterical than amused. "You don't know my father."

"We don't owe anything to our fathers. All that matters is what we want to do."

"What about your brothers? And my sisters?"

A pained expression crossed his face. "This isn't their decision to make. It's ours. I need your help, Eve. My children need a mother. Please say yes."

She was tempted. The children gave her the perfect excuse to marry Connor, if she needed one. But the real reason the idea appealed to her so strongly was that she'd have a lot better chance of Connor falling in love with her if they lived under the same roof than if they ended up across the country from each other.

"All right," she said. "I'll do it."

"I'm glad."

Eve felt a qualm when he merely looked relieved, rather than happy. "How are we going to introduce the idea of a marriage between us to our families?"

"We'll have to tell them something soon," he said. "I suspect Mrs. Stack has already spread the word of our notorious engagement."

"What's your father going to think about you getting married barely a year after Molly's death?" Eve asked.

"He won't understand," Connor said flatly.

"Why not?"

"My mother died when Devon was born. I always wished my dad would remarry, so I could have a mom like other kids. When I asked him about it, he said he could never love another woman as much as he loved my mother, so what was the point?"

Eve felt the blood draining from her face. Was it a case of like father, like son? Was that why Connor was so willing to settle for a marriage of convenience? Had his heart been irreparably broken by Molly's death? Was he unwilling to fall in love again?

Eve realized the terrible position she was putting herself in. She already loved the children, and she would only love them more as time passed. What if Connor never fell in love with her? Staying married to him would be agony. Leaving the children would be even worse. She might be making a terrible mistake. But it was a risk she had to take.

"Are you sure you want to do this?" she asked, giving Connor one last chance to back out.

"I think this will work for both of us. I'm game if you are."

Eve could hardly believe they were going through with this crazy scheme. *I'm going to marry Connor Flynn.* She felt giddy. *And terrifed.* And hopeful. *And terrified.*

"What are your plans for today?" she asked.

"Just moving your mustangs onto the ranch. How do you want to do that?"

"Let's drop the kids off with Leah. That way I can help you with the roundup."

"What's Leah going to think about getting stuck babysitting my kids?"

"Who do you think took care of Brooke and Sawyer when you were overseas and Molly and I went out for the evening?"

"Leah?" he guessed. "I suppose the kids know her and love her."

"Everyone loves Leah."

"Not my brother Aiden," Connor muttered under his breath.

"What did you say?"

"Nothing."

Connor's unwitting revelation suggested that it was Aiden, the eldest son, who'd given Leah such a hatred of Flynns. Where had Aiden and Leah crossed paths? When had their romance occurred? And what had she and the other Brats been doing that they'd never noticed Leah's pain?

Eve felt discouraged. How could she expect King and Angus to forgive and forget when, now that she knew the pain Connor's brother had caused Leah, she wanted to hurt him back.

"Since we'll be at Kingdom Come to collect my mustangs, I suppose we should stop by the Big House and break the news of our engagement to my family," she said.

"Are you sure that's a good idea?"

"You said yourself our engagement isn't likely to be a secret for long."

Connor shoved his hands into his pockets, then pulled them out and shoved them through his hair. "When was the last time a Flynn crossed your threshold?"

"When your aunt Jane left for the last time."

"You can see why I might be a little leery of stopping off to say, 'Oh, by the way, King, I'm going to marry one of your daughters.'"

Eve looked into Connor's worried blue eyes and shrugged. "What's the worst he can do?"

"I shudder to think."

"There's nothing more he can take from me," Eve said, realizing as she said it that it was true. "My sisters love me. They want me to be happy. They'll go along with whatever I decide."

"And if they don't? Can you be happy with just me and the kids?"

Eve wished he hadn't asked. "I think so. I hope so."

"You don't sound very sure."

"What do you want me to say, Connor?"

He was silent for a long time. Finally he said, "If you agree to marry me, Eve, I promise I will do everything in my power to make you happy."

Eve wondered if that included loving her as much as he'd loved Molly. But she didn't ask.

Chapter 10

"I ABSOLUTELY FORBID it!"

"I'm engaged to marry Connor Flynn, and there's nothing you can do about it."

Eve's heart was battering against her chest as she confronted her father. She hadn't gotten the chance to break the news to him gently. One of his cronies had called to guffaw about the fact that one of his daughters was marrying one of those wild Flynn boys. King had called her and demanded an explanation.

Eve had refused to talk over the phone. From past experience she knew her father was far more likely to be lenient—that is to say, she was far more likely to get her own way—when he could see her slumped shoulders and repentant tears while her voice cracked with regret. Except, in this instance, she felt a great deal more confrontational than contrite.

"Let me come with you," Connor offered when she told him what had happened. "We should broach him together."

Eve recognized the humor of the situation. Connor was talking as though King stood atop a castle wall that had to be knocked down to reach him. "I wouldn't put it past my father to aim a shotgun at you to keep you out of his house," she replied. "Let me do this. I know my father. King Grayhawk doesn't like to be thwarted, but he can be made to see reason."

When she arrived at Kingdom Come, alone, Leah met her at the kitchen door with her balled fists on her hips and said, "What have you done? King's on the warpath."

"I'll talk to you later," she answered, pausing only long enough to throw her coat on a wooden rack inside the back door. She headed straight to the library and found her father sitting in his favorite cowhide chair behind an ancient, spur-scarred oak desk, a whiskey in hand.

Eve had often faced her father across that desk as a quivering child. King's word was law, and when the law was broken, punishment was quick and certain. She'd realized at a young age that King was far less likely to be upset if it was somebody else's laws she'd transgressed. So long as she obeyed his rules, she could pretty much do as she pleased.

Unfortunately, his most important rule was *Stay away from those Flynn boys,* and she'd broken that law with a vengeance.

"Please, Daddy," she said, placing her hands flat on his desk and leaning toward him, "won't you listen to why I got engaged?"

He shooed her away with his free hand as though she were a bothersome fly. "Your reasons don't matter. I refuse to be related in any way, shape, or form to that conniving scoundrel who's done his best to make my life a nightmare ever since I divorced his sister."

Eve settled in the sturdy leather chair in front of King's desk, which was purposely low enough to make whoever sat in it feel like he was a supplicant to the throne. "I'm engaged to marry Connor because his children need a mother. I don't love him."

"Is that supposed to make me feel better?" he said, slamming his emptied whiskey glass on the desk so hard the ice cubes clinked against the crystal. "What the hell kind of marriage is that?"

"The practical kind," she retorted. "In case you've forgotten, I no longer have a home. I no longer have a place to range my mustangs. I need both, and Connor's offered to provide them."

"So he's buying your cooperation?"

Eve's face flamed, but she kept her voice steady as she said, "We're each getting something we want. And I love his children."

"But not their father?" King queried.

When she didn't reply, he said, "Don't do it, Eve. I've been down that road. I promise you, you'll regret it."

It was the first time her father had revealed any sort of regret over his multiple marriages. Even so, she wasn't sure if he meant she'd regret marrying Connor, or that he'd make her regret marrying Connor.

"There's nothing more you can do to hurt me, Daddy." The angst in her voice made it plain that he'd already done enough to hurt her plenty.

Eve saw the frustration on her father's face when he realized he had nothing to use for leverage to get her to obey him. She had no trust fund he could control. He'd already kicked her out of house and home.

Matt had forced her to move her mustangs off the ranch. There was no other pressure he could bring to bear to enforce his will.

Eve suddenly noticed two small feet sticking out from under the curtains that were pulled back from the large picture window behind King. She pointed and said, "Were you aware we have company?"

"What?" King swiveled his chair around to face the curtains and frowned at the pair of small cowboy boots that stuck out from beneath them. "Come out and show yourself, boy."

For a moment, Matt's son didn't move. Then he shoved his way out from behind the forest-green brocade drapes and stood with his hip cocked so the shorter leg held most of his weight. He was dressed in a miniature version of western gear, including a long-sleeved western plaid shirt, Levi's held up by a tooled leather belt, and ostrich cowboy boots.

"How long have you been hiding back there?" King asked, his voice stern.

"A little while," Matt's son replied in a quavering voice. "I was playing hide-and-seek."

"With whom?" King demanded in a booming voice.

"Nobody," the boy admitted. "I just like to hide and see how long I can stand still before I'm discovered."

"It's not polite to eavesdrop on a private conversation," King said. "Does your father approve of this kind of behavior?"

"He doesn't like it. But since he's gone most of the time working, and Pippa is usually busy, I get away with a lot of stuff."

Eve wondered if the six-year-old knew how much he'd revealed in that little speech. A father gone most of the time working? A sister too busy to keep an eye on him? He sounded like an abandoned child. It seemed Matt was following in King's footsteps in more ways than one.

King reached out a hand. "Come here, boy."

"My name isn't 'boy.' It's Nathan."

Eve watched the smile flicker across her father's lips before he said, "Come here, Nathan."

The boy took two halting steps that put him even with King's knees before King picked him up and sat him on one.

"Do you know how to ride horseback, Nathan?" King asked.

The boy nodded. "But I don't ride anymore."

"Why not?"

"I got thrown and broke my leg. That's why I limp."

"Would you like to go riding with me sometime?" King asked.

Nathan shook his head. "I'm afraid of horses. My dad says I'm foolish. That you have to face your fears. But I'm too scared to ride."

Eve met her father's gaze above Nathan's head. How often had she heard *You have to face your fears* from her father's lips? More times than she could count.

"You have any objection to cleaning out stalls?" King asked.

The little boy looked at King with wide eyes. "No, sir."

Eve noticed the appended "sir" and recognized

that form of address as something else she'd grown up with. King had wanted that label of respect added to every response. Eve had never done it, not if she could help it. She'd answered "yes" and hesitated, waiting for King to demand the "sir." Half the time he let it slide, because that was easier than making an issue of the fact that she was defying him.

Maybe there was a reason she was considering marriage to a Flynn when none of her sisters had dared. Eve had a sudden thought. Was that why Leah had ended up with a broken heart? Because she wasn't ready to defy King and marry a Flynn? Knowing Leah as she did, it seemed far more likely that Aiden had backed away, unwilling to fight his father to marry a Grayhawk.

Eve wondered how her marriage to Connor would affect all the bad blood between his siblings and hers. Make it better? Make it worse? The possibilities were mind-boggling.

Eve realized she'd lost track of King's conversation with Matt's son.

"You're big enough to have a job," King said to Nathan.

"I am?"

King nodded. "From now on, every morning after breakfast, I want you to show up at the stable."

The little boy's wide eyes were focused steadily on King. "Why?"

"Because it's going to be your job to help muck out the stalls."

"I'm too little—"

"You're six, right?" King said.

"I will be in April," Nathan replied. "That's why I'm not in first grade yet."

"What about kindergarten?" Eve asked.

"Dad said I didn't have to go back to kindergarten again this year. I can just start first grade in the fall."

Eve thought that was shortsighted. Nathan might not need what he would learn in kindergarten, but he would have met kids his own age with whom he could play and become friends, so he wasn't so alone in a new place. Unless Matt didn't plan to be here that long. Was there any chance he didn't plan to stay the whole year? Could Matt have come here for reasons that had nothing to do with claiming the ranch?

Eve was still examining that novel idea when she heard Pippa yelling for her brother.

"Nathan! Where are you?"

The library door flew open, and Pippa stopped cold in the doorway. Her jaw dropped when she saw where Nathan was sitting. "You're supposed to be playing in your room," she chided. "Come on. Let's go."

Without a word, Nathan slid off King's knee and headed for the door. When he got there, he stopped and turned back to King. "Are you gonna be there?"

"Be where?"

"At the stables, to show me what to do."

"Of course," King said. "How else are you going to learn how to do it right?"

Pippa put a hand on her brother's shoulder and ushered him from the room without saying another word, closing the door quietly behind her.

"Are you seriously going to muck out stalls to-morrow morning with that little boy?" Eve asked.

"That little boy is my grandson, and that's as good a way as any to spend time with him. He's going to need to be able to ride if he's going to take over this ranch one day. The more time he spends around horses, the sooner he'll get over his fear of them."

Eve stared at her father in disbelief. "Do you really believe Matt's going to stay? That he won't sell this place the moment it's his?"

"Mark my words: He won't sell. My family's been on this ranch for generations. A Grayhawk should be running it when I die."

"What about me? What about Taylor or Vick? What about Leah, for heaven's sake? Didn't you think one of us might like to run the ranch?"

He looked stunned, as though the idea had not, in fact, occurred to him. "I figured you'd all get married and be mothers and—"

"What century are you living in?"

"This one!" he snapped. "Are you or are you not about to get married and become a mother?"

He had her there. Eve glared at him. If she hadn't been desperate because of King's deal with Matt, she might not have ended up in the situation she was in. Honestly, she wouldn't have wanted to run the ranch, but she felt sure Leah would have jumped at the chance. And if one of her sisters had ended up owning the ranch, she knew she would always have been welcome there.

Which wasn't the case now.

It hurt to know that her father favored Matt and his son over his daughters and stepdaughter. She felt envious of the six-year-old who was going to muck out stalls with her father. It sounded dumb, but King had never done anything remotely like that with her or her sisters.

It must have been the bout with cancer that had changed him. All this talk about ranching dynasties and inheritances and having a Grayhawk at Kingdom Come had started up after he'd come face-to-face with his mortality and survived. But he *had* survived, so why all this planning for a future when he wouldn't be around?

She blurted, "Is the cancer back?"

"What makes you ask that?"

"I notice you didn't deny it," she said, over the sudden constriction in her throat.

"Don't worry about me," he said, again avoiding the question. "Worry about yourself. Think long and hard before you marry Connor Flynn. That man has problems you can't imagine."

"What are you talking about?"

"Why do you think he's running that ranch of his as a refuge for troubled vets?"

Eve was shocked that her father knew Connor had a ranch, let alone that he'd planned it as a sanctuary for veterans. "He has a kind heart," Eve said.

"He killed his best friend."

Eve's stomach clenched. She didn't contradict her father, because she couldn't. She'd known Connor had been a tortured soul since returning home, but she hadn't known why. "Where did you hear that?" she asked in a measured voice.

"I have my sources. Just be careful, girl. Connor Flynn is a man fighting demons."

She rose without another word and left the library. Who was King Grayhawk to be accusing Connor of being a disturbed veteran? If anyone had been acting crazy, it was her father.

Eve raced toward the kitchen and the certain hope of comfort from Leah. She was fighting panic by the time she shoved her way through the swinging door. She opened her mouth to complain about King and snapped it shut again.

Leah wasn't alone.

Chapter 11

TO EVE'S DISMAY, Leah was standing in the middle of the kitchen floor arguing with Connor, who was still wearing his coat. Brooke and Sawyer weren't with him.

"What are you doing here?" She'd been regretting her decision to leave Connor at home and wishing she had his strong arms around her, and suddenly, there he was.

Connor whipped his head around, took one look at the tears swimming in her eyes, and said, "What the hell did he do to you?" He scowled as the first tear trickled onto her cheek. "I should never have left you to face your father alone."

Connor opened his arms, and Eve walked right into them, seeking the comfort he offered. She slid her arms around his waist and pressed her nose against his throat, loving the feel of his solid strength supporting her and the intimacy of his bristled cheek against her skin.

This was what she'd imagined it might be like all those years when she'd stood on the sidelines wanting what she couldn't have. The reality was even better than she'd imagined.

"Are you all right?" he whispered in her ear.

"I'm fine. Where are the kids?" she asked as she leaned back to look into his concerned eyes.

"I left them with Aiden and Brian."

From the corner of her eye, Eve saw Leah wince at the mention of Aiden's name. Eve felt a wave of compassion for her sister but remained in the circle of Connor's arms.

Connor continued, "When I dropped the kids off my family was still in the dark about our engagement. I figured we could give them the news when we pick up the kids."

Eve's heart sank. She had no desire to be cordial to that male wolf pack, but since she was now engaged to one of them, she couldn't very well show up snarling. This marriage business was getting really complicated really fast. She made herself step back, so Connor's arms fell away. "We'd better go."

Connor grabbed her coat from the rack and held it so she could put her arms into the sleeves, a courtesy she'd seen him perform for Molly on countless occasions. His gaze remained on her face as he adjusted the collar. Eve felt warm all over. She hadn't realized that once Connor felt committed he would treat her with all the care and attention he would have given to her if she were already his wife.

She felt like a traitor to her family, because she liked one of those awful Flynn boys a lot. Okay. Fine. She *loved* one of those awful Flynn boys. Only he wasn't awful. Not anymore. Not to her.

Eve saw the frown on Leah's face and knew her sister thought Connor was acting, that his behavior was false, that no Flynn could be trusted. Eve couldn't allow such doubts to take hold. She had to give all of herself to Connor and believe that, in the end, he would be able to love her. Otherwise, this marriage was doomed from the start.

Connor was reaching for the doorknob when Matt pushed the door open and stepped inside the kitchen. The shoulders of his shearling coat were layered with snowflakes, and he pulled off his Stetson and slapped it against his jeans to rid it of the snow caught on the brim. He stopped cold when he saw who'd come to visit.

"Well, well. How are you, Connor?"

The two men did one of those male embraces where they bumped shoulders and slapped each other on the back, big smiles on both faces.

"Long time no see," Connor said. "I figured I'd let you get settled before I gave you a call. How are you, Matt?"

Matt shot a look at Leah and Eve before he said, "Not bad."

Eve had been expecting animosity, but the two men had greeted each other like old friends. Then it hit her. Matt's mother and Connor's father had been sister and brother, which made the two men cousins. It had never occurred to her that her elder Grayhawk siblings might not share King's aggrieved attitude—which had become her attitude, and that of her sisters—toward Angus Flynn and his sons. She'd never considered the fact that, before her father divorced Jane Flynn, the cousins might have been close.

"Are you two friends?" Eve blurted.

Connor turned to her and said, "Matt's mom— my aunt—was living with us—" He cut himself off, hesitated, then finished, "At the end. Matt shared many a supper at our table."

Eve shot a look at Matt. It was the first information any of them had gleaned about Matt's life before he'd left home. No wonder Angus was so angry at King. Apparently he'd been a witness to his sister's deterioration and, very likely, her death.

Eve did the math and realized Connor would have been a ten-year-old when Matt left home at seventeen, which was the same year Matt's mother died. Connor had been old enough to grieve the loss of his aunt, with whom it seemed all of the Flynn boys had been close.

"We've missed you, Matt," Connor said. "What have you been doing with yourself all these years?"

"This and that."

Eve wasn't sure whether Matt had been vague because it would have taken too much time to explain, or because she and Leah were standing there.

"Eve and I just got engaged," Connor announced.

"Congratulations." Matt reached out to shake Connor's hand. "I hope you know what you're doing."

She saw Connor's lips twist ruefully, conceding the difficulties that were bound to result from a Grayhawk hitching up with a Flynn, not to mention the sheer number of compromises and changes that occurred when two people married.

"Eve just told King the good news," Connor said.

Matt eyed her speculatively. "How did that go?"

"About how you'd expect." She wasn't any more willing to share information with Matt than he was with her.

"Don't forget I need those mustangs off my land this week," Matt said.

Eve bristled to hear him call Kingdom Come "my land." But she simply said, "Don't worry. My herd will be gone by the end of the day."

"Maybe not," Connor said.

"What's the problem?" Eve asked.

"I made arrangements to use a friend's tractor-trailer, since we're moving twenty-two animals. I just got a call that it's not available until tomorrow."

"There'll be a foot of snow on the ground by tomorrow," Matt said, glancing out the kitchen window, where snow was falling in large, beautiful flakes.

A spring snowstorm was nothing out of the ordinary in Wyoming, but it was going to make rounding up her mustangs a lot harder if they had to do it with a lot of fresh snow on the ground.

"Daddy has a tractor-trailer," Leah said.

Eve turned to Matt. "Any problem if we use that?"

She felt her blood pressure rise every second Matt hesitated. To her surprise, the answer didn't come from Matt.

"Use it," Leah said. She looked at Matt and arched a brow. "Do you want those mustangs gone, or not?"

"Take it!" Matt snapped.

"I'll make sure it's parked by the loading pens when you get there," Leah said, ignoring Matt.

Eve was halfway out the door when Connor turned back to Matt. "You shouldn't have come back, Matt. You can't undo what happened."

He'd already pulled the door closed behind him before Eve had a chance to react to what he'd said.

She stopped on the covered back porch. "Why shouldn't Matt have come back?"

"If Matt wants you to know why he left, or why he came back for that matter, he'll tell you."

"You shouldn't have said anything if you weren't going to spill the beans," she said irritably. "I don't like secrets."

"I'll remember that," he said with a wry smile. "No secrets."

Eve felt a spurt of guilt. She'd been keeping a pretty big one for a very long time. Maybe Connor had, too, if her father was right and he'd killed his best friend. An accident? Friendly fire? Or did her father mean *killed* figuratively, as in, something Connor had done had resulted in his friend's death.

"We'd better get moving if we're going to beat the snow," Connor said, making her shiver when he set his hand on her nape. He ushered her to her pickup and opened the door, then lifted her with both hands at her waist, as though she weighed nothing, and gently settled her in the driver's seat.

Eve had never felt so precious. She wanted to reach out and smooth the lock of hair from Connor's forehead, but it felt like something only a lover would do. She held herself back because she didn't want to give him any reason to suspect that her feelings ran much deeper than his. She felt far too vulnerable to show him she cared. Besides, he might begin to wonder just when her feelings for him had grown so strong.

It took an hour for them to get back to Safe Haven in their separate vehicles, and another thirty minutes to collect three volunteer cowhands and trailer the horses they would be riding on the roundup.

"The snow's really falling hard," Eve said, biting her lip as she surveyed the landscape on the drive back to Kingdom Come. The wind had whipped up, and visibility was poor.

"You want to ask Matt for extra time to move your mustangs?" Connor asked. "After all, what can he do if they're not gone in a week?"

"Have them picked up and sent to slaughter," Eve replied. "I'm not taking any chances. We do it today."

"I don't remember Matt being as ruthless as you're painting him," Connor said.

"Maybe he wasn't then. He is now. What happened to him? Why did he leave? Can you at least tell me that?"

Connor shook his head. "It isn't my story to tell. Ask Matt. Or your father."

Eve shot Connor a sideways look. Her father must have done something horrible to Matt, as Leah had suggested. What could be so bad that Matt would run so far and be gone so long? She had no more time to contemplate the matter, because they'd arrived at the pasture where the horses were kept.

Eve glanced at the pickup following them that contained Frank and the two wannabe cowboys. "I'm a little worried about using those greenhorns to get this done."

"The guys who volunteered said they can ride. Besides, we don't have much choice. We need the help."

"What if someone gets lost in this snowstorm? What if someone gets hurt?"

Connor chuckled. "You're forgetting who you're talking about, Eve. These are men who've been shot at—and who've shot back. They've lived in terrible conditions for months at a time, been bored silly one moment and fighting for their lives the next. I think they can handle a horseback ride in the snow."

Eve pursed her lips and shrugged. "I don't want to be responsible if one of them gets injured."

A shadow crossed Connor's eyes. "I know what you mean."

Eve considered asking Connor about his friend who'd died, but she didn't want to cause him more pain. Instead she said, "I'm surprised you felt comfortable leaving Brooke and Sawyer with your brothers." Because she'd spent so much time with Molly, Eve knew the kids had spent very little time with their uncles while Connor was gone.

"Brian's great with kids," Connor said. "I suspect it's because he makes so many visits to local schools dressed up as a fireman."

"I thought Brian lived in town. Did he come to the ranch just to spend time with your kids?"

Connor shook his head. "His wife got the house in the divorce. He's been living at the ranch when he isn't on duty at the fire station. Brian always wanted kids, but his wife didn't. It's another reason they weren't a good fit."

"Do you want more kids?" Eve asked.

Connor looked surprised by the question. "I haven't thought about it. Do you?"

"I'd love to have a sister for Brooke and a brother for Sawyer, but I'd be happy with two more healthy children whatever their sex."

"So four kids in all?"

Eve nodded. It was something she'd imagined her whole life. A family where the father and mother sat down to dinner together with their children. Idyllic maybe, but it never hurt to dream.

"We'll have to work on that when you're ready," Connor said with a smile.

Eve felt her face heat and knew she was blushing. She tried to meet Connor's gaze but was too aware of the desire in his eyes to hold it for long. The idea of making a child with him, something that had been a fantasy her whole life, was suddenly very real. But she wasn't willing to take that giant leap until she saw how their "convenient" marriage played out. Which meant continuing the contraceptives she'd been taking the past three months since Connor had come home. She'd told herself there was very little chance that she and Connor would end up making love. But she was practical enough—and hopeful enough?—to have taken precautions anyway. Now she was glad she had.

They parked at the pasture gate, unloaded the horses, tightened cinches on saddles, and mounted up.

"How hard are these mustangs going to be to find?" Connor asked as the five of them headed across the rolling terrain on horseback.

"They'll likely be along the back fence where there's a stand of pines and evergreens to cut the wind."

That was where they found them. There was no stallion with her herd. Her twenty-two mustangs consisted of sixteen mares, two of which were pregnant, five gelded yearlings, and a colt that had been born shortly before she'd bought the herd.

The mustangs were still wild, and their instincts were honed to survive attacks by wolves, bears, and mountain lions, so they were alert and running the instant they caught sight of the riders.

Eve reined her mount to a halt, her heart in her throat as she watched the wild horses take flight, manes and tails flying. They looked majestic, harking back to a bygone day when there had been millions of wild horses on the plains, just as there had once been millions of wild buffalo. The sight of her small band of mustangs galloping across the snow, their pounding hooves sending powder flying, was breathtaking.

Eve wished she had her camera with her. Taking photographs of wild herds was how she'd fallen in love with mustangs in the first place. Her small herd included three golden palominos, two stunning brown-and-white pintos, one gray, and one chestnut. The rest were browns, some with stars on their foreheads, a few with white stockings, but most just as ordinary as ordinary could be. Eve dreamed of the day that the single colt, which was black with a white star on its forehead, would take its place as leader of the band.

Except, by the time the colt was full grown, there would be no herd. These horses were all destined to be tamed and sold as saddle horses. If the colt had been born into a wild herd, it would eventually have fought another stallion for the right to become patriarch. But as far as most folks were concerned, there was no reason to keep him as a stud when all he could pass along were mustang genes.

Before her father had given away his ranch, Eve had imagined her small herd of mustangs roaming free forever. But their lives were going to change, just as hers was changing.

Living with Connor, loving Connor, was a dream

come true—except for the part where he didn't love her back. Eve didn't know if there was a way to make someone fall in love with you. All she could do was be the best wife and mother she could be and hope love would grow. There was a great deal of risk in laying her heart on the line. But if she wanted the gold ring, she had to reach out and grab for it.

Eve waited for Connor to mount up. Once he was on his horse, she met his gaze and said, "If we're going to get married, I think we should do it tomorrow."

Chapter 12

EVE RODE THE whole way back to Safe Haven with her heart in her throat, wondering what Connor thought of her suggestion, wondering if she'd made a mistake. There had been no opportunity for him to respond during the trip home, because Frank had joined them in Connor's pickup. Eve had trouble concentrating on Frank's ideas for the best way to involve the vets with taming her mustangs, because every molecule in her body was on tenterhooks awaiting Connor's answer.

As they unloaded the last of the mustangs at Safe Haven, Eve kept glancing at Connor, trying to get a sense of what he was feeling, but he never once looked at her. She felt her stomach clench as the moment approached when they would be alone again. She wondered why it mattered so much to her whether they started their marriage now or six weeks from now. It didn't take much soul-searching to find the answer.

That brief moment of closeness at Kingdom Come, when Connor had offered support and solace, had shown her what she'd been missing all these years. It seemed like forever that she'd wanted to be Connor's wife. Now that the way was open for them to marry, what was the point of waiting even one day longer?

The sooner they were husband and wife, the sooner Connor could start falling in love with her. Even more than the joining of their bodies, she craved Connor's love. Eve wanted to see the glow in his eyes when he looked at her that she'd seen when he looked at Molly. Most of all, she wanted the freedom, at long last, to express her love for him.

"Thanks for your help, Frank," she said. "Connor and I couldn't have done it without you and your friends."

"There they go," Connor called out as he put a booted foot on the lowest wooden rail of the pasture gate at Safe Haven and leaned his arms on the top rail. Eve stepped onto the lowest rail beside him, steadying herself with her hands on the top rail, close enough to touch but not actually touching, and watched the last of her mustangs trot off, their tails to the wintry wind.

"I'll start working with that pinto mare in the morning," Frank said. "I'll check with the men and let you know how many of them want to participate."

"Thanks, Frank," Eve said. "I appreciate this more than you know."

"We're the ones who appreciate your willingness to let us work with your mustangs." Frank gave her a snappy salute against the brim of his Stetson. "See you later."

"We'd better go pick up the kids," Connor said as he slid an arm around Eve's waist to help her down. "Aiden and Brian must be worn to the bone by now."

Eve felt her heart beat a little harder, not just because Connor's arm remained around her waist as they headed back toward his pickup, but because making sure she was safely down from her perch was one more indication of how considerate and caring he was toward the woman in his life.

She glanced at Connor, looking for even a little of the anxiety she felt, but saw none. Eve wasn't sorry she'd jumped the gun. She'd listened to her intuition all her life, and her instincts told her that getting married now was the right thing to do.

Her heart skipped a beat when Connor asked, "Do you really want to get married tomorrow?"

Eve's reply had nothing to do with wanting to be married to the man she loved. Instead she said, "The sooner we're married, the less chance for either of our fathers to try to stop us."

"Is that your only reason for the rush?"

She should have known Connor wouldn't settle for the easy answer. Did he want her feelings to be a part of the decision? She couldn't admit to loving him. Not now. Not yet. Then she realized the perfect answer was right under her nose.

"I want to be a mother to Brooke and Sawyer. I want to be a part of what you're doing at Safe Haven. And I want my mustangs to have a home. Those three desires aren't going to change."

"Do you want our families to be there?"

Eve made a face. "For a make-believe marriage?"

"It's not make-believe, Eve. It's convenient. It's practical. But it's entirely real."

Eve could feel her pulse beating frantically in her throat. *Entirely real.* She wanted everything those words suggested. Love. Laughter. Happily ever after.

"It would be difficult under the best of circumstances to get our families into the same room together without some kind of clash," she said. "I would rather have just you, me, and the kids there."

"You won't miss having a big wedding?" he said as he opened the passenger door of his pickup and set his hand under her elbow to help her inside.

She'd never dreamed of a white wedding dress or a bouquet of white roses and baby's breath or her sisters dressed up as bridesmaids, because by the time she was eighteen the man she loved was already married to another woman. It had never made much sense to imagine her wedding in any kind of detail when there was no groom she wanted to marry.

"I'd be happy with a simple civil ceremony," she replied, meeting his gaze as he put the truck in gear.

"All right. We can do whatever paperwork is necessary in town this afternoon."

Eve's throat was swollen with emotion. It was hard to believe that by this time tomorrow she would no longer be Eve Grayhawk. She would be Eve Flynn. Mrs. Connor Flynn. As a teenager she'd written those names, embellished by flowers and hearts, in her spiral notebook over and over again. She turned to stare out the window so Connor wouldn't see the tears brimming in her eyes and stinging her nose. How often did your dreams really come true? Eve felt a smile forming on her face and let herself feel the happiness bubbling up inside her.

The ride to the Flynn ranch seemed short, probably because her mind and heart were both racing with excitement. "Will your father be home?"

"He's always home."

As opposed to her father, who was almost never at home.

"What's he going to think of this marriage?"

"It doesn't matter what he thinks. We don't need his permission or approval."

"He doesn't control your trust fund?"

"He does, but he's never interfered with it before. I don't see why he should start now."

Eve wondered if Connor was being naïve. Her father was more than willing to apply financial pressure to get what he wanted. It was hard to believe Angus wouldn't do the same.

Would he be able to talk Connor out of the marriage based on the enmity between their families? Or threaten him with financial consequences if he married a Grayhawk?

"I can't believe he won't have something to say about us getting married," Eve said.

"Dad might have objections, but only because he's worried about my happiness," Connor said.

It was hard to imagine Angus the Ogre, as she and her sisters had often referred to him, as a loving, caring father.

"What do you mean?"

"My father is convinced that you three Brats are spoiled rotten. He wouldn't want me to end up with a wife who isn't responsible enough to be an equal partner."

There was just enough truth in the accusation to make Eve defensive. "I've grown up a lot over the past couple of years."

Connor laughed. "I'm not the one making those claims. It's been a few years, but you have to admit, that last stunt you and your sisters pulled was pretty childish."

Eve flushed. "You Flynn boys deserved it after you Saran-wrapped Leah's pickup in town. It took her an hour to unwrap it—at night, in below-zero weather—before she could drive home."

Connor laughed. "You should have seen the look on Aiden's face when he came out to the mudroom in his stocking feet the next morning to put on his boots, and they were glued to the porch. He was mad as a peeled rattler."

Taylor had discovered that the Flynns left their boots on the screened-in back porch to keep the mud and manure out of the house, which had made the prank easy to accomplish.

The more Eve thought about it, the more she could understand at least one of Angus's concerns. It was her own fault that she hadn't moved away from Kingdom Come and started a life independent of her father. Inertia had kept her living at home. She'd told Connor she was a responsible adult, which was true, but she'd never been responsible for anyone but herself. Eve wasn't lazy, but she'd never had to work really hard at anything, either. She'd been capricious as a child and a thrill-seeker as a teenager, but she'd grown up and out of the sort of behavior that had gotten her labeled as one of King's Brats. At least, she thought she had.

But wasn't this marriage the sort of crazy leap across a giant chasm that she and her sisters used to attempt, with calamity waiting at the bottom of the crevasse?

Eve wondered if her sudden angst about getting

married so quickly arose from the fear that she wouldn't measure up to Molly, who'd been a great mother and a perfect wife.

"Do you have any second thoughts about getting married in such a hurry?" she asked.

Connor's lips pressed flat for a moment, and he shook his head slightly. Eve waited for him to meet her gaze, but he kept his eyes on the road as he spoke. "In an ideal world, I'd rather spend more time getting to know you. I have an idea of who you are in my head, but that doesn't mean it's who you really are." He met her gaze at last and added, "I like the woman I know. I hope that's who you turn out to be."

Eve remained silent, because the good friend to Molly and godmother to his children she'd let him see wasn't the sinful woman she felt like inside. That woman had coveted Molly's husband. That woman couldn't help feeling guilty for the joy she expected to feel as Connor's wife.

Eve wondered if she should confess all now. Tell the truth, and let the chips fall where they may. But she was too ashamed—and too desirous of the life that finally seemed within reach—to speak. So maybe Angus Flynn wasn't so wrong to worry that one of King's Brats might not be such a good wife for one of his sons.

"We're here," Connor announced as he shut off the engine.

"I've always wondered what your bachelor abode looks like inside," Eve said.

"What are you expecting?"

"Spartan furnishings. Leather and liniment on every surface. Dishes in the sink."

Connor laughed. "Come inside and see."

Chapter 13

CONNOR REALIZED IT wasn't exactly true that his father had never interfered with his trust fund. Angus hadn't revoked the trust, but he'd threatened to do so if Connor didn't leave the army. He hadn't bowed to his father's wishes, but he wondered now if the only reason Angus hadn't cut him off was because Molly had died. He felt a shiver of foreboding run down his spine. What if Angus forbade the marriage?

Connor forced his thoughts away from the worst-case scenario. Angus hated King for what he'd done to Aunt Jane, but he'd never gone after King's daughters. It was Connor and his brothers who'd done that. Connor wasn't sure how his father would react when he presented Eve Grayhawk as his fiancée.

The subject of marriage between the two families had never come up, not even when Aiden had gone out a few times with Leah. Their relationship hadn't lasted very long, and once it ended, Aiden acted like it had never happened. He'd known his brother had suffered precisely because Aiden had never spoken of it.

He and Eve came in through the back door, which was where everyone entered a frontier home. The door was never locked, harking back to a day when men alone on horseback, or with families in Conestoga wagons, found a welcome and often necessary refuge at any homestead on the plains.

When they got to the mudroom off the kitchen, Connor said, "Leave your boots here." He grinned and said, "With any luck, you'll be able to retrieve them when you leave."

Eve laughed as she toed off her cowboy boots. She padded into the immaculate kitchen, with its stainless steel appliances, black granite counters, and oak floor, in her stocking feet.

"Hey!" he called out. "Anybody home?"

Sawyer came running, yelling the whole way until Connor caught him and lifted him high into the air before setting him on his feet again. His son giggled and said, "Uncle Brian is fun!"

Connor forced himself not to take offense at the suggestion that while Brian was fun, *he* was not. He was pleased that Sawyer, who had few memories of him, had come running straight to him and leapt into his arms. But it suddenly dawned on him that to Sawyer, he wasn't anyone special. He wasn't "Daddy." He was just another friendly face.

Connor's heart nearly broke right then, right there.

He knew he'd done the wrong thing avoiding his children after his wife's death. But seeing how Brooke cocked her head like a small bird when she didn't understand something, the same way Molly always had, or seeing Sawyer's unbounded enthusiasm for life, which Molly had also possessed, made him ache for the loss of his wife.

It also fed his guilt that he'd spent so little time

with her during their marriage. He'd just never imagined that she wouldn't always be there. He was the one living in danger's path. He was the one who should have died.

Connor glanced at Eve. He had a second chance to be a better husband. He had a second chance to share more of himself—and his troubles—with his wife. He hadn't wanted to worry Molly, so he hadn't told her most of what had happened to him in Afghanistan. But he knew she'd been hurt by his unwillingness to explain the nightmares that had plagued him.

He wanted to do better this time. He just wasn't sure he could admit the truth about Patrick Daniel's death to anyone, especially a woman whose admiration he hoped to gain, because of his part in the tragedy. But if he wanted Eve to be open with him, he owed her the same honesty.

Connor's stomach knotted. Telling the story of his best friend's death meant reliving it all over again. But that tragedy was the reason he'd been willing to give up being a soldier. The reason he'd started Safe Haven. The reason he wanted to change his life and be a better husband and father. He needed to tell Eve what had happened.

Soon, he promised himself. When they knew each other a little better he would find the courage to tell Eve the truth. Then she would have to judge for herself whether, after what he'd done, he was a man worth loving.

Connor noticed that Brooke hung back by Brian's side. Seeing her cling to his brother gave him comfort—

and made his throat ache with unshed tears. She spotted Eve and ran to her, keeping her distance from him.

Connor didn't understand why the child who knew him best skirted him most. Was Brooke old enough, at four, to blame him for being gone so much and leaving her behind? To blame him for not being there to hold and comfort her when her mother died? Surely not. But he had no other explanation for why his daughter so persistently rejected him.

Connor realized he'd been holding his breath and released the air in his lungs in a silent sigh. He'd earned the love and respect of his men in combat. This fight was no less important. He would try harder and hope that cherishing his children and caring for them would be enough to earn their love.

When Aiden entered the room, Connor could sense Eve stiffening beside him. "Where's Dad?" he asked.

"Where he always is," Aiden replied.

Aside from all the time spent on horseback in order to run a ranch the size of the Lucky 7, a great deal of business had to be done from behind a desk. Every rancher Connor knew had an office with a picture window so he could still see the sky when he was stuck inside working. His dad was no different.

"I'd like him to meet Eve."

"He already knows you're engaged," Brian said. "After you dropped off the kids, he got a call from the owner of the café where he meets up with his friends for breakfast on Friday mornings."

"And?" Connor said when Brian stopped himself from saying more.

Brian smirked. "I had no idea he knew some of

the words he used." He eyed Eve but made no effort to greet her.

Connor noticed Eve's face was the color of parchment and grasped her hand in case she toppled over. It was cold as ice.

She stared first at Aiden, then at Brian, and finally at him, and murmured, "I can't get over how much you Flynn brothers look alike."

"If you say so." Connor knew why people had that impression. Except for Devon, they were all over six feet tall with black hair and blue eyes. Devon, the youngest, wasn't quite six feet and had dark brown hair and gray-green eyes. Aside from their looks, the three eldest brothers were nothing alike, not in personality, not in attitudes, and certainly not in the sort of women they preferred.

Then Eve made the mistake of saying to Brian, "I've seen you with your wife at a couple of charity functions."

Brian's countenance turned dark. "Don't mention that bi—" He cut himself off as he glanced at the children. "We're divorced," he said brusquely.

"I know," Eve said, taken aback. "I just—"

"And better off for it." Brian went down on one knee in front of Brooke and gave her a hug, then stood and tweaked Sawyer's chin. "I gotta go be a fireman. See you urchins soon, I hope."

"Bye, Uncle Brian. I had a really good time," Brooke said.

Sawyer waved and said, "Bye, Uncle Brian."

Brian left without a word to Eve. Connor stopped him at the door by saying, "This is going to happen, Brian."

Brian turned back, his eyes bleak, and said, "Then I'm sorry for you both."

A moment later, Connor heard Brian's boots thumping as he put them on in the mudroom. He met Eve's gaze and saw she looked as shaken as he felt by Brian's ominous prediction. He turned to Eve and said, "I think we should take the kids with us when you meet my dad."

"You just don't want him to be able to say what he's thinking," she replied.

"That thought had crossed my mind," Connor said with a smile meant to put her at ease.

"That's not a good idea," Aiden interjected.

Connor had forgotten his eldest brother was still in the room. "Why not?"

"You need to be able to talk. You won't be able to do that with kids in the room."

Connor pursed his lips. It seemed Aiden was no more optimistic about the chances of this marriage succeeding than Brian. "Can you keep an eye on Brooke and Sawyer for a few more minutes?"

Aiden squatted down level with the kids. "I've got some chocolate chip cookies and milk, if anyone wants some."

"I do!" Sawyer said.

"Can I have a glass of water with my cookie instead of milk?" Brooke asked, taking the hand Aiden reached out to her.

"Sure, pumpkin," Aiden said.

"She's not a pumpkin," Sawyer said, seeming amused at his uncle's mistake. "She's a girl."

"Let's go," Connor whispered to Eve. "Before they notice we're missing."

Connor kept his hand on the small of Eve's back, directing her past the Great Room, with the inevitable spectacular view of the snowcapped Grand Tetons through floor-to-cathedral-ceiling windows, past the grand staircase that led upstairs to the many bedrooms, all the way to the opposite end of the house. He felt the increasing tension under his hand as they closed in on his father's study.

"He's just a man, Eve," he said in an attempt to ease her anxiety.

"He's a monster of mythic proportions," she countered.

He stopped outside the study door, tipped her chin up, and, on impulse, kissed her. She seemed startled, and stared at him in confusion. He felt a little confused himself. Why had he done it? To comfort her? Or to reassure himself?

"We're engaged," he said. "We're going to be married. We need to present at least the pretense of caring for one another or my father will eat us both alive."

"What do you want me to do?" she said irritably. "We're getting married for purely practical reasons. Any suggestion of affection between us *is* all pretense! Your father's no idiot."

Connor pulled Eve into his arms and hugged her close. "This isn't easy for me, either," he admitted. "I guess what I'm suggesting is that we make it clear to him that we're committed to making this work." He leaned back and looked into her troubled eyes. "That much is true, right?"

She nodded.

"What can I do to make this easier for you?"

She leaned her cheek against his chest and slid her arms around his waist. "This helps a lot."

He held her close, feeling comforted as he gave comfort. "Ready?" he whispered in her ear.

"As I'll ever be."

Connor wasn't. His body had responded eagerly to the feel of Eve's, which was pressed against him from breast to hips. *Too many unrequited dreams of making love to her,* he thought. He suffered a pang of guilt at how glad he was that Eve didn't want to wait to get married. At how happy he was that someday soon she'd be sharing his bed.

He was a widower. He had to go on living, so there was no reason to feel remorse over desiring Eve. He just wasn't sure what he'd done to deserve a woman he'd wanted ever since he was seventeen. The only way to repay such a gift was to be happy, which likely meant allowing himself to love her.

Even if she can't love you back?

Connor had no answer for that. How could he expect his wife's best friend to think of him in romantic terms? If love blossomed at all, it was going to take time.

Connor slid an arm around Eve's waist so they would appear as a couple when they entered his father's study. He could feel the apprehension in her body and see it in the furrow on her brow.

"Take a deep breath," he said.

She did.

As she let it out he said, "One more." He waited while she took another deep breath and asked, "Ready now?"

She nodded.

"All right. Let's do this."

Connor knocked and waited until Angus said, "Come in, Aiden." He didn't correct his father's mistake before he opened the door and stepped inside.

Angus was facing out the window with his back to the door and his head bent over a stack of papers in his lap. "I've got the bastard," he chortled. "It's taken me twenty years, but, by God, this time I've got him. He's invested everything. If I play my cards right, he'll be ruined."

There was no doubt in Connor's mind, or in Eve's, he was sure, who the "bastard" was. He was sorry to have revealed to Eve that his father was still fixated, twenty years after Aunt Jane's death, on getting revenge.

"It's me, Dad," he said, to cut off any further revelations.

As Angus swiveled his chair around and slapped the papers on his desk, Connor tightened his hold on Eve's waist. He was struck by how much Angus had changed since the first time he'd gone overseas. His father's jowls sagged and his eyelids were heavy with age. His once-black hair had turned completely white, making his blue eyes look even bluer.

His posture remained erect, and although his body had thickened, Connor was willing to wager that Angus Flynn could hold his own against many a younger man. In short, he was still a formidable opponent. There was a flare of anger in his eyes at the sight of Eve.

"Did you hear all that, young lady?"

Eve's chin came up. "I did."

He turned to Connor and said, "You could have

told me she was in the room, boy." He sneered. "Doesn't matter. There's nothing she or anybody else can do to help King now. I've won."

Connor had felt the verbal slap but knew better than to react to it. As the third son, he'd been lost in the middle of the pack and ignored. The only way to get noticed was to act out, which he'd done in spades. He'd gotten more spankings than all of his brothers combined, but he'd taken his licks and come back for more, because at least that meant he had his father's full attention.

"I understand you've already heard about our engagement."

"I have." Angus rose from his chair and said, "Come here, girl, and let me take a closer look at you."

His father's eyesight was just fine, so Connor had no idea why he needed to take a closer look. Nevertheless, he let go of Eve, who crossed the room and stood before his father's desk. He wondered if her heart was beating as hard as his own. Whatever nerves she'd suffered on the way here were absent in her demeanor as she greeted his father.

"Hello, Mr. Flynn. I've known of you for a very long time. It's nice to meet you at last."

He looked her up and down as though she were a brood mare he was planning to buy, then turned his piercing gaze on Connor. "This is your choice of bride? One of King's Brats?"

Connor flushed as he took the few steps to join Eve and slid his arm protectively around her waist. "Eve has agreed to marry me."

"And make you the happiest of men? I didn't

think that was possible, when you so recently lost your wife."

Angus's eyes bored into Connor's during the silence that fell between them.

He should have known better than to think Angus would accept his decision to wed, let alone his choice of wife. He was tempted to turn and walk from the room without defending either choice. If it were only him, he'd gladly close the door between himself and his father. But his children loved their grandfather.

"We aren't asking for your permission or your approval. We only came to let you know we intend to marry."

"What does your father have to say about this?" Angus asked Eve.

"He wasn't any happier than you appear to be," Eve admitted.

Angus snorted. "I want to see his face when the son of a bitch realizes he's going to have *Flynn* grandkids."

"Please don't refer to my father that way," Eve said. "Otherwise, the son of a bitch will end up having Grayhawk *hyphen* Flynn grandkids."

His father laughed. "The girl has moxie, my boy. Go and let me get back to work," he said, waving them out of the room.

"That's it?" Connor said, stunned by the dismissal. *You don't have anything else to say? Or any blessing to give?*

His father looked him in the eye. "I think you're making a big mistake. But it's your life. And your mistake."

Connor didn't waste his breath arguing. He turned

and ushered Eve from the room. There were no hugs for him or his future wife as there had been with Molly. There were no good wishes. But none of that mattered. He was doing the right thing, whether his father thought so or not. Having a wife would make his life and his children's lives better.

Once they were out of his father's study with the door closed behind them, he muttered, "Thank God that's over."

Eve stared at him, her eyes swimming in tears. "You don't get it, do you?"

"Get what?"

"Nothing's *over*. All the digs, all the slights, all the words of hate uttered by my father toward you, and your father toward me, and ultimately by both of them toward our children, it's all just *beginning*."

"You're wrong, Eve. None of that has to be a part of our lives."

"How can it not?" she cried. "I'm a Grayhawk, and you're a Flynn. Your father just admitted he's been plotting revenge against my father for years—and maybe, at last, has managed to ruin him." She threw her hands up in frustration. "I can't do this, Connor. I can't! It just won't work."

Long after she'd disappeared from view he was still standing there, wondering where he was supposed to go from here.

Chapter 14

EVE STOPPED BEFORE she reached the kitchen to choke back her sobs and compose herself so she wouldn't upset the children or give Aiden Flynn any hint of how devastated she felt. She ignored Aiden's perusal of her reddened eyes and put an arm around each of the children, who were sitting on bar stools at the kitchen counter. "Are you ready to go home?"

"Uh-huh," Brooke said.

"Where's Daddy?" Sawyer asked.

"He'll be here in a minute."

"Are you going to live with us forever and always?" Brooke asked.

Eve's heart jumped to her throat. "Who told you that?"

"Mrs. Stack said you and Daddy are getting married and that you're going to be our new mother."

"When did she tell you that?" Eve asked, appalled. How was she going to back out of this marriage when the children already knew about it?

"This morning. When she talked to us in my bedroom."

Eve had completely forgotten about the social worker. Forgotten about the very real possibility that

Connor could lose his children if he didn't provide them with a safe, loving home. Completely forgotten that they'd already announced their engagement to Mrs. Stack. What would it say about Connor if he was abandoned by a woman who'd already agreed to marry him, even if it was a marriage of convenience? She couldn't do that to him, even if it meant putting up with a thousand nasty comments from both their fathers.

"Would you like me to be your new mother?" she asked Brooke tentatively. She loved Brooke, and she thought Brooke loved her. But would the little girl be willing to accept her as a replacement for her mother?

"What if you die, too?"

That response told Eve a great deal. Brooke wanted a mother she could love, but was afraid to love someone who might leave her again. Eve hugged the little girl. And made up her mind. "Oh, baby, I'm not going anywhere."

"I'm not a baby. Sawyer's a baby."

Eve laughed. "If you say so." She realized that while Sawyer had been listening to their conversation, he hadn't weighed in. He'd only been a year old when Molly died. He would never have any memory of his mother that he didn't get from pictures or stories that Eve and Connor told him about her. Likely, he had no idea what role a mother was supposed to play in his life. It would be up to her to teach him.

"Eve's going to be our new mother," Brooke said when her father appeared in the kitchen doorway.

Eve saw that Connor was shocked by this announcement, especially after what she'd said outside his father's study. She met his troubled gaze and explained, "Mrs. Stack told the children that we're getting married, and that I'm going to be living with them from now on."

"She did?"

Eve nodded along with Brooke.

"Um. That's nice," Connor said.

Eve felt like laughing and crying at the same time. She'd gotten herself into—and out of—a lot of messes in the past. But there was no escaping this one, so she might as well make the best of it. She sobered, wondering if she should tell her father what Angus had revealed. Leah's words came back to her: *He doesn't have the money.* It was entirely likely King was aware of the trap Angus had set for him. But had it already snapped shut? Or was there still a way for her father to escape?

Eve suddenly wondered if Angus's financial manipulation was going to affect Matt's possession of the ranch. Maybe Matt wasn't going to own everything a year from now after all. Maybe it was all going to belong to Angus Flynn.

She eyed Aiden, who was pouring himself a cup of coffee on the other side of the kitchen, then said quietly to Connor, "I have to call my father. I need to tell him what your father said, in case there's a way he can fix things."

"You still want to go through with this marriage, after all the discouraging things my family said?"

"I wish your family felt differently, but none of my reasons for marrying you have changed. In fact, if my father's ruined, I need this marriage more than ever."

"Then we'd better get moving," Connor said. "We have errands to run in town." He exchanged a significant look with Eve, reminding her that they still needed to get their marriage license.

Eve felt a welling of sadness. It was one thing to imagine Matt living at Kingdom Come. It was another thing entirely to imagine it lost forever to Angus Flynn. But it seemed whatever financial Armageddon was going to occur had already happened. And in that case, it made sense to marry quickly and quietly.

Connor crossed to Aiden and said, "Thanks for taking care of the kids today."

"My pleasure. Everything okay with you?"

"I'm hanging in there."

At Aiden's question, Eve took a closer look at Connor, and saw that his face looked drawn and his eyes looked wounded. He appeared to be a man on the edge of exhaustion. She wondered just how much sleep he'd been getting in the days before he'd gotten his children back. Clearly, he needed the help she'd offered and then snatched away. Clearly, he was relieved to have it offered again.

Eve picked up Brooke while Connor retrieved Sawyer, and the kids waved at their uncle as they headed out the back door. She helped Connor buckle the kids into their car seats and watched them fall asleep as soon as they got on the road.

"The kids must have worn themselves out playing with Aiden and Brian," Connor said, eyeing the sleeping children in the rearview mirror.

"They were up in the middle of the night and then missed their naps," Eve replied.

He glanced at her and asked, "What changed your mind, Eve?"

She sighed. "Mrs. Stack put me on the spot when

she told the kids we were getting married. I realized I'd regret it if I let you down. And I didn't want to disappoint Brooke, who seems to want another mother but who's worried I might die. Sawyer, bless his heart, doesn't seem to know what a mother is."

"If you don't want to do this, don't do it."

Eve's heart skipped a beat. She glanced at Connor, whose hands had tightened on the steering wheel until his knuckles were white. "Are *you* having second thoughts?"

"Second, third, and fourth thoughts. I haven't changed my mind, but I don't want to force you into anything."

"I want to marry you," she said, realizing that if she wasn't careful, she would lose the man she loved to his sense of chivalry. "I want to be a mother to Brooke and Sawyer. And I want to have more children with you. It's just that—"

"Our families are a problem," he finished for her. "We don't have to let them interfere in our lives. We can set boundaries and refuse to listen when one bad-mouths the other."

"You're dreaming if you think you can draw a line in the sand that our families won't cross."

"They can't hurt us if we stick together," Connor insisted. "So. Do you still want to do this tomorrow? Or not?"

She felt her heart squeeze. It seemed it was up to her whether this wedding was going to happen. She swallowed to relieve the sudden constriction in her throat and said, "Could we have the kids with us when we marry? I think Brooke might like to be part of the ceremony, and it might help Sawyer to understand a little better that you and I are going to be partners from now on."

"Partners sounds good."

Eve didn't reply. As far as she was concerned, *partners* was just a place to start.

A half hour later she was questioning her ability to step into Molly's shoes—at least as far as parenting was concerned. Both kids were whiny and tired and didn't want the mac and cheese Connor had fixed them for supper, despite the fact that it was their favorite meal. Brooke fought with Sawyer over the toys in the tub and didn't like the SpongeBob pajamas Eve picked out for her. Sawyer wanted to sleep in Eve's bedroom and cried when she made him stay in his own bed.

Connor was beside himself, because he'd never dealt with the kids without Molly's help when they were this contrary. "Are they like this often?"

"Often enough," Eve replied. "It'll help if we keep them on a schedule like Molly did, so they get naps and have a regular bedtime."

"You promised me a story tonight," Brooke reminded her father.

Connor found a Dr. Seuss book and started reading it, but Brooke said, "Not that one. I want *Are You My Mother?*"

Eve and Connor both searched for the book, but neither of them could locate it.

"I'm sorry, Brooke, it isn't here," Connor said.

Brooke started crying and wouldn't stop. What she moaned wasn't "I want my book." It was "I want my mommy."

"What do I say to her?" Connor said, his voice raw with pain. "What will make it better?"

Eve slipped off her shoes, lay down beside Brooke, and pulled the little girl into her arms. "I'm here, sweetheart."

Brooke slung her arms around Eve's neck and cried, "Mommy, Mommy, Mommy."

Eve met Connor's agonized gaze and said, "Why don't you go check on Sawyer?"

Eve just about had Brooke calmed down when Connor returned with a weeping Sawyer in his arms. He didn't say a word, just slid Sawyer under the covers in the middle of the bed, kicked off his boots, and crowded under the covers with the rest of them.

Eve was facing the center of the bed, so she could see Connor's eyes above the children's heads. He looked both desperate and disappointed that his children weren't comfortable sleeping in their own rooms. He reached over, turned off the light, and said, "Time for bed, everybody."

A very short while later the sniffles stopped. A little while after that both children could be heard breathing slowly and steadily, signaling they were asleep.

"Do we dare leave them?" Eve whispered to Connor in the dark.

"I'm not willing to take the chance. You're welcome to go."

"If it's all the same to you, I'll stay, too. Good night, Connor."

"Good night, Eve."

She was just drifting off to sleep when she heard him mutter, "Somehow, this isn't how I imagined our first night in bed together."

Chapter 15

EVE WAS STARTLED awake and found Connor tossing and making fretful noises in his sleep, clearly in the throes of some sort of nightmare. She debated whether to wake him, but realized if she didn't, he might disturb the children. She slipped out of bed and crouched beside him.

"Connor," she whispered.

He made a guttural sound and struggled beneath the sheets. She put a hand on his shoulder, and he sat bolt upright. To her surprise, he didn't make a sound, just grabbed for something—which wasn't there. A weapon?

Eve held her breath as Sawyer, who was closest to Connor, rolled over, but the little boy settled again without waking.

"Connor," she said quietly. "You were having a nightmare."

His eyes finally found her face in the moonlight, and she saw a look of agony that made her stomach churn.

"I need to get out of here," he muttered.

He rose as silently as a wraith, and Eve followed him down the hall all the way to his bedroom. He sat on his bed without turning on a light, then palmed his eyes as he dropped back on it. "God. That was awful."

Eve didn't think, she just acted. She crossed the moonlit room and crawled onto the bed beside him. She lay close and put an arm across his chest, offering comfort. A moment later he turned on his side and pulled her into his embrace, their legs tangling as he pressed his nose against her throat.

She could feel him trembling and held him tighter. She waited for him to speak, to share whatever it was that had shaken him so badly, wanting to help.

She ran her hand through his hair and rested it on his cheek. "I'm here, Connor. Are you all right?"

He swallowed hard. "Molly used to ask me what was wrong." His next words seemed to be wrenched from him. "I never told her."

Eve remained silent. If he hadn't told Molly what was troubling him, he wasn't likely to share it with her. She ran a soothing hand over his shoulder, holding him close.

"I should have told her what caused the nightmares," he said. "I promised myself I would tell you. I just didn't plan on doing it this soon." He rolled over onto his back again, separating them, and threw an arm across his eyes.

Eve stayed on her side facing him. "You don't have to explain if you'd rather not."

He sat up, keeping the distance between them, his eyes glittering in the moonlight. "I figure I owe it to you to let you know just who you're marrying. In case you want to back out."

Eve sat up, too, her heart thumping hard in her

chest, and stared at him. "I don't think I want to hear this."

"I got my best friend killed."

Eve held herself still. That was a very different statement from *I killed my best friend,* but all the same, Connor obviously blamed himself for his friend's death.

"I sent Paddy out on a patrol I should have taken myself. I told him I was exhausted, and he volunteered to go in my stead." He sighed and shoved an agitated hand through his hair. "I wasn't tired. I'd had a couple of really close calls—got grazed by a bullet, caught a little shrapnel from an IED—and I figured my luck couldn't last. I was just plain scared."

"Was it anything in particular that scared you?"

"Coming home without arms or legs. Coming home with a traumatic brain injury. Coming home burned beyond recognition. Not coming home at all."

"That would do it," Eve said, seeing the grisly humor in his recitation of the dangers he and every other soldier faced.

"The risk of getting wounded or killed is part of the deal," Connor said in a harsh voice. "You fight anyway. You do your duty for the sake of your buddies." He rubbed both hands over his face. "That day, I didn't. And Paddy died. I heard his radio calls for help. I heard him scream when he got hit. I heard him dying."

Eve didn't know what to say. Was Connor to blame? Had he done something cowardly? Or had a soldier who'd seen too much war simply reached his limit? "You kept on fighting," she pointed out. "You didn't quit."

"I felt too guilty to quit," he said flatly. "I was alive and Paddy was dead."

"You can't blame yourself. He was a soldier. Things happen in war."

"It should have been me!" Connor said in a tormented voice. "There's no going back. There's no undoing what's done. My weakness—"

Before he could finish Eve was in Connor's lap, her legs around his hips, her arms around his neck. She pressed her cheek against his and said, "You're not weak! You were a good soldier. You have the medals to prove it." She leaned back and looked into his eyes. "Have you ever thought that your friend must have seen what you were feeling, that he *wanted* to go in your stead? That Paddy went because he cared about you, and it was the best way—maybe the only way—he could help?"

She wasn't expecting the kiss. It came along with a murmured "Thank you, Eve."

Eve tried to speak again, but their lips caught and the kiss lingered. They were sitting in a pose so intimate she couldn't help feeling his arousal, warm and hard, pulsing against the heart of her.

"Let me love you," he whispered. She shivered as he moved her T-shirt aside and kissed her naked shoulder. His other hand slid up under the cloth to close possessively around her breast.

Eve's whole body tingled with anticipation. All her high-minded vows to wait for true love flew out the window. Connor's tongue slid into her mouth, tasting and teasing, and she returned the favor. All of her dreams were finally coming true and the reality was even better than the fantasy.

She could feel the muscle and sinew in his back and arms as she caressed him. Her hand brushed across a scar on his side, and she paused and traced it again.

He froze, then dropped his head against her shoulder. His hand let go of her breast and fell away to the bed.

Eve realized that the demons that plagued him had taken hold again. She held him closer, wanting to comfort, wanting to ease his pain.

"Was this where the bullet grazed you?" she asked as she traced a wound under his arm.

He shook his head. "That was shrapnel." He took her hand and placed it on an indentation at his waist where flesh was missing. "The bullet tore a chunk out of me."

She ran her hand over the spot and felt him flinch. "Does it still hurt?"

He smiled wryly. "You tickled me."

"Oh. Where did the shrapnel hit?" She'd seen the wounds on his chest, but she wanted to feel them with her hands. It was the only way she could think of to share his pain and to ease it.

He unbuttoned a couple of buttons on his shirt, then pulled it off over his head. He sat unmoving, allowing her to examine the scars slanting across his chest, which gleamed white in the moonlight.

Eve traced several of them in turn, then reached for the one over his heart. "This one was close."

"A quarter inch deeper and I'd be dead."

"I'm glad you were spared. I'm so glad you came home to . . ." She was about to say "me" and substituted "us." She leaned forward to kiss the scar and felt him quiver when her lips touched his flesh. Eve draped her arms around Connor's neck and leaned her head against his shoulder, loving the feeling of closeness to him that was more than physical. "Did you start Safe Haven in memory of your friend?"

Connor shook his head. "I started it for guys like me, who have to go back again and again to fight. Guys who need a respite from killing and death. Guys who need a break from the constant wariness of watching for the bullet or bomb that's going to get you. Paddy's sacrifice forced me to acknowledge that even a man like me, with medals for valor, has limits. That soldiers sometimes desperately need a place to rest, so they can fight again."

Eve kissed his throat. "You're doing a good thing, Connor."

"I think what you're doing for those mustangs is pretty special, too," he replied. "What got you started?"

Eve took advantage of the opportunity to touch Connor, and brushed the stubborn lock of hair off his forehead. "A friend asked me to take photos of a herd of wild mustangs a week before they were scheduled to be removed from land where they'd been running wild all their lives. They were going to be rounded up and placed in corrals."

"Why?" Connor asked.

Her body quivered with anger. "According to the Bureau of Land Management the grassland where the mustangs lived was 'overpopulated' for the available food and water."

"And it wasn't?"

"It wouldn't have been if the wild mustangs weren't sharing it with a herd of cattle."

"Whose cattle?"

"Whoever leased the land from the government at rock-bottom prices." She leaned back to look into his eyes. "Oh, Connor, they were so beautiful in the wild! So playful. So utterly fascinating to watch. The week I spent with that herd I took some of the best photographs I've ever taken in my life.

"My friend invited me back a month later to see the same herd—or rather, what was left of it—in pens waiting to be adopted and turned into saddle horses." Eve sighed heavily. "They stood canted on three legs, uninterested in their surroundings—no need to graze, no need to be wary of predators—in a dirt corral with no available shade. The life had gone out of their eyes. I stayed for the sale of the mustangs that hadn't been adopted the third time around, the ones sold to 'kill buyers.' The ones headed to slaughter."

She shuddered and felt Connor's arms tighten around her. "Then I made the mistake of following the kill buyer's truck as it left. When I passed it on the highway, I saw a wild horse that was clearly in distress, the whites of his eyes showing, his mouth open wide to reveal bared teeth as he shrieked—that's the word that comes to mind—shrieked in terror. Did he know what was coming? I don't know. I raced to get in front of the truck, then slammed on my brakes so the driver had to screech to a halt to keep from hitting me. I bought every animal in that truck. Twenty-two mustangs."

"Your herd."

She nodded, her head moving against his chest. "It took every penny I had in savings, but it was worth it. You've seen them running free, how proud they are, how majestic."

"I'm surprised you're letting the vets break them to saddle," Connor said.

"If I were wealthy, if I had the land, I'd keep them free. But they won't be unhappy as saddle horses, not if they get good homes. Horses and men have been partners for eons. Besides, there are a lot more mustangs out there that need to be rescued."

"I guess you and I have at least one thing in common," Connor said.

"What's that?"

"We want to save the world."

Eve laughed. "Not the world. Just a few wild horses."

"And a few good men."

Eve had never felt closer to another human being than she felt to Connor right then. The amazing thing was that there was nothing sexual about their closeness. Was this what marriage was like? Was this what their life would be like in the years to come?

Eve realized that although Connor had said "Let me love you," it had been a request for the physical act. What they'd shared had been far more profound. He'd told her something he'd never shared with Molly. What did it mean?

"I'm sorry my nightmare woke you," Connor said. "You must be whipped. Do you want to sleep here with me or go join the kids?"

Eve wanted very much to stay with Connor, but she was afraid they'd end up making love after all. They were going to be married tomorrow, and even if she wasn't going to have a fancy wedding, it was still possible to have a wedding night.

"I need to go back to my own bed," she said. "I don't want the kids to wake up and find me gone."

Connor kissed her quickly on the lips and stood as he eased her out of his lap and onto her feet. Eve realized he wanted her out of the bedroom before he gave in to temptation. There was a certain look to his features, a heaviness of lids, a fullness of lips, that told her he was ready and willing to make love to her right then, right there.

Eve glanced at Connor once over her shoulder before she turned and ran down the hall. She was careful not to wake the kids when she slipped under the covers. But if she thought she could fall asleep, she was very much mistaken. Thoughts of her wedding night, and hopes and expectations for the future, kept her awake long past when she should have been soundly sleeping.

Chapter 16

EVE WOKE THE next morning to the sound of a land-line ringing somewhere in the house and discovered that she was alone in bed. When she'd returned to her room last night, she'd changed out of her clothes and put on a knee-length, Swiss-dotted, baby-blue night-gown so she wouldn't get caught half dressed if the kids wanted her help in the morning.

When she'd finally managed to doze off, she hadn't slept well. Brooke's elbows and knees stabbed her every time the little girl rolled over, and the kids had sprawled across so much of the bed, she'd spent the night clinging to the edge, hoping not to fall off. By the time dawn arrived, she was exhausted. She could hear the kids in the kitchen with Connor and blessed him for letting her sleep in.

She was in the middle of a lazy stretch, groaning with enjoyment as she extended her fingers wide, her hands high over her head and her toes arched toward the foot of the bed, when Connor appeared in the doorway, phone in hand.

"It's for you."

Eve felt self-conscious because, with mascara clumped on her eyelashes and her hair spiked every whichaway, she looked like something the cat dragged in.

Connor must have just gotten out of the shower. A lock of damp hair fell over his scarred forehead, and he was freshly shaven. He was dressed in a short-sleeved black T-shirt that showed off his powerful biceps and jeans faded with age that lovingly cupped the proof of his sex, which happened to be at eye level.

She had a vivid recollection of what it felt like to have that warm, hard part of him nested against her own softness and felt her body quicken. Eve ran her hands through her tangled hair to keep from reaching out to touch. "Hardly anyone knows I'm here. Who is it?"

He handed her the phone. "I don't know. Some woman asking for you."

Eve tried to imagine who it could be, but came up blank. She started to slide out of bed and realized her nightgown had gaped open at the top. She grabbed at it and shook her head in chagrin as she met Connor's gaze.

He grinned and waggled his eyebrows, acknowledging that he'd enjoyed the view.

Eve playfully swatted his arm as she took the phone from him. "This is Eve Grayhawk."

She could feel Connor's eyes on her as she listened and then replied to the speaker on the other end of the line. "Um, yes. I see. How soon? Yes. How long? Thank you. I'll be in touch."

She clicked off the phone and dropped it on the bed, too stunned for a moment to speak. She looked at him with amazement and said, "That was *National*

Geographic. They loved my photographs. They have another assignment for me."

Connor's smile was instant and infectious. He lifted her into his arms and swung her in a circle. "Congratulations! I told you your work was good."

She was laughing by the time he set her down. "I still can't believe this is happening. It's a dream come true." It just didn't seem possible that she'd been offered something that she'd been working toward ever since she'd first picked up a camera at thirteen.

She'd told Mrs. Stack about the project she'd done for *National Geographic* as though she took photographs for the magazine all the time. In truth, it was her first job with them, and she'd been waiting on pins and needles to hear how much of her work they were actually going to use. Now she'd gotten this wonderful, life-altering call.

"I'll be photographing mustangs in the wild," she said, her voice filled with enthusiasm.

"Here in Wyoming?"

"In Nevada."

After a long hesitation, Connor asked, "When?"

"Six weeks from now, in May."

"For how long?"

"As long as it takes." She couldn't keep the smile of delight off her face. It wasn't just taking photographs for one of the premier magazines in the world, it was photographing the wild mustangs she was so passionate about saving. Her evocative photos could move hearts and change minds. They could be the impetus to keep more mustangs in the wild.

"I'll be following a herd of mustangs with several

pregnant mares until they give birth and then taking photographs of the foals as they grow."

"So you'll likely be gone for several weeks. Or maybe months."

Eve nodded. She was still on cloud nine when Connor said, "How does that fit in with our plan to be married today?"

The smile disappeared from Eve's face as though she'd clicked a camera shutter. It had never been necessary in the past to balance her life between the people she loved and the work she loved. She took a deep breath and let it out. "I don't know."

Connor's expression was unreadable, but his hip was canted, and he'd stuck his hands into his back pockets. "I suppose there's a big payday for this job," he said. "Big enough to help you relocate your horses and afford a place to live."

Eve crossed her arms protectively over her chest. "I guess, yes." The amount she'd been offered for this single project was as much as she'd made in an entire year selling her photographs locally.

"If I'm not mistaken, once folks see your photographs—which I'm guessing will be spectacular—you're going to be deluged with offers to take pictures all over the world."

Eve felt flattered by Connor's estimation of her work. She stayed silent because she was beginning to realize the full scope of the opportunities she was going to have—and how they might take her away from the man and the children she loved.

"You no longer need to marry me to have a home and save your mustangs," he concluded.

Eve's throat constricted at the thought of giving

up a life with Connor and Brooke and Sawyer. Surely she didn't have to choose. Surely she could have both her work and a family to love. "Nothing's changed, Connor."

"Everything's changed." He looked at her with wounded eyes. "I'm not going to steal your dream from you, Eve. The deal was that I'd get something and you'd get something. That's no longer true. Don't worry about me and the kids. We'll figure out some way to get along without you. I'm glad for you. I'm just sorry things turned out this way."

He turned to leave, but she grabbed his arm to stop him. "Wait!" Why did he have to be so noble? Didn't he want to marry her? Was she really so easy to dismiss from his life?

Eve could feel something important, something vital to her happiness, slipping away. "I don't have to leave for six weeks. I can still help you get through this adjustment period with Brooke and Sawyer."

He whirled to face her, and her hand fell away. "Then what? The whole point of getting married— and staying married—was to give the kids two parents they can count on."

"I love them. I don't want to leave them." Eve saw Connor flinch and realized what she hadn't said. That she loved *him*. That she didn't want to leave *him*. But it was too soon to exchange words like those, even though she yearned to say them.

"Getting married to me is only going to tie you down and hold you back," he said. "Why would you want to do it?"

Because I love you. Because I've always wanted to be your wife. "You seem to think a home for my-

self and my mustangs is all I'd be getting out of marriage to you. I love those children," she said fiercely.
"I want to be their mother." *And I want a life with
you.* "Lots of women balance careers and families. At
least let me try!"

"What are the kids supposed to do when you
take off? They've already lost their mother. They'll be
devastated if they lose you, too."

"They won't be losing me. I can talk with them
on the phone. I can Skype. They'll know I'm still there
for them, and that I'll be coming back."

"If you do a good job—and I have no doubt you
will—won't this just be the first of many assignments
that take you away from home? What about having
more kids? Can you have babies and take on more
projects like this?"

He was asking good questions, none of which
she'd had time to consider. "I don't have all the answers, Connor. I just got the offer a few minutes ago.
I haven't even agreed to take the job."

"Why not?"

"They gave me time to consider whether I wanted
the work. I'm supposed to get back to them."

"When?"

"I need to give them a month's notice, so two
weeks from now."

He rubbed a hand across his nape. "I want you to
have the life you've always dreamed of having. I don't
want you giving that up to help me out."

If only she could tell him the truth. If only she
could say, You're *the dream I've had all my life.*
You're *the dream I don't want to lose.* She loved taking photographs, and she could never give up the

work that gave her life so much meaning, but she was more willing to compromise than Connor seemed to believe. "I'll always want to take photographs, but I won't always have to leave you and the kids to do it. Give me a chance. Give us a chance."

"What are you saying?"

She met his gaze, her heart in her throat, and said, "I want to go through with the wedding."

He didn't respond for several long moments. "All right," he said at last, his voice rough with emotion. "Let's go get married."

Chapter 17

CONNOR STOOD BESIDE Eve, listening to the magistrate read the words that made them husband and wife, wondering if he was making a mistake marrying a woman who loved his kids—but not him. He hadn't realized until it seemed he might lose Eve just how much he wanted to be married to her.

It was the vow to try and be a better husband that had caused him to share his feelings of guilt and shame for Paddy's death with Eve. He hadn't realized how good it would feel to have her absolve and defend him or how moved he would be when she shared an important turning point in her life.

He felt a tug on his jeans and looked down into his son's cherubic face. "Pick me up, Daddy."

He picked up his son and held him close. He knew how precious and fleeting these moments with his children were. Molly's death had proved there were no promises in life. He had to reach for happiness if he hoped to have any chance of achieving it. Which meant marrying a woman he'd loved most of his life, even though she didn't love him. He fought the ache in his throat so he'd be able to speak when the time came.

Eve smiled at him as he settled Sawyer against his waist.

Brooke stood between them, a bright blue ribbon tied around her ponytail and a small bouquet of wild-flowers in her hands. She was listening carefully to everything the magistrate said.

Brooke looked up at Eve when she said, "I will," and then up at him when he said, "I will."

The magistrate said, "I now pronounce you husband and wife." He grinned. "I have to say I'm surprised to see you two here under these circum-stances." Both Connor and Eve had appeared before the magistrate more than once as teenagers to atone for mischief they'd caused.

Eve shot Connor an embarrassed look, and Con-nor grinned and shrugged back.

The balding man, who sported an impressive han-dlebar mustache, continued, "Never thought I'd see the day when I'd marry one of you wild Flynn boys to one of King's Brats. My best wishes to you both."

He shook hands with Connor, then with Eve, and when Brooke lifted her hand, he shook hands with the little girl, and finally, of course, with Sawyer, who didn't want to be left out.

"Where are you folks headed now?" the magis-trate asked.

"Back home," Connor said.

"To the Lucky 7?" the magistrate asked. "Or to Kingdom Come?"

"To my ranch," Connor said. "Safe Haven."

"It seems a shame not to celebrate in town first," the magistrate said. "Or maybe with your families?" He looked from Connor to Eve and back again.

With no one from either of their families present at the simple ceremony, the magistrate was obviously fishing for information about whether either of their fathers knew what they'd just done. Connor wasn't about to satisfy the old man's curiosity, not after all the times the magistrate had ordered him to perform a hundred hours of community service.

The truth was they hadn't told either parent they were getting married today. After their visits yesterday, Angus and King knew their children intended to wed. He and Eve had thought it better to present their fathers with a fait accompli.

"Oh, I nearly forgot," the magistrate said with an impish grin. "You may kiss your bride."

Connor was caught off guard. He set Sawyer down, then turned to Eve, who looked vulnerable and afraid. As he leaned forward, her eyes slid closed. He hesitated a breath away from her lips, his heart full of emotion.

"Kiss her! Kiss her! Kiss her!"

Connor was startled into lifting his head. He stared at his daughter, who was laughing and clapping her hands. The chant was something Brooke used to do when he'd teased Molly before kissing her. The shocking reminder of his first wife at his second wedding was like a punch in the gut.

Sawyer picked up Brooke's chant, which had gotten louder, and Connor realized that the only way to get them to stop was to kiss his bride.

He took his time. He owed Eve that.

He captured her face between his hands, feeling the warm flush in her cheeks with his fingertips. He somehow knew it was bashfulness rather than reluctance that made his new wife lower her gaze. He pressed his lips against Eve's and felt them trembling. He slid one hand around her nape, holding her captive as he deepened the kiss. She leaned into him, surrending to his desire, and he suddenly envisioned a world of possibilities in their life together.

He felt a sharp jerk on his jeans, followed by Sawyer's demand, "Time for pizza, Daddy." Connor broke the kiss reluctantly and searched Eve's face to see how she was faring after this strange wedding. He felt his heart jump when he saw a look that felt like love in her eyes. It was gone an instant later, and he wondered if he'd imagined it.

"Daddy!" Sawyer said insistently. "Pizza!"

Eve looked away first. She dropped to one knee, gave Sawyer a hug, and laughed as she yelled, "Pizza!"

Sawyer chortled and hugged her around the neck as she picked him up.

It had been Eve's idea to bribe Sawyer by promising him that if he was quiet during the brief ceremony he'd be rewarded with pepperoni pizza, which would serve as their wedding dinner.

Connor thought back to his first wedding, from the elaborate floral decorations in the church, to Molly's exquisite white dress and veil and her cascading bouquet of lilies, to the lengthy Catholic wedding ceremony, and finally to the outdoor barbecue and dance for five hundred guests.

If he didn't have the marriage license tucked in his pocket, Connor could almost believe they'd appeared before the magistrate this afternoon for stealing antlers from one of the arches that decorated the four corners of the town square.

He was wearing jeans, a white western shirt, and cowboy boots. So was Eve. Brooke was holding the only flowers in the room, which they'd picked from around the porch this morning before they'd gotten into his pickup to drive to town. They'd exchanged no rings. Two children dressed in play clothes had been their only attendants as they said their vows, and they were about to eat pizza as a wedding supper.

What was wrong with this picture?

Connor studied Eve looking for signs of dissatisfaction. She was smiling, her eyes crinkled at the corners, as she ushered the kids out of the magistrate's office. He couldn't imagine any other woman he knew, certainly not Molly, agreeing to marry him without all the usual bells and whistles. And yet, Eve had. Didn't all girls dream of their wedding day and imagine a thousand ways they could make it dazzling?

Five minutes later, as they settled at one of the tables at Mountain High Pizza Pie, the kids busy with coloring books that Eve had thoughtfully brought along, Connor leaned over and asked quietly, "Are you okay?"

She angled her head as though he'd asked a peculiar question. "Why wouldn't I be?"

"You didn't find that wedding . . . odd?"

"Different, certainly," she agreed. "But I loved the simplicity of it. Didn't you?"

"Of course. But I feel like you got cheated."

She laughed. "Cheated of all those agonizing weeks of planning and all that last-minute panic worrying that everything wasn't perfect? Thanks, but no thanks. I like the way we did it."

"We don't have a single picture of our wedding," he said, appalled at the oversight.

"I have my cell phone with me. Want to come over here and take a selfie with me?" she said with a grin.

"You're really okay with this, aren't you?"

She nodded, and then sobered. "It would have felt strange if we'd had a fancy wedding. How could I top the beautiful wedding you and Molly had?"

It dawned on him that she'd been there as Molly's maid of honor. Eve would have gone through all the angst of planning the thing with Molly in the three weeks between his proposal and his return to Afghanistan and been a part of all the frantic preparations for a last-minute barbecue for five hundred of their parents' closest friends and acquaintances.

"This was nice." She rubbed her bare ring finger and added, "I would like to have a ring, but there's no rush."

"What kind of ring do you want?"

"Something I can wear when I'm running around in the wilderness."

"Taking pictures of mustangs?"

"That, too," she said. "Do you want a new ring? Or do you want to keep that one?"

Connor realized he was still wearing his original wedding ring, a plain gold band he'd worn constantly since the day he was married and hadn't taken off after Molly's death. It was almost like another part of him. He brushed the underside of the band with his thumb, something he'd often done when he was away from home that made him feel closer to Molly. "Do you mind that I'm still wearing it?"

She laid her ringless left hand over his. "That ring has sentimental value for me, too. I was with Molly when she picked it out. I remember how happy and excited she was to be marrying you." She glanced at Brooke and Sawyer. "Molly will always be a part of our lives. I think it's wonderful that you don't want to take it off."

Connor made up his mind then and there to find the perfect ring for Eve and to put it on her hand so she was wearing it when she took off for Nevada. Maybe it would remind her that he was waiting for her to return.

The pizza was delicious, but it added to the surreal feeling of their bizarre wedding day. He was the one who'd set this strange day in motion with his suggestion of a "marriage of convenience." He hadn't realized it would also result in such a "convenient marriage."

Connor could see nothing in Eve's demeanor that suggested she had any regrets, but he couldn't help wondering if she would be sorry later that they hadn't made their wedding more special. He smiled to himself. It had been a memorable day, if for no other reason than the fact that they'd skipped all the traditional ways to celebrate. He wondered if they were going to forgo the wedding night, too.

He eyed Eve and realized he didn't want to do that. He wanted to make love to his wife. Last night had only given him a taste of what was in store. He didn't want to fall any deeper in love with her when they didn't know whether they had a future together. But he couldn't help hoping that Eve would be willing to make their wedding night an occasion worth re-membering.

Out of the blue, Brooke asked Eve, "Are you my mother now, Aunt Eve?"

Eve shot him a startled look before answering, "Do you want me to be your mother?"

Brooke pulled a slice of pepperoni off her pizza, popped it into her mouth, and began chewing as she answered, "I guess so."

"Then the first thing I have to say to you, young lady, is chew with your mouth closed!"

Brooke's mouth dropped open in surprise and then snapped shut as she chewed vigorously, her eyes sparkling and her cheeks puffed out by her smile. After she'd swallowed, she said, "Mommy used to say that all the time."

Eve brushed Brooke's bangs off her forehead in what Connor realized was a caress. "I know, sweet-heart. Your mom was very nice and very wise. I hope I can be even half as good a mother to you as she was."

"Are you gonna be my mommy, too?" Sawyer asked.

"You bet," Eve said, shoving the wayward lock of hair off his forehead with another fond caress.

"Now do Daddy's hair," Brooke said.

Eve stared at the little girl in disbelief, then glanced at Connor.

"Go ahead," he said with a grin.

She reached out tentatively, and he felt the soft brush of her fingertips across the scar on his forehead.

"Now you do Aunt Eve," Brooke said to him.

Eve's bangs were long, so he settled for tucking

them behind one ear, feeling her shiver slightly before he removed his hand. When he looked into her eyes, he saw that her pupils were dilated and her skin was flushed.

Connor felt his heart knocking against his ribs. The sooner he got the kids home and tucked into bed, the sooner he could begin the seduction of his bride. He jumped up from the table and announced, "Time to go home."

"You said we could go to the movies," Brooke reminded him.

"When did I say that?"

"You said if I was good—"

"I remember now." Sawyer's bribe was pizza. Brooke had insisted on the latest cartoon movie. "All right. Let's go." It was the sing-along version, where the audience joined the on-screen characters in belting out the songs. Connor had pretty much learned the words to the theme song, since Brooke sang it endlessly.

He met Eve's gaze over Brooke's and Sawyer's heads, wondering if she felt any of the growing anticipation he felt as their wedding day wore on. He wondered if she was also looking forward to the moment when the children were asleep and they would finally be alone together as husband and wife. Their wedding day might be spent in ordinary ways, he thought, but there was no reason they couldn't have an extraordinary wedding night.

Chapter 18

E<small>VE</small> <small>COULDN'T REMEMBER</small> when she'd enjoyed a day more, even though she'd spent most of it wondering about the night to come. Would Connor want to make love to her? Was she willing to make love to him, even though he wasn't in love with her? They'd come very close to having sex last night, and all day she'd carried the feeling with her of something important left unfinished.

The children were a welcome distraction, fun and funny, especially during the movie sing-along. She'd been enchanted when Connor, who knew all the words to Brooke's favorite song, joined in.

By the time the children got fussy, they were already on their way home. She and Connor gave them their baths and put them right to bed. The copy of *Are You My Mother?* had been found, and Eve read that to Brooke, while Connor read *Horton Hears a Who!* to Sawyer.

When Eve left Brooke's room she found Connor waiting for her in the hallway.

"How about a glass of champagne?" he said.

"I'd like that." Eve felt a frisson roll down her spine at the suggestion of what more might be in store

on her wedding day: a wedding night. She followed
Connor into the kitchen, but he said, "Make yourself
comfortable on the couch."

She was too nervous to sit. She crossed to the fireplace and held out her hands to warm them. Except,
she wasn't the least bit cold. In fact, she felt warm all
over. She wanted to be held and loved by Connor.
She wanted to hold him and love him back. But she
hadn't forgotten what had happened the first time
they'd kissed. She hadn't forgotten their aborted lovemaking last night. She wondered if they could really
get through their wedding night without Molly somehow ending up in bed between them.

Eve was still standing by the flickering fire, which
provided the only light in the living room, when Connor held out a flute of champagne. She took it and
turned to face him. His hooded eyes gleamed in the
firelight, and his lips were full. She felt her heartbeat
ratchet up as she recognized the signs of desire.

"To second chances," he said.

She clinked glasses with him and drank, laughing
when the bubbles tickled her nose. Connor's toast reminded Eve that she didn't want to make the same
mistake again. She had a better chance of getting what
she wanted if she reached for it with both hands.
If she wanted Connor to make love to her, she had to
let him know it.

Before she could say a word, Connor captured
her nape and drew her close. His tongue slid along
the seam of her mouth seeking entrance, and she
opened to him, feeling her blood surge as desire blossomed. Eve smiled as she tasted buttered popcorn and
champagne. He still smelled faintly of the woodsy

aftershave he'd put on earlier in the day and another scent that was very male and recognizably Connor.

He broke the kiss to set his glass on the mantel, then took her glass and set it beside his. "All day long I've wanted to hold you." His strong arms closed around her until her breasts were pressed against his muscular chest and her hips were cradled against the length and hardness of him.

Eve had enjoyed sex in the past, but she'd never made love to a man she loved. She'd been curious enough to try sex to see what it was like, and smart enough not to keep having sex just because she could. She'd been waiting for this moment. Waiting for Connor.

She took his hand and said, "Come with me."

He followed her readily enough, but when they arrived at his bedroom door he stopped. "Are you sure you're okay with this?"

There was no way he could know how long she'd been waiting for this moment. She smiled as she said, "I've never been more certain of anything in my life."

She laughed in surprise when he picked her up, and she held on tight as they entered his bedroom. Connor hadn't carried her over the threshold when they returned home after their wedding, but transporting her to his bed was equally reminiscent of those long-ago stolen brides brought home by the warriors who'd won them in battle.

When Connor set her down, Eve realized he must have come here to prepare the room while she was dressing Brooke for bed. The covers had been carefully turned down. A pine-scented candle burned on the chest across from the bed, and a sprig of mountain columbine rested between the pillows.

Eve felt her heart wrench with gratitude. "This is lovely, Connor. Thank you."

A flush rose under his skin. "I wanted something about this day to be special for you, Eve."

"I loved my wedding day." She met his gaze. "And I'm very much looking forward to my wedding night."

As Connor took her in his arms, she slid her hands into his hair, loving the softness of it. He took his time. Kissing her temples. Kissing her closed eyes. Kissing her cheeks. And finally kissing first one edge of her mouth, and then the other. Eve's heart was pounding, and her body was tensed in expectation.

He brushed the callused pad of his thumb over her lips, and Eve opened her mouth slightly in response. A moment later, his mouth claimed hers. Their tongues parried as they tasted one another, and Eve's body came alive as Connor palmed a breast and then teased her nipple into a hard bud. She explored the strength in his shoulders and arms, loving the feel of muscle and sinew under her fingertips.

She could hardly believe where she was, what she was doing, who she was doing it with. She felt a kind of euphoria she could never have imagined, knowing Connor wanted her. At the same time, there was a knot of fear in her belly that something would break the spell, and her dream of happiness with him would end before it had even begun.

"I want to see you," he rasped.

Connor undid the buttons on her shirt, while she returned the favor. She tugged his shirt out of his jeans as he did the same for her. His shirt had the sleeves rolled up, so it came off without a problem. She was imprisoned for a few moments by her sleeves, but she held her wrists up, forcing a wobbly smile as he undid the buttons, holding her breath as her shirt slid to the floor.

She'd worn jeans instead of a wedding dress for the ceremony, but Eve had been aware this moment might come. She stood before her new husband in a white demi-cup bra that lifted her breasts up like a delectable feast. A wave of pleasure washed through her when Connor's eyes lit with desire. He cupped her breasts in both hands and leaned down to kiss the crest of each one before he reached for the snap on her jeans.

White bikini underwear trimmed in feminine lace appeared as her zipper came down. Eve was having trouble catching her breath. Having trouble keeping her heart from beating right out of her chest. She was excited. And terrified.

What if she didn't please him? What if he compared her to Molly and found her wanting?

Eve stood there trembling, afraid to move forward, unwilling to move back, her jeans caught on her hips, as Connor unbuckled his belt and pulled it through the loops, then reached for the snap on his jeans. The sound his zipper made as it came down sent a shiver of expectation rushing the length of her spine.

Connor chuckled as he stared down at his Levi's, which had pooled atop his cowboy boots. "Okay. We can do this the hard way or the easy way."

"What?"

He was laughing as he said, "My jeans aren't coming off until I get out of these boots. Neither are yours. Any suggestions?"

The humor in his eyes eased the tight knot in her belly and unfroze her limbs. "I vote for the easy way." She dropped onto the edge of the bed and stuck both feet into the air.

Connor grinned as he pulled off her boots and then her socks. Her boots hit the floor with two thumps, and he tossed her socks after them, then pulled her jeans down her legs, leaving her dressed in nothing but the sexy underwear that had been her only concession to the fact that this was her wedding day.

Eve told herself it was silly to feel self-conscious in front of Connor, but her heart didn't get the message. She could feel her pulse thrumming wildly in her throat. He couldn't help but compare her with Molly. To postpone the moment, she jumped up and gave Connor a little shove so he plopped onto the bed, then turned her back to him to pull off each of his boots, dropping them with much louder thumps. She pulled off his socks and threw them over her shoulder as though she were flipping her hair back behind her.

He laughed as she grabbed the legs of his jeans and pulled them off. He was wearing long gray Jockey shorts that fit him like a second skin and left nothing to the imagination. She no longer doubted that he wanted her. The proof was barely constrained by the fabric that covered him. She tried not to stare, but it was a few moments before she raised her gaze to meet his. From the visible pulse in his throat, she realized his heart must be racing as fast as her own.

Connor sobered as he stood and took the few steps to join her. In a low, guttural voice he said, "Just a few more scraps to go," and released the front clasp on her bra.

Eve didn't react quickly enough to stop Connor, but she instinctively caught the two halves and held them in place.

He dropped his hands to his sides and raised a questioning brow.

Eve wished she had enough confidence to tease him, to play the femme fatale, but she cared too much what he thought, and she was too aware that she wasn't Molly. Molly had been short, with small breasts and narrow hips. Her shape was very different.

It took all of Eve's courage to let go of the bra and allow the straps to slide down her arms. She lowered her gaze, unable to bear the tension of wondering whether she pleased him.

Eve felt Connor's knuckle under her chin and lifted her head until their eyes met.

"You are so beautiful you take my breath away," he said in a gruff voice.

Eve felt the knot inside loosening a little more. She laid her hands on his bare chest and said, "You're beautiful, too."

He shook his head. "That's the wrong word for a man."

She didn't contradict him, just let him see the admiration in her eyes.

As he reached for her panties, she took a step back and said, "Let me." Her gaze lowered shyly as she shoved them down over her hips. When they reached the floor she stepped out of them. Then, and only then, did she meet Connor's gaze again.

His pupils were huge and dark in his blue eyes, his lips full. She felt her body flooding with the need to be held by him, to be touched by him, to be joined with him, and said in a voice she hardly recognized as her own, "Your turn."

All his life Connor must have cursed his light skin, which revealed a sudden blush as he stripped off his shorts and kicked them aside. It took her a moment to realize that he was as anxious for her approval as she'd been for his. She tried to smile to show she was satisfied, or to say something to let him know that the sight of his body pleased her. But her mouth wouldn't move, and her throat was too thick with emotion to speak.

Eve kept her gaze focused on Connor's face as she took the few steps to reach him. She ran her hands across his chest, reveling in the feel of muscle and bone. "I've wanted to touch your naked flesh all day."

She didn't know where that low, throaty voice had come from, but she felt Connor's muscles tense under her fingertips.

His hands circled her waist, urging her closer until they were pressed together body to body. She heard his low growl of satisfaction as she slid her arms around his neck. When she laid her cheek against his powerful chest she could hear his galloping heartbeat, which matched the pace of her own eager heart.

Connor used a fingertip to nudge her chin up so their lips could meet. His tongue searched deep for honey, mimicking the sex act and making her body throb. His hands were both gentle and insistent as they forayed across her back and up her spine. Without warning he picked her up and carried her to the bed. He reverently laid her down and then joined her there.

Connor held the weight of his body on his arms as he kissed her face, her throat, and finally found her mouth with his. One hand cupped her breast and teased the nipple before sliding down her belly toward the ache below. His mouth replaced his hand on her breast, and Eve found herself arching toward the exquisite pleasure. She bit his shoulder as his fingertips worked their magic on her body.

Eve hadn't realized what a difference it would make to love the man caressing her. Hadn't realized how much she would crave his touch. Hadn't realized the joy she would experience when he made a guttural sound to express his appreciation as she searched out the places on his body that brought him the most pleasure.

"Molly, I—"

Eve froze as Connor spoke her best friend's name, then shoved at Connor's shoulders to move him away. "Connor, stop!"

Connor rolled over onto his back and slung an arm across his eyes. He was breathing as heavily as she was, and he was still aroused.

Eve's throat tightened so it was hard to swallow. She grabbed for the sheet to cover her nakedness, as though she were that first Eve, hiding herself because she'd sinned.

Oh, God. She'd known this would happen! She'd feared this would happen. What did it mean? What should she do? Ignore it? *Impossible*. Discuss it? *Impossible*.

She heard him swallow noisily before he said, "Eve, I'm sorry."

She said nothing. She had no idea what to say.

"You're nothing like Molly," he said into the silence. "I don't know why I said her name."

Eve cringed. His comment made it seem like she was missing something that Molly had. She wanted to run and hide, but where could she go? She was Connor's wife. This was her home. This was her bed.

"I swear I wasn't thinking of Molly," Connor said.

"Except it was her name you said."

He sighed but said nothing.

Molly would always be a part of their lives, a beloved wife and best friend. Neither of them really wanted her gone. So where did that leave them?

"Maybe you haven't finished grieving," Eve said.

Connor said nothing, just continued to lie beside her with his arm covering his eyes.

"Or maybe it isn't me you really want," she said into the silence. When he didn't immediately contradict her she added, "It's all right if you don't."

Connor lifted his head and looked down at her, his brow furrowed. "I hope you don't mean that, Eve. I hope it matters to you whether I desire you."

Eve blushed. "It's just . . . I half expected something like this to happen. For Molly to be here with us."

"I didn't." Connor's eyes bored into hers. "I knew exactly who I was holding in my arms." He shoved the sheet out of his way and slid his arms around her naked body, tucking her in a close embrace.

"You don't have to do this," she said.

"I don't have to. I want to."

A sudden raucous clash of metal on metal caused Connor to clutch her tighter, then roll them both off the bed. As soon as they were on the floor, he crouched on one knee, using the bed as a shield.

Eve grabbed at the sheet, pulling it off the bed to cover herself as she stared at Connor. "What just happened?"

He shot her a sheepish look. "I still haven't stopped ducking for cover when I hear anything that sounds like a gunshot."

Eve stared appreciatively at Connor's lean flanks and buttocks as he rose and strode, completely naked, toward the window. Before he got there, he retrieved his shorts and pulled them on.

The clamor intensified as he shoved open the window and stuck his head out. "I don't believe it!"

"What is it?" Eve asked, her whole body tensed for action.

He turned back to her, shaking his head in disbelief. "A shivaree."

"A what?"

"Old frontier custom," he explained. "The neighbors get together to serenade a newly married couple— with pots and pans—and generally interrupt the wedding night."

They'd done a pretty good job of that on their own, Eve thought. "Who's out there?"

"No idea, but they aren't going away until we give them something to eat and drink."

Two small forms appeared in the doorway clutched together.

"What is that?" Brooke asked fearfully.

"I'm scared," Sawyer said.

Connor pulled on his jeans as he said, "Some folks are wishing me and Eve noisy congratulations on getting married." He grabbed his shirt and headed for the door. "Let's let Eve get dressed while we go say hello. Then you two can head back to bed."

Eve hurried to put her clothes on, regretting that they hadn't made love, but feeling more encouraged than she had in a very long time. Connor might not love her, but he wanted her. She hoped whoever it was didn't stay long, because she very much wanted to finish what they'd started.

Eve heard what sounded like a violent quarrel as she headed down the hall. She recognized Taylor's voice. And Victoria's. And several male voices arguing back. Connor's brothers?

Eve ran for the kitchen, hoping she was in time to keep blood from being shed.

Chapter 19

EVE WAS APPALLED to discover her eldest sister, Taylor, with her balled fists on her hips confronting Brian Connor. Taylor was the beautiful sister, the one who looked the most like their stunning mother, Jill. Taylor was tall, with posture like a ballerina. She had long, lustrous, movie-star-blond hair and dazzling blue eyes that left men speechless when they met her for the first time.

Brian and Taylor weren't alone. Leah and Victoria stood to either side of Taylor while Aiden and Devon braced Brian. They were all still wearing their coats. Connor was situated between the kids, who were sitting on stools at the kitchen counter.

"It doesn't surprise me that you'd choose this way to celebrate a wedding between my sister and your brother," Taylor said. "Bad judgment seems to run in your family."

"What are you doing here? Tell me that?" Brian shot back.

"I came to wish my sister well."

"I did the same for my brother," Brian said. "Connor knows a shivaree is all in good fun."

"It's awful!" Taylor said. "Look at those two poor

quivering children." She pointed toward Brooke and Sawyer.

Unfortunately, at that moment the children were laughing at something Aiden was saying.

Brian snorted. "Yeah, they look real scared."

Leah spoke quietly to Connor, and he helped the children down from their stools. After a single wave goodbye from Brooke in the direction of the adults in the kitchen, Leah escorted the two children down the hall toward their bedrooms.

As Taylor watched them go she said, "Well, they *were* scared when they showed up here in the kitchen. I guess you Flynns can be hilarious when you want to be."

"You would know," Brian said.

"How dare you bring that up!"

Eve saw tears spring to Taylor's eyes and wondered what had happened between Brian and Taylor in the past that had caused her sister such anguish. Brian's blue eyes were as dark as his soul seemed to be.

She wasn't given the opportunity to sympathize with her sister, because the instant Taylor caught sight of Eve, she blurted, "I can't believe you got married without inviting any of us!"

"Without giving us a chance to stand up with you," Victoria added.

Eve's only defense was the truth, that it was a marriage of convenience, and as such, anything fancier would have been absurd. But she didn't know whether Connor wanted his brothers to know why they'd married so abruptly, and the more people who knew the real story, the better chance the truth would have of getting back to the social worker. "We both thought a simple wedding was best."

"This wedding wasn't just simple," Taylor accused. "It was a travesty."

Brian turned to Connor and said, "A speedy wedding without family present seems pretty suspicious to me." He turned to Eve and asked, "Are you pregnant?"

Connor hit his brother in the jaw. "That's my wife you're talking about. Watch your mouth!"

Eve gaped.

Devon had caught Brian as he stumbled backward and kept him upright. Brian rubbed his sore jaw with his hand as his gaze shifted from Connor to Eve and back again. "I notice you didn't answer my question."

"Why, you—"

Aiden caught Connor's cocked fist before he could punch Brian again. He let him go, then said in a voice that demanded obedience, "That's enough."

Eve was caught off guard when Leah asked, "Well, are you?"

She hadn't seen her sister return to the room.

"No, I'm not!" Eve opened her mouth to explain that they'd gotten married so quickly for the sake of the children and snapped it shut again. They didn't owe their siblings any explanation. "We had a lovely wedding and a lovely wedding day—that is, until the six of you showed up. Be happy for us."

She crossed to Connor, slid an arm around his waist, and looked up at him with all the love she felt. "We want to be together. Is that so hard to believe?"

Brian snorted again. "Yeah, it is." He shot a glance

in Taylor's direction before he said, "Grayhawks and Flynns are notoriously incapable of getting along."

"That's because all Flynns are liars," Taylor snapped back.

Eve stiffened. "I can't let you get away with that. Connor's never been anything but straightforward with me."

Leah put a comforting arm around Taylor's shoulders and said, "I think we should wish the newlyweds well and take our leave."

"Nothing good can come of this," Taylor replied.

"That doesn't mean we can't hope for the best," Leah said.

Eve's stomach churned. Was it really so impossible for her sisters to believe that she could be happy with Connor simply because he was a Flynn? She wasn't the only one of her sisters to have interacted with one of "those wild Flynn boys," but it seemed she was the only one who hadn't been wounded by the experience. Or at least, whatever pain she'd suffered because of falling in love with Connor wasn't his fault.

"By the way, your buttons are off-kilter," Victoria said, pointing to Eve's shirt.

Eve looked down and self-consciously grabbed a handful of her shirt where a button was in the wrong hole.

"Your shirt isn't buttoned at all," Devon said to Connor with a grin. He quirked an amused brow as he surveyed the two gathered sets of siblings. "Looks like these two are getting along a lot better than the rest of us."

Eve flushed to the roots of her hair. A quick glance at Connor's fair skin revealed an equal rush of blood to his cheeks, although he did nothing to close the shirt that gaped open down the center of his chest.

"Let's let these two get back to whatever it was they were doing," Aiden said with a chuckle.

"We should go, too," Leah said. She crossed to Eve and kissed her cheek. "If you're happy, I'm happy for you."

"Me, too," Victoria said as she kissed Eve's cheek.

"I wish I could believe this will end happily ever after," Taylor said. "But I don't." She grimaced at the admonishing look Leah shot her and added, "I love you, Eve. I hope you know what you're doing."

Eve watched Leah stiffen as Aiden stepped in front of her on her way to the door. He said something low that Eve couldn't hear, which resulted in Leah's looking up at him with troubled eyes. Her sister quickly lowered her gaze and moved past Connor's brother without touching him and without saying anything. Aiden followed Leah with his eyes until she was gone from the house.

Devon shook Connor's hand and said, "Congratulations. I wish the best for both of you."

Then he did something that surprised Eve. He leaned over and kissed her cheek, much as her sisters had done. It was only then it dawned on her that none of her sisters had offered Connor their best wishes. She wanted to call them back and demand that they do so, but it would only have pointed a finger at their lack of courtesy.

She tried to make up for it by being especially cordial to Connor's brother. She smiled as radiantly as she could and said, "Thank you, Devon."

Her goodwill toward the Flynn brothers was

quickly extinguished when Brian appeared before Connor, gripped his hand, and said, "You're making a big mistake." He turned to look at her and added, "Both of you."

"Thanks for your concern," Connor replied in what Eve thought was an amazingly level voice. "I know how unhappy you were in your marriage, so I understand your pessimism. I'm satisfied with the choice I made, and I hope you can be happy for me."

Connor never let go of Brian's hand the entire time he was talking. When he was done, he made the extraordinary gesture of hugging his brother. He whispered something in Brian's ear that made his brother scowl. The moment Brian was free, he turned without another word and headed for the door.

Aiden was the last to speak to them. "This marriage of yours caught Dad by surprise. He knew you were engaged, but he never suspected you'd jump the gun like this."

"How did he find out?" Connor asked.

"The magistrate called him."

Eve made a disgusted sound in her throat. Nothing important that happened in Jackson Hole escaped the many eyes and ears devoted to keeping King Grayhawk and Angus Flynn informed. She'd wondered how her sisters knew about the wedding. It seemed logical to assume that if the magistrate had called Angus he would have called King as well. Either King had told Leah, who'd told her sisters, or Leah had intercepted the call and told them.

"Angus was pissed," Aiden said.

"Too bad," Connor replied.

Aiden eyed Eve with what appeared to be concern before he said, "Seems he was only cordial to the two of you when you announced your engagement because he figured he'd have plenty of time to talk you out of getting married. He was ranting about taking away your trust fund if you don't have this marriage annulled."

Eve searched Connor's face to see his reaction to this potentially devastating news. A crease formed between his eyes, his mouth flattened, and a muscle worked in his jaw.

"You can tell him for me that I'm married, and I'm staying married."

Aiden grimaced. "I'll do what I can to smooth things over, but I doubt it'll do any good. Dad seems pretty rabid on the subject of any son of his being married to any daughter of King's."

"It's already done," Connor said.

Aiden turned his attention to Eve, and she saw what Leah might have found attractive about Connor's eldest brother. When he focused his full attention on her, she felt almost breathless at the impression he gave of pride and power.

"I think my brother should have hired a good babysitter instead of marrying you. Try not to break his heart."

"This isn't a love match," Eve blurted. "It's a marriage for mutual convenience."

Aiden frowned at Connor. "What the hell have you done?"

"Nothing that needs to concern you," Connor replied.

"You're about to lose your trust fund, little brother."

"That's not your problem."

"I happen to think that what you're doing here at this ranch is a good thing," Aiden replied. "I'd hate to see all that come to an end because you needed a baby-sitter."

Eve watched Connor's fists bunch, but he didn't take a swing at his brother. Instead he said, "I think you should leave."

"I'm trying to help."

"I know what I want."

"And King Grayhawk's daughter—and all the trouble that comes along with her—is what you want?" Aiden persisted.

"She is."

Aiden's brow furrowed as he looked at Connor, then at Eve, and back at Connor again. "Have I missed something here? Do you love her?"

"Of course—" Connor clamped his mouth shut before finishing the sentence.

Of course not. Eve was pretty sure that was what he'd intended to say. But that would only have been adding fuel to his brother's fire.

Insistent pounding on the door interrupted the squabble.

Connor left his brother standing where he was and hurried to the front door. When he opened it, Frank was standing there breathing hard, his eyes frightened. "It's one of the men," he said. "He heard all that banging early on and went a little crazy. I haven't been able to calm him down."

Connor turned to Aiden. "I know you think of me as your little brother, but I don't need your help with my life or my marriage."

"What about Dad's threat?"

Connor's mouth turned down in a ferocious frown. "I'll deal with Dad on my own."

A moment later Connor and Frank were gone, and Eve was left alone with Aiden Flynn.

"Do you love him?"

The question shocked Eve. She stared wide-eyed at Connor's brother, not sure what answer to give.

"I saw how you looked at him. I think you love him. I think you've loved him for a long time."

"Connor was married to my best friend," Eve said quietly.

"Yeah. He was. I think you grabbed at this chance to get him to marry you."

She felt Aiden's speculative gaze on her and wasn't able to control the hot blush that grew on her cheeks. She looked up at him defiantly. "I won't hurt him."

"You can't promise that. What if he never falls in love with you? What then? How are either one of you going to be happy?" He shook his head in disgust and muttered, "It's that fatal temptation Grayhawk women wield over Flynn men."

"What are you talking about?"

"Tell one of us he can't have something, and that's exactly what he wants," Aiden said.

"I won't hurt him," Eve repeated.

"I hope not. Because if you do, it's going to make the chance of happily ever after for any of the rest of us an uphill climb."

He headed for the door without another word.

Eve was left standing with her mouth hanging open. Was Aiden talking about himself and Leah? Was he still interested in her sister, even though they'd stopped dating? She couldn't imagine what else he could mean.

Eve was left with a great deal of food for thought.

"Is everybody gone? Where's Daddy?"

Eve turned to find Brooke standing in the middle of the hallway. She crossed and knelt before the little girl. "Your daddy had to go help one of the visiting soldiers."

"Oh. When is he coming back?"

"Soon, I'm sure."

"Can I sleep with you?"

"I don't have my own bed anymore. I'll be sleeping with your daddy in his bed."

"Oh."

Eve realized that Brooke hadn't said anything—positive or negative—about finding her in Connor's bed earlier in the evening. She wondered how much the four-year-old understood about the ceremony she'd witnessed earlier in the day. "Do you understand what it means to be married, Brooke?"

"Uh-huh."

"What do you think it means?"

"You and Daddy get to kiss each other and sleep in the same bed."

Eve was amused by the simple explanation. "Is that all right with you?"

"Uh-huh. Daddy smiles more now that you're here."

Eve hugged the little girl. "I think he smiles more because *you're* here. You and Sawyer."

The little girl looked thoughtful for a moment. Then she laughed and said, "Daddy's happy because we're a family again. Me and Sawyer and you and Daddy and Mommy."

Eve wasn't sure what to make of what Brooke had said, but she couldn't let it stand without speaking. As gently as she could, she said, "Your mommy's not coming back, Brooke."

"I know that. She's in heaven. But she's watching over us every day."

Eve rocked Brooke in her arms. "Yes, she is." Maybe the secret to forgiving herself for coveting Connor all those years was to keep Molly's memory alive for her children. She led Brooke back to her canopied bed and joined her there, then began telling Molly's daughter the story of her mother's first date with her father at the Sadie Hawkins dance.

A little while later, Eve awoke in Brooke's bed, aware she must have dozed. She checked on Brooke and saw that the little girl was sound asleep. She looked at the Hello Kitty clock on the side table and realized that nearly two hours had passed since Connor had left for the bunkhouse. Where was he? And what had happened to keep him away so long?

Chapter 20

CONNOR HAD SET his own worries aside until he was sure the spooked vet was back on an even keel, but if anything, tonight's events had proved just how necessary a place like Safe Haven was. As he left the cabin, where the young soldier was now relaxed and joking with Frank and a couple of the other vets, Connor realized that the sanctuary would be in big trouble if his father revoked his trust fund. And Angus was just vindictive enough to do it if he didn't get his way.

Connor's lips pressed into a grim line. His father didn't know him very well if he thought he would give up his new wife without a fight. Which made him wonder why he was so determined to keep Eve, especially in light of the way he'd sabotaged their lovemaking. Why on earth had he called out Molly's name?

Because you replaced Molly with a woman that you've always lusted after. Because you felt guilty about enjoying the taste and the feel of her. Because you didn't believe you deserved the joy of having Eve Grayhawk in your bed.

At least he'd had a chance to make amends for his faux pas before his brothers and Eve's sisters had interrupted their wedding night. Connor wasn't sure what it was about Eve that made his body sing whenever he was anywhere near her, but sing it did. He craved her in a way that seemed somehow sinful, because his desire was so strong.

All he had to do was recall the softness of her skin, the scent of her flowery shampoo, the taste of her kisses, and he was hard as a rock. Connor's body throbbed, and he wondered if it might be possible to resume their wedding night. He checked his watch and was surprised to discover that it was nearly midnight. In all likelihood, his bride was sound asleep.

But what if she wasn't?

The house was dark except for a single light in his bedroom. Connor felt his heartbeat speed up as he headed silently down the hall.

"Eve?"

His new-made wife sat up abruptly in bed and rubbed her eyes. She looked delightfully, delectably disheveled. One strap of her baby-doll pajamas had fallen off her shoulder, leaving it bare, and revealing the rounded crest of one luscious breast.

He closed the bedroom door and locked it, then crossed and sat down beside her.

"What time is it?" she asked in a throaty voice.

He couldn't tell if she was aroused or just sleepy. He leaned over to kiss her bare shoulder, feeling her shiver when the air hit the damp spot his lips had left on her skin. He sat up and focused his gaze on the bow of her upper lip. "It's still our wedding night for another ten minutes."

"Is the soldier who was upset okay?" She lifted

her arms to shove her hands through her hair, causing her breasts to rise into peaks beneath the thin cotton.

Connor had trouble keeping his voice even as he replied, "He's fine. He was just startled." He brushed a thumb across one of her nipples and heard her sharp intake of breath. "I wasn't sure you'd be awake."

She lowered her hands. Her blue eyes, as warm as Caribbean waters, never left his. "I am now."

He began unbuttoning his shirt, pulling the tails out of his jeans. "I could use a shower." He hesitated, then said, "Would you like to join me?"

She looked uncertain, but she didn't say no, so he rose and headed for the bathroom. He didn't close the bathroom door, leaving it open as an invitation he hoped she would accept. He was already in the shower, steam rising to fill the room, when he spied her standing in the doorway. She was naked. The shy smile on her face made his heart jump.

"I decided I could use a shower, too."

His pulse leapt as his shaft hardened. He shoved aside the clear shower curtain and held out his hand to her. "As you can see, I'm glad you decided to join me."

She laughed and took his hand so he could help her climb into the ancient, claw-footed tub.

He pulled her close so the hard length of him pressed against her belly. The joy in Eve's eyes sent adrenaline spiking through his veins. He caught a handful of her hair in his fist and angled her head for his kiss. She opened to him, welcoming the lash of his tongue as his wet hand slid across her breast, his fingers caressing a nipple that had formed into a hard bud.

She thrust her hands into his wet hair as he lowered his head and sucked the nipple into his mouth.

Eve moaned, and Connor replied with a guttural sound of satisfaction. His mouth was on hers again a moment later, as his hand slid down her belly between her legs, forcing them wide for his intrusion. He made another sound of appreciation when he felt how wet she was inside, and his fingers plucked at her like a harpist, making heavenly music. Eve made whimpering sounds and writhed in his arms, reaching for any part of him she could find. She brushed her hands across his nipples, which had become hard nubs, through the diamond of rough black hair in the center of his chest, and down past his naval. Before she could reach what she sought, Connor lifted her into his arms. He turned both of them into the spray of water and said, "Shut that off."

Eve twisted the knob and threw the shower curtain aside almost in the same motion. Connor stepped out of the tub and headed for the bed. He laid her on the sheets, spreading her legs with his knees as he thrust himself inside her to the hilt.

She made a low sound of satisfaction in her throat, and he met it with a growl of his own.

She wrapped her legs around his hips as he lifted her buttocks to give him better purchase. He took what he wanted and gave pleasure in return. Eve arched into him, and he thrust deeper, groaning as her body captured him after each powerful thrust, only to release him to thrust again.

Her eyes had turned the dark blue of storm-ridden skies, and remained intent on his. He didn't say her

name. He didn't speak at all. But he was aware every second of the woman to whom he was making love.

Connor's heart skipped a beat. *Making love.* It surprised him that he'd thought those words. He felt a great deal for Eve, more than he wanted to feel. More than he should have felt for a woman who'd become his wife as a matter of convenience. He was left with the uncomfortable thought that he might have had feelings for Eve—something more than lustful desire—when he was married to his wife.

Connor stopped thinking and concentrated on feeling. Everything. Every touch of Eve's lips. Every caress of her fingertips. She gave all of herself to him. She took all of him. She arched upward into his body, her fingernails clawing his shoulders as her body began to convulse. A raw sound issued from her throat and was met by an equally ragged cry of his own. They clutched each other in the throes of something rare, a sharing of ecstasy that magnified the joy and pleasure of both.

As Connor eased himself to her side, his lungs heaving, she chuckled.

"What's so funny?"

Eve laughed, a happy sound, and said, "I need a shower."

Connor smiled as he pulled her into his arms, holding her close. "We'll get one in the morning."

"Where are the covers?" she asked.

"Who cares?"

"The sheets are sopping wet."

"Fortunes of war."

She snuggled close, her nose against his throat,

her belly aligned with his. "So long as you don't mind keeping me warm all night."

His arms surrounded her and he leaned down to kiss her beneath her ear. "I don't mind at all."

"Connor."

"What?" he murmured.

"We have to put on some clothes. Or find the covers."

"Why?"

"The kids."

"I locked the door."

He heard her sigh and felt her relax. "Meanwhile," he said, "I have you exactly where I want you." His shaft stirred against her belly.

Her eyes opened wide. "Again?"

Connor shot her a smug grin. "Still."

He hissed in a breath as Eve rubbed her breasts against the bristly hair on his chest. She smiled coyly and said, "I'm ready if you are."

Connor took her at her word. He lifted her on top of him, her legs splayed on either side of his waist.

She seemed startled but delighted to be in control of their lovemaking. "Don't move," she ordered. "Not until I tell you it's okay."

She impaled herself on his erection, taking her time, moving to bring herself the most satisfaction, her eyes avid, her eyelids heavy.

Connor grasped her hips tightly, but he didn't try to control her, just held on and lay still, afraid he would explode if he moved. As she leaned over him, his hands left her hips and he reached up to knead her breasts, playing with them and taking one in his mouth to suck, strong and hard.

Eve cried out as her body began to spasm. Connor's hands caught her hips again to thrust hard and deep, and he gave a cry of exultation as he spilled his seed.

She collapsed onto his chest, her lungs sucking air as his bellowed beneath her. He closed his eyes and held her close, but he said nothing. This was no love match, so there were no love words to be spoken.

Chapter 21

"MY WIFE'S STILL in bed," Eve heard Connor say from somewhere down the hall. "She didn't get much sleep last night."

There was long, terrible silence before she heard a hearty female laugh, a vigorous laugh, a totally engaging and funny laugh. Then Eve heard a voice she recognized as belonging to Mrs. Stack say, "Well, well, Mr. Flynn. I wondered whether this was a real marriage. I guess I have my answer."

Eve smiled and stretched languorously, arching her toes and stretching her fingers wide. She was in a *real* marriage. She stopped mid-stretch and jumped out of bed. A *real* wife would be in the kitchen right now helping to make breakfast. She wrapped her naked body in a sheet and ran down the hall barefoot, ducking into her former bedroom to put on a robe and slippers before continuing her journey to the kitchen. She found Mrs. Stack sitting on one of the bar stools with Sawyer on her lap. Brooke occupied the other stool, while Connor stood at the stove making pancakes.

When he saw her he said, "Good morning, sleepyhead."

A hot blush rose on her cheeks in response to the eloquent look he gave her. She ruffled her hands through her hair before tucking it neatly behind her ears. "Good morning."

"Hi, Aunt Eve," Brooke said.

"Hi, Aunt Eve," Sawyer said. "Want some pancakes?"

"I sure do." She exchanged another look with Connor, who had the audacity to arch a knowing brow, reminding her of the reason she was so hungry.

"I was just telling Mr. Flynn it won't be necessary for me to check in as often, now that you two are married."

"That's good to hear." Eve wondered what the social worker was going to think when she took off for Nevada in six weeks. *Am I really going to leave Connor and the kids?* How could she not go? It was what she'd worked for all her life.

What if you give up your dream, and Connor ends up having to annul the marriage to save his dream? Eve found it hard to believe, after what had happened between them last night, that Connor would do such a thing. The lovemaking had been exactly that— making love to each other. No words of love had been spoken by either of them, but Connor had revered her and made her feel adored. And she'd finally, at long last, been able to touch and tease and torment him in ways that had given them both unbelievable pleasure. Surely he couldn't make love to her with such tenderness and then walk away.

Unless he had no other choice.

If Angus cut Connor off, even what she earned from *National Geographic* wasn't going to be enough to make up for the lost income from his trust fund. And he was every bit as passionate about what he was trying to accomplish at Safe Haven as she was about saving wild mustangs from slaughter.

Eve stared at Connor's back as he chatted with the social worker, wondering if her happily ever after was about to be ended, not by a wicked old witch, but by a wicked old man.

"The judge authorized supervision for six months," Mrs. Stack was explaining to Connor, "or for a shorter period if I'm satisfied that the children are in a safe, happy home." Mrs. Stack glanced from Connor to Eve and said, "I'm willing to give the two of you the benefit of the doubt. Of course, I have the option to revisit my decision if circumstances change."

Eve's heart sank. She met Connor's gaze and saw the concern there. He wasn't out of the woods yet.

"Those pancakes are burning," Mrs. Stack said.

Connor pulled the pan off the fire and dumped the burned pancakes in the sink. "I've got plenty of batter," he said with a hard-won smile. "I'll have another batch ready in a jiffy."

"With blueberries?" Brooke asked.

"Yep," Connor replied.

Eve had shopped for blueberries before they returned from town yesterday, along with eggs and milk and enough fruits and vegetables to satisfy someone as particular as Mrs. Stack, while Connor ran some errands.

"Will you be staying for breakfast?" Eve asked.

As Mrs. Stack stood, Eve took Sawyer from the social worker, setting him on her hip.

"I've got to get back to town," Mrs. Stack said. "You folks enjoy your breakfast."

A moment later she was gone. Eve joined Connor at the stove. She looked into his troubled eyes and said quietly enough so the children wouldn't hear, "What's she going to think about me leaving to work in Nevada?"

"We'll deal with that when the time comes."

Eve took a deep breath and asked, "What are you going to do about the ultimatum from your father?"

"Nothing."

"Nothing? Aren't you worried that he'll rescind your trust fund?"

"My father can do what he wants. I'm not going to let him dictate my life. We're going to have breakfast, and then, if it's all right with you, we can take the kids for a horseback ride and enjoy a picnic lunch. We're entitled to a honeymoon. I say we enjoy it."

Eve couldn't believe Connor was so nonchalant about the potential calamity he faced if his father took away the funds he needed to support Safe Haven. But he knew Angus better than she did. Maybe when push came to shove, Angus wouldn't—couldn't— hurt his son like that. Or maybe Connor had some other source of income she didn't know about.

"A horseback ride and picnic sound wonderful," she said.

Brooke could ride by herself, and Sawyer was completely comfortable on horseback in the lap of an adult. Then it dawned on her that she and Connor were taking two little kids on their "honeymoon" picnic. And that she was looking forward to it.

The reality of life with Connor and the children

was turning out to be every bit as wonderful as she'd imagined. There were a few glitches, of course. Like needing to leave her new husband and family so soon to pursue a professional dream come true. And Connor perhaps ending up broke.

Eve was doing her best not to wallow in guilt about getting what she'd always coveted. But she wondered if the sudden obstacles to her fairy-tale ending meant that she didn't deserve what she was getting, and that, in fact, she might not, after all, live so happily ever after.

Like most women she knew, Eve wanted it all: to be a superb wife and mother and have a satisfying professional life. She was discovering that the balancing act required wasn't easy. And that there were no simple answers.

All she could do was live each day as it came and make the choice at each turning point that seemed most likely to make her happy. Right now, nothing could make her happier than spending the day with Connor and the children, especially since she could take along her camera.

Eve grinned. It seemed like a good omen that for today, at least, she could have her cake and eat it, too.

"What has you grinning like the Cheshire cat?" Connor asked.

Eve shook her head, unwilling to explain that, in a life that had become very complicated, all her choices this morning had been easy. Instead she said, "I'm just happy."

Within the hour, they'd packed a lunch and saddled the horses, Eve had collected the black canvas bag that contained all her camera equipment, and they were on their way.

"Where are we going?" Eve asked as they mounted up at the stable, Sawyer settled in Connor's lap.

"Before I bought the ranch I rode most of the trails. One of them leads to a mountain meadow, which ought to be filled with wildflowers about now."

It was a perfect Wyoming spring day, the sun warm and the wind absent. Eve had her camera slung around her neck so she could easily take pictures. She looped her knotted reins around the saddle horn so she would have both hands free to take a photograph of Connor and his son.

Sawyer was leaning back against Connor's chest looking up at his father, while Connor's head was bent to answer whatever question his son was asking.

Click.

Connor looked up at the sound and smiled self-consciously.

"Don't mind me," Eve said, giving her horse a nudge with her heels to keep him moving along with the other animals.

"Take my picture, Aunt Eve," Brooke said.

"Ride up beside your father," Eve encouraged the little girl.

"Here I come." Brooke smiled for the camera and dug her heels into her pony's side, prodding him to a trot.

Click.

The three of them stopped to wait for Eve to catch up, and Sawyer leaned way over to pat the neck of Brooke's pony.

Click.

"Look!" As Connor pointed, Sawyer sat upright and both children lifted their eyes skyward. Brooke shaded her eyes with her hand to observe the eagle soaring overhead.

Click.

Connor turned around in the saddle and said, "Are you coming, Eve?"

"Don't worry about me. I'll catch up."

Connor took her at her word and kicked his horse into a slow trot. Eve let them get a little farther ahead, angling her horse to the side so she could get a shot of the riders on horseback with the unending green forest and cloudless blue sky in the distance.

Click.

Holding the camera in one hand and the reins in the other, she urged her horse into a lope to catch up to them.

"I figured you brought your camera along to take pictures of wildlife, not pictures of us," Connor said.

"You're a different kind of wildlife," Eve teased. "Besides, I've got an eagle in one of those shots, not to mention a couple of horses."

Connor laughed. "Touché. Click away."

Eve did exactly that, saving moments of love and laughter along the trail that she and Connor could enjoy long after the children were grown. Eve realized that she didn't want this fairy tale to end. There had to be a way, there just had to be a way, to make it all work out—the job and the kids and the husband and the unborn babies they would have someday in the future. But how?

After two hours on the trail, they emerged from

the forest onto a grassy meadow filled with colorful wildflowers, hundreds of yellow butterflies flittering and fluttering among them.

Eve gasped. "Oh, Connor. How lovely!"

"I'm glad you like it," he said as he lowered Sawyer to the ground, then dismounted himself. The little boy took off at a run following his sister, who'd slid off her pony the moment they reached the meadow, chasing after butterflies.

"Stay where I can see you," he called to the two children. "We'll be eating lunch soon."

"Okay," Brooke called back without stopping.

Eve untied the blanket behind her saddle and loosened the cinch, staking her horse, along with Brooke's, on a long line so they could munch on the mountain grass and not stray. Connor did the same with his horse before retrieving the saddlebags that contained their picnic lunch.

Connor set the saddlebags on a rock outcropping, then took the blanket from Eve and flung it open so it settled on a level spot in the grass. She straightened the edges before dropping to her knees on the blanket. Connor transferred the saddlebags onto the blanket and joined her there.

From the corner of her eye, Eve had been keeping track of the children. "They're going to be exhausted if they keep running around like that."

"Good. Maybe they'll take a nap after lunch."

Eve felt her face flush when she met Connor's gaze. It was perfectly clear what *he* would like to do to *her* after lunch.

"Brooke! Sawyer!" he called. "Time to eat."

The children must have been hungry, because they

came running. By the time they reached the blanket, Eve had peanut butter and jelly sandwiches and apple slices set out on paper plates and small juice boxes affixed with straws. The kids arrived breathless and plopped onto the blanket.

"Here, Aunt Eve," Brooke said, handing Eve a bunch of wildflowers she'd picked. "These are for you."

"Here, Aunt Eve," Sawyer said, dropping a handful of flowers without stems into her lap. "For you."

Eve felt tears sting her eyes. "They're beautiful. Thank you both." She gave each child a kiss to show her gratitude, but they were more interested in the plates of food, digging in as though they hadn't finished breakfast a mere three hours ago.

Eve suddenly realized that the children had given all the flowers to her, rather than sharing them with their father. "You deserve a few of these," she said to Connor, holding out the bouquet Brooke had handed to her.

He plucked one of the flowers from her hand and sniffed it, then looked into her eyes and said, "I'd rather enjoy the sight of you holding them."

Was he *flirting* with her?

Connor got distracted when Sawyer dripped jelly onto his shirt. He grabbed a napkin and swiped up the blob, then unwrapped his own sandwich and began eating.

Eve was still staring at him, enjoying the thrill of being admired by a man who'd married her for practical reasons that had nothing to do with admiration.

"Here," he said, tossing her a sandwich in a completely unloverlike way. "Better hurry up and eat. I have a feeling that when they're done we'll all be chasing butterflies. Personally, I'd rather be picking flowers."

He shot her a mischievous look, and Eve felt a frisson of excitement race down her spine. *Picking flowers?* Or did he mean plucking buds of an entirely different sort?

When they were done eating, the kids were still bouncing with energy, so Eve suggested a game of tag.

"That's a great idea," Connor said. "You're it!"

Eve decided to tag Brooke and raced after the laughing girl. Brooke was so agile, and made such quick stops and starts and turns, it took Eve several breathless minutes to catch up to her. "Tag!" she shouted when she finally tapped Brooke's shoulder. "You're it."

Eve turned and ran to escape before she could be tagged back, and Brooke looked for Sawyer, who would be an easy target. Unfortunately for her, Connor had picked up the little boy and was running with him in his arms. Sawyer giggled as Connor weaved back and forth to avoid his daughter, and Eve joined in as she dodged and darted to stay out of Brooke's way.

Eve was surprised when Connor didn't slow down to let the little girl catch him. She was equally surprised when Brooke didn't give up, just kept pursuing Connor until he tripped in a gopher hole and almost fell, going down on one knee to be sure Sawyer didn't take a tumble.

"Tag!" Brooke said triumphantly as she touched his arm. "You're it."

Connor set Sawyer on his feet, then held out his

curved hands like some clawed monster and said, "Watch out, everybody. Here I come!"

Brooke and Sawyer turned, laughing and shrieking, and ran full tilt in opposite directions.

Eve figured Connor would chase after the kids, making sure he didn't catch them too soon. To her astonishment, he headed straight for her.

Eve turned and bolted, laughing and shrieking as loudly as the kids, zigzagging to keep from getting caught.

But catch her he did. By then, they'd reached the tree line on the opposite side of the meadow from the kids. "Tag!" he shouted. "You're it."

But instead of merely touching her arm, he pressed her back against the closest pine so they were aligned, body to body. Her heart was pounding from all the running and she was laughing, having enjoyed the game. Hidden from the children, his hands came up to caress her breasts. Eve trembled with excitement, her body instantly aroused and ready.

"What are you doing?" she asked breathlessly. "The kids—"

"Will be here any second. Until then, I want to touch you."

Eve could feel the hard length of him between her thighs. His hot breath fanned her cheek, and she angled her head so their lips could meet.

He claimed her mouth as though he might never have another chance, the kiss almost savage, then let her go abruptly and stepped back.

He met her gaze, his eyes clouded with pain, then turned his face sharply away.

"Are you all right?" she asked. "Is something wrong?"

She heard him swallow hard before he said, "Nothing's wrong. I just wish . . ."

Eve finished the sentence for herself. *Molly were here.* Jealousy ran through her veins like molten lava. *Molly's dead. It's my turn!*

Eve's whole body flamed with red-hot rage. She'd always been jealous of Molly, but she'd kept that jealousy under tight control. Now, when it seemed Connor might be hers at last, it seemed her best friend was still holding the man Eve loved in thrall. She struggled, without success, to control the green-eyed monster that had reared its ugly head. She felt her hands curl into fighting claws. But how did you fight a ghost?

When is it my turn, Molly? Let him go, so he can love me.

"Wish what, Connor?" she said, her throat so swollen with emotion that she thought she might choke. "That Molly were here instead of me?"

He shook his head as he whirled to face her, his blue eyes dark and bleak. "No! I wish Molly and I had spent more time doing things like this together when she was alive." He grimaced. "But she wasn't big on picnics. And I wasn't around to go on one anyway. The truth is, I'd never have played tag with the kids if it weren't for you."

Eve was thrown for a loop. Connor wasn't wishing for Molly? Connor was giving her credit for making the day special?

He took a step to close the distance between them and drew her into his embrace again. Eve felt the adrenaline draining from her body, leaving her totally enervated. She put her arms around Connor's neck and clung to him to keep from falling down.

"I'm glad you're a part of our lives," he whispered in her ear.

"Me, too," Eve said.

A moment later he separated them again, setting her a short distance away. "Before those two imps show up I have something to give you."

He reached into his jeans pocket and came out with a ring. "I searched every store in town yesterday while you were shopping for groceries and found this."

Eve stared at the simple gold band with a tiny diamond leaf embedded in it. She felt the tears coming and couldn't keep them from falling. "Oh, Connor."

"Don't cry," he said, with a lopsided smile. "Give me your hand."

Both hands were covering her mouth as she tried to keep from sobbing, but she let him have the left one, which shook as he slipped the ring on her finger.

"It's beautiful."

"So are you," he said.

"Hey!" Brooke said, arriving breathlessly at Eve's side. "Are we gonna play some more?"

"I think you and Sawyer need to rest for a little while," Connor said.

"I'm not tired!" Brooke protested.

"Five minutes," Connor said.

He took Eve's hand, the one with the wedding band on it, as Brooke reached for Eve's other hand, and the three of them headed back toward where they'd left the horses. They met Sawyer on the way, and Connor picked up the exhausted toddler and carried him back to the blanket, where he set him down beside Brooke.

"Close your eyes, and I'll tell you a story," Eve said, as she dropped onto the blanket beside the children.

"This I've got to hear," Connor said as he settled across from her.

"Once upon a time," Eve began, "there was a beautiful princess." Before long, both children were sound asleep.

"Good story," Connor said.

Eve stretched her legs out so she could lie on her side.

"Would you like me to tell you how it ends?" she asked coyly.

Connor chuckled. "I think I know how it ends." He lay down facing her, his head supported on his hand. "The jealous witch—"

Eve sat up abruptly. That word, *jealous,* brought back all those ugly feelings she'd experienced, and which she never wanted to experience again. "I have something I need to say."

Connor sat up across from her, a concerned look on his face.

Eve had no idea where to start, so she simply dove in. "I'm jealous of Molly."

Connor looked confused. "What?"

"I know it's silly. I know she's gone. But I used to have a crush on you in high school, and I guess I never got over losing you to my best friend."

He opened his mouth to speak, but she kept on

talking, certain that if she stopped, she'd never get started again.

"I know you miss Molly. I miss her too. But I can't help wanting you to want me instead of her. So when you start a sentence with 'I wish Molly' it makes me a little crazy." She swallowed over the knot in her throat and added, "Jealous, I mean."

Eve fought to lift her eyes to meet Connor's gaze, afraid of the censure she might find there, but needing to know his reaction to what she'd just admitted.

His blue eyes were narrowed. Not a good sign. "You had a crush on me in high school?"

Eve couldn't speak, so she nodded.

"And you still set me up to go with Molly to that dance?"

Eve nodded again. She felt sick to her stomach. Maybe this hadn't been such a good idea.

"I liked you, too, Eve. A lot."

Eve gaped. "You did?"

Connor rubbed a hand across his nape and shook his head. "What a clusterfuck."

Eve was shocked at the word he'd chosen to describe their crossed wires in high school. "Why didn't you say something to me?" she asked.

"It wasn't possible. Not with the way our families hated each other."

"They still hate each other. How is the situation different now?"

"I was a boy then. I didn't know any better."

And he was a man now, willing to defy his father and his family to marry her, Eve suddenly realized.

She knew her feelings hadn't changed, but what about his? She'd admitted to a crush. He'd admitted to liking her. A lot. But liking was a long way from loving. Had his feelings ever run deeper? Perhaps not, Eve realized. After all, he'd been a grown man when he'd married Molly, and he'd chosen her best friend over her.

"You don't need to be jealous of Molly," Connor said. "I loved her. I won't ever forget her. I won't ever let the children forget her. But there's certainly a place in my life for another woman. For you."

Eve noticed he'd said "my life" and not "my heart." Could he fall in love again? Eve took comfort from the fact that he'd married her in defiance of both their families.

She rubbed the gold ring on her finger with her thumb. She wanted to ask if he still had feelings for her. Wanted to admit that she'd always loved him. But she'd come as far as she dared. It would be awkward to admit to feelings Connor didn't share. So she remained silent.

Brooke rubbed her eyes and sat up. "Can we play tag again?"

"Not today," Connor said. "We have to get started home." He looked at Eve as he said, "But we'll do this again. Soon." He grinned and added, "There are a few games your mom and I didn't get a chance to play."

Eve blushed. And laughed. And then realized what Connor had said. *Your mom.* Her heart felt full. This was where she belonged. This was what she wanted to be doing with her life. She didn't want to leave Connor or the children to go take pictures in another state, not so soon and not for so long. There had to be a way to take pictures for *National Geographic* and be a wife and mother, too.

Then, like a flashbulb going off, it dawned on her that she had a herd of mustangs that included two pregnant mares. And a young colt. And five rambunctious yearlings.

On the other hand, she had no mustang stallion. And technically, her herd was no longer running wild.

Would *National Geographic* be willing to compromise? The only way to find out was to ask.

Chapter 22

DURING THE RIDE home from the meadow, Eve kept the children engaged in conversation, giving Connor time to think. What he thought about was Eve.

Until Eve's confession, Connor hadn't been willing to admit that what he felt for her, what he'd always felt for her, was more than lust. It was a yearning for what might have been if he'd pursued Eve instead of Molly. If he'd married Eve instead of Molly. When he'd walked away from Eve, who was still holding the strawberry ice cream cone he'd bought for her, he'd known he was leaving something precious behind.

Those thoughts felt disrespectful to his late wife, and he was having trouble dealing with them. But last night, when he'd made love to Eve, it had felt as though a dark, yawning space inside him was filled with light . . . and with love.

He wondered how he'd gotten so lucky. What were the chances that a woman like Eve Grayhawk, with more attributes than he could name in a single breath, would still be single at twenty-six when her best friend had married at eighteen? And not just single, but single without a steady boyfriend. Had she been too committed to her career to marry? Or simply not found a man she loved enough to marry? But if Eve had stayed single for either of those reasons, why had she so readily married him?

Connor thought of his own teenage feelings, which had continued into adulthood, and wondered if Eve's "crush" might have survived as well. Had they each been harboring feelings for the other all these years? Was it possible that she hadn't married another man because she was in love with *him*?

If he allowed himself to believe that bit of fantasy, Connor was left with the intriguing possibility that Eve had loved him while he was married to her best friend. He would never ask her for the truth of his supposition, but if he was right, she'd managed to keep her feelings completely hidden, both from him and, as far as he knew, from Molly. He watched her chatter with the children and wondered what it must have been like for her, knowing her feelings would never be returned. No wonder she'd confessed to being jealous when he'd mentioned Molly's name.

So where did he go from here?

The answer was simple. *Love Eve and hope she loves me back*. He might be asking for heartbreak, but he thought the risk was worth it. He had six weeks before she had to leave for Nevada. Six weeks to make sure that she loved him enough to come back home, no matter how many times she had to leave again to do her amazing work.

They were unsaddling their horses when Frank came trotting up to the corral. "You've got a call at the house, Connor. It's your dad. I told him you'd call him back, but he said it was important and he'd wait."

Connor felt his gut clench. He'd told Eve his father didn't run his life. But it was still possible for Angus to *ruin* it. "Thanks, Frank."

Connor hadn't taken two steps toward the house when he realized Eve was beside him. "What do you think you're doing?"

"Coming with you."

"The kids—"

"Are helping brush down the horses."

"I don't need your help handling my father."

"Too bad. I'm part of this family."

"For now, anyway," he muttered. He was dying for a good, knock-down, drag-out fight. Determined to start one. Pushing as hard as he could to send Eve over the edge. Into his arms? Away from him for good? He just wanted everything settled, once and for all.

"Six weeks," she said through gritted teeth. "Then I'm gone, and you can have your life back just the way you want it."

"You think this is what I want?" he snarled, turning on her. "My kids lost their mom. I lost my wife. I married a woman who lights my fire like no other woman I've ever known—including my late wife—and she has plans of her own that don't include me or my kids. That is *not* the life I planned for myself. That is *not* what I want!"

He stalked away, leaving her standing with her jaw agape, mad at himself for having revealed so much. He yanked open the back door and stomped his way to the phone in the kitchen. He picked it up and said, "You don't run my life. Take your money and stuff it where the sun don't shine." Then he slammed the phone back in the cradle.

A moment later Eve reached his side, breathless from running to catch up, her voice strident. "You're not the only one who had a different life planned. This isn't what I wanted, either. I miss my best friend. I wish she was here. I wish there was more than just this physical . . . thing . . . between us. I wish—"

That was as far as she got before Connor's arms locked around her. It took him a moment to realize she was fighting him. He let her go and stared down at her, his body so hard it hurt.

Her chin was quivering, and her eyes looked wounded. "This isn't going to make things better."

"Can't make them any worse," he quipped.

"Please don't."

A painful knot formed in his throat. He met her gaze and nodded his capitulation, because it was impossible to speak.

"You need to go see your father," she said. "You can't blow him off like that."

"Too late. Angus Flynn doesn't forgive or forget."

"We'll go see him together."

"Bad idea."

"We have to do something. We can't leave things the way they are."

"Why not?"

"Why not annul the marriage? I have to leave anyway."

"I refuse to give him the satisfaction."

"Connor, be reasonable. Why don't we just admit

that this isn't going to work, and go our separate ways?"

"Because I don't want to end this marriage."

"Why not?"

Because I have feelings for you. "Because I hate giving up. On anything."

"We're running out of time," she reminded him.

"Trust me. I'll work it out." He'd plan some kind of fund-raiser, or get a loan and use the ranch as security, or borrow money until he could make the ranch self-sufficient.

"If you don't go talk to him, I will," Eve threatened.

"If you care at all for me, you won't do that."

She looked chastened. "All right. But I think you're making a mistake."

"It's my mistake. I'll deal with it." And he would. He just had to figure out how.

Chapter 23

FOR THE NEXT two weeks, Eve deferred to Connor's wish to deal with his father on his own. The problem was, as far as she could tell, he'd dealt with the issue by ignoring it.

She'd kept her fingers crossed that *National Geographic* would go for her idea of photographing the mustangs at Safe Haven, but it hadn't worked out. The editor had been apologetic, but she'd pointed out to Eve that they needed photographs of an actual band of *wild* mustangs. Otherwise, what was the point? If Eve wanted the job it was hers, but she would have to take her photographs in Nevada. And the deadline for her answer was looming.

Eve had another day or so to make her decision, but she didn't see how she could turn down the job. Especially in light of Connor's situation. The only thing she could think to do was force a confrontation with Angus Flynn and get him to back down.

When Sunday morning came around again, Eve got up early and dressed the children and herself for church. She announced to Connor, who sat in front of the fire with a cup of coffee and *Fortune* magazine,

"The kids and I are going to church this morning. Care to join us?"

He didn't even look up when he answered. "God and I aren't on speaking terms at the moment."

That was a complication Eve hadn't foreseen. "Because of Molly?"

"That's one reason."

He glanced at her, a line etched between his brows, and Eve realized he hadn't made peace with God over Paddy's death, either.

He pursed his lips. "Which church are you planning to attend?"

"The one your children have always attended."

"You're taking them to St. Michael's?"

"Your children are Catholic, Connor. Of course I'm taking them to St. Michael's."

"My family will be there."

"Most likely, yes, they will."

"Where are you planning to sit?"

"With them, of course."

Connor scowled. "Angus won't like it."

"It won't be easy for him to throw us out," Eve said. "I'm his daughter-in-law and Brooke and Sawyer are his grandchildren."

"In other words, you'd be perfectly happy to make a scene."

"What I'm telling you is that *he* won't make a scene. Not with the children there and all his friends watching."

"You don't know my father," Connor muttered.

"Are you going to let some old bully get away with keeping your wife and children from sitting with your family?" Eve challenged.

Connor sat up abruptly, spewing a mouthful of coffee. "Did you just call my father an *old bully*?"

"If the shoe fits—"

"Hell and damnation! You're liable to start World War Three if I let you go there by yourself."

She saw the moment Connor realized that he'd just been manipulated into going to church.

He shot her a rueful look as he stood and swiped at the coffee on his T-shirt. "I need a shower and a shave."

She smiled sweetly. "We'll wait. We have plenty of time."

He glanced at the antique clock on the mantel and made a disgusted sound. "We need to leave in the next fifteen minutes if we're not going to be late."

"You were a Delta sergeant. It takes you five minutes to shower and shave."

Connor scowled, crossed the room to set his coffee cup on the breakfast bar, and headed for the bathroom. "All right. You win."

"I'm not playing games," Eve shouted after him.

"Tell that to my dad," he called back to her.

Eve was more anxious about the upcoming meeting with Angus than she'd let on. She was counting on Connor's father wanting to keep up appearances, which meant there would be a window where he would be forced to speak with civility to his son and his son's wife.

Since the day was warm, she'd sent the kids out onto the porch to play and joined them there to wait for Connor. He showed up eight minutes later wearing a pale blue oxford-cloth shirt with a striped tie, a navy sport coat, khaki trousers, and brown loafers.

"Wow." Eve felt her insides flutter at the sight of

him, his face freshly shaven, his blue eyes bright, his hair still damp, with that dashing hank of hair falling on his brow.

Connor smirked in response to her awestruck expression. "I figured it you were going to dress up and look good enough to eat, I should, too." He gestured toward the pickup. "Shall we?"

Eve took Sawyer's hand in one of hers, but when she reached for Brooke's hand the little girl said, "I always hold Daddy's hand when we go to church."

Eve saw the shocked look on Connor's face before he reached out to take his daughter's small hand in his large one. Brooke had played tag with Connor during their picnic, but for weeks she'd avoided addressing him directly. Eve had seen his frustration grow as time passed, and nothing he'd done had melted his daughter's reserve.

All it had taken was a willingness to do something he and Brooke and Sawyer and Molly must have done every Sunday morning he was at home during Brooke's entire short life to remind his daughter that he was indeed her father.

Connor looked at Eve with dawning understanding. He obviously hadn't been to church since he'd returned from Afghanistan or Brooke would have insisted he take her hand long before now. He reached down and picked up his daughter and held her close. The little girl threw her arms around Connor's neck and held tight, her nose pressed against his throat.

Eve felt her throat swell with emotion as tears suddenly appeared in Connor's eyes.

He croaked, "I guess we . . ." He cleared his throat and finished, "better go."

Chapter 24

Connor didn't want to let go of his daughter to put her in her car seat. If only he'd known that something as simple as attending church with Brooke would be the key to melting her heart or winning her trust or whatever it was that had made her finally reach out to him. Did this mean she would allow him to hug her from now on? That she would be giving him butterfly kisses at bedtime?

A painful knot was still caught in his throat as he finished attaching the belts on Brooke's car seat. He exchanged a grateful look with Eve over the children's heads. She was the reason he'd broken his vow not to return to church until he could forgive God for taking Paddy, for taking Molly, and for all the death and destruction he'd witnessed during three tours in Afghanistan. If not for Eve, he might still be estranged from his daughter.

He spent the entire hour drive to town listening as Eve sang children's songs with the kids. He glanced at her often, amazed at the smile that remained on her face as they sang song after song, none of which he knew.

His mind was focused on figuring out what to say to Angus.

Keeping the sanctuary up and running was important not just for the sake of the vets, but so that Eve didn't need to take that assignment in Nevada in order to support her mustangs. Not that she might not decide to go anyway, but they would both have more choices if the trip weren't financially necessary.

Brooke interrupted his contemplation with the command, "Sing, Daddy!"

He realized the other three were belting out "Let It Go." He would have done anything his daughter asked to reinforce the new accord between them. He grinned at Eve and began to sing.

They had just finished, laughing and off-key, when they pulled up in front of St. Michael's. The old stone church sat in the shadow of the Grand Tetons surrounded by a windbreak of spruces and pines. As he turned off the engine, Connor asked Eve, "Do we take the kids with us to church? Or leave them in child care?"

"Let's take Brooke with us. She's old enough to sit through the service."

And affectionate enough to melt his father's cold, cold heart, Connor thought. "And Sawyer?" he asked.

"He'll do better in child care."

Connor held his breath as he released the belts on Brooke's car seat. Would she come into his arms again? Or would she reach for Eve?

When his daughter held out her arms to him, Connor lifted her into his embrace and felt his heart swell with love for his child. He dared so far as to kiss Brooke's cheek and saw her sudden glance sideways at him. He waited for some protest, but she merely slid her arms around him and snuggled close.

He set her down, and the four of them walked hand in hand toward the church.

Connor felt a moment of apprehension when they arrived at the door to the nursery. He wasn't sure how Sawyer would react to being left behind. His son ran toward one of the other little boys, calling out his name. "I guess he isn't going to miss us," he said with a chagrined smile.

Eve laughed. "No, he won't. Mrs. Robertson runs the nursery."

Connor was both shocked and dismayed. "What?"

Eve nodded toward a short, slender, dark-haired woman with her back to them, bending over a small child holding up a toy truck. "She has for the past six months. I guess you wouldn't know that. Molly brought the kids to St. Michael's every Sunday and usually put Sawyer in the nursery. He knows all the kids."

Sawyer left his friend's side and charged over to his grandmother, who picked him up and gave him a hug. Mrs. Robertson turned in the direction Sawyer pointed, and Connor saw the same wariness in her face that he felt himself. As she walked toward them Brooke called out a jubilant "Nana!" She pulled free of his grasp and raced toward her grandmother.

Mrs. Robertson talked briefly to both children, who seemed excited to see her, then took Brooke's hand and led her back to Connor.

"Hello," she said. "The children look well."

"Did you think they wouldn't?" Connor heard the antagonism in his voice and felt Eve's hand on his arm in the same instant.

"It's nice to see you, Mrs. Robertson," Eve said. "You're looking well, too."

That wasn't exactly true, Connor realized. Molly's mother looked tired, as though she weren't sleeping. And sad, which he could understand. He felt a spurt of sympathy and tamped it down. This woman had tried to steal his children.

Connor felt Eve's fingers twine with his, felt the reassuring pressure of her grasp, and let the anger and resentment seep out of him. He had his children back. He could afford to be generous.

"Will you be leaving Sawyer here today?" Mrs. Robertson asked.

Connor nodded curtly.

"And Brooke?"

"Brooke's going to church with us," Eve said.

Molly's mother looked disappointed, but she merely patted Brooke's chestnut curls and said, "I'll see you after the service, sweetheart."

"Bye, Nana," Brooke said as she ran back to Connor, her arms outstretched to be picked up.

As he let go of Eve's hand to scoop his daughter into his arms, Connor realized that Brooke was totally unaware of the tension arcing between him and her grandmother. Maybe he should make sure it stayed that way.

"We'll see you after the service," he said.

Mrs. Robertson looked surprised at the neutral tone of his voice, but also relieved. "Yes. See you then."

As they turned to leave, Eve whispered in his ear, "I'm proud of you."

He frowned. "For what?"

"For giving her a chance. For having an open heart. For doing what you know is right."

Connor made a face. But it felt good to hear Eve's words of praise.

"Just a moment, Eve."

Connor and Eve both turned back to Mrs. Robertson.

"I have something for you," the older woman said. "I've been carrying it around with me, hoping I would see you in town. If you don't mind coming with me a moment, I can give it to you now."

"Of course." Eve followed Mrs. Robertson toward the back of the nursery, where Molly's mother retrieved her purse from a shelf. She rooted through it, then handed Eve a small book with a flowered cloth cover.

Connor saw the surprise on Eve's face, her attempt to return the book, and Mrs. Robertson forcing it back into her hands.

Eve finally tucked the book into her purse and rejoined him.

As they left the nursery and headed back down the hall to the church, he asked, "What did she give you?"

"A book."

"I could see that. What kind of book?"

"It belonged to Molly."

"Are you going to make me keep asking questions, or are you going to tell me what it is?"

"It's a diary."

Connor stopped in his tracks and turned to face her. "Molly's diary?"

"No, Mrs. Robertson's diary." She snorted at the

stunned look on his face. "Of course it's Molly's diary!"

"Why did she give it to you?" *And not me?*

"She said there are a few passages in it I should read. She marked them for me."

Connor waited for Eve to share more of whatever reason Mrs. Robertson had given for handing over Molly's diary, but she remained stubbornly mute. "Fine. Don't tell me anything. I probably don't want to know what's in the damned thing anyway."

Eve looked unhappy. "No, I don't think you do."

"If Molly wrote something bad about me—"

"It's not about you," she said, interrupting him. "It's about me."

Connor stared at her a long moment, then felt Brooke tugging on his hand.

"Come on, Daddy. Church is starting."

He searched Eve's face one more time for any sign that she might relent, then said, "We better get to church."

He took one of Brooke's hands and Eve took the other as they walked down the center aisle to the Flynn pew on the right-hand side at the front of the church. Angus sat on the aisle. Aiden, Brian, and Devon were spread out, leaving no room for anyone else. "Scoot over," Connor said to Aiden.

Aiden turned to Brian and said, "Move over."

Brian said to Devon, "Make some room."

The three brothers edged farther down the pew to make room between Aiden and Angus to fit Connor and Eve. Connor watched his father's back stiffen and his shoulders square as Eve stepped past Angus and settled on the cushioned pew beside Aiden. Connor sat to Eve's left, next to his father, and held Brooke on his lap.

Connor didn't hear much of the liturgy. He was too busy wondering what Molly had said in her diary. Then he realized he hadn't asked Eve the most important question. What year had the diary been written? During Molly's youth? Or since their marriage?

He realized he had far bigger problems than Molly's diary. His father sat rigid as a fence post beside him. Angus hadn't said another word after "Hummmph" when Connor sat down next to him. Connor was pretty good at reading body language, and Angus's said, "You're toast."

Connor let Brooke fiddle with the handkerchief in his pocket, with the buttons on his suit coat, and with the clasp that held his tie. He let her draw with a pencil provided by the church on one of the church's attendance cards. He held her in his arms when they rose to sing hymns, and when the time came, he helped her to kneel on the prie-dieu beside him.

It was all familiar behavior. The only thing missing was Molly. But for the first time since her death, Connor had hope that he might find happiness again after the loss of his wife. His wedding night—and all the nights since then—had been a revelation, in more ways than one. Surely Eve couldn't make love to him night after night, often several times a night, if she didn't have feelings for him.

Since Aiden hadn't moved down enough to give Eve much room, her thigh was pressed against Connor's. He caught her hand in his and held it, knowing that she was as unlikely to make a scene in church as his father. He wasn't just making a statement to his father, he actually enjoyed holding her hand.

His father held the hymnal where Connor could see it, but the instant the song was done, he slapped it closed and set it back in the rack behind the pew.

When it came time to take Communion, Connor settled Brooke in Eve's lap and followed his father to the rail, his brothers behind him. Connor found surprising solace in taking Communion. It was one more step toward letting go of all the anger he felt at having his life turned upside down.

To his surprise, as soon as his family was seated again, Brooke scooted from Eve's lap onto her grandfather's lap. In the past Connor had brought his daughter to both church and the Lucky 7 frequently, so he knew Angus had a soft spot for his first grandchild.

Connor was content to let Brooke sit with his father for the rest of the service. He watched as Angus pulled his cell phone from his pocket and handed it to Brooke, who immediately began playing a digital game. Connor was astonished at how adept his four-year-old daughter was at handling the complicated cell phone. His child's world had definitely moved on while he'd been overseas.

Since the Flynns sat at the front of the church, they were the last to leave. Angus didn't get up, he simply handed Brooke to Eve and said, "Connor and I will meet you out front later."

Eve eyed Connor sideways as she stood and left the church with Aiden, Brian, and Devon. Once they were alone, Angus focused his steely gaze on Connor and said, "If you expected this spectacle of familial harmony to change my mind, you're badly mistaken."

"I brought my wife and daughter to worship with my father and brothers. I'd hardly call that a spectacle."

"She's a *Grayhawk*." He made the word an epithet. "Her father killed my sister. That's something I can never—will never—forgive."

"Aunt Jane's been gone a long time, Dad. Why don't you let it go?"

"Because he got Matt back!"

Connor was confused. "What does Matt have to do with anything?"

"King doesn't deserve that boy's love."

"From what I've heard, Matt's only here until he can take possession of Kingdom Come."

"King will never give him the ranch—assuming, of course, that he owns it a year from now."

"There's a chance he won't?"

Angus sneered. "A very good chance. But if he does, that slimy son of a bitch will find some excuse to call off the deal."

"I can't believe Matt wouldn't have asked for something in writing before he came all this way."

"You can bet whatever King signed is unenforceable," Angus said. "It's what I'd do. Whatever else I think about that snake in the grass, he's every bit as crafty as I am."

"Why are you so cynical?" Connor asked. "Why can't you believe King just wants his son back and is willing to pay the price to make it happen?"

"Because that bastard never did a generous, loving thing for anyone in his whole miserable life."

"Dad, listen to yourself. This has to stop. No

one's all bad. King Grayhawk is my wife's father. Nothing is going to change that."

"I don't want his blood mixed with mine. I want that marriage annulled before she—"

"No."

He saw the shocked look on his father's face before his cheeks reddened with anger. "Are you daring me to cut you off?"

"If you're forcing me to choose between Safe Haven and my wife, I'll take Eve."

"What's got into you?"

"I don't want to lose her."

"You hardly know the woman."

"She's a fantastic mother. She's a great photographer. And she's going to be a damned good wife."

Angus lifted a bushy black brow. "Is the girl pregnant? Is that why you're being so obstinate?"

"No, Dad," Connor said in disgust. "I'm not asking you to give me anything that isn't already mine, but I need that trust fund."

A pained expression crossed Angus's face.

"I'm not asking for myself. I'm asking for the veterans who come to Safe Haven."

Connor watched the creases in his father's brow deepen before he said, "Get rid of that Grayhawk woman, and you can keep your trust fund. Otherwise, my lawyer will start the paperwork to rescind it starting bright and early tomorrow morning."

Connor didn't argue. Angus was obstinate, used to getting his way as only a very powerful and wealthy man could be. He was going to have to figure out another way for his sanctuary to thrive.

"Goodbye, Dad. If we're going to use family relationships as weapons against each other, you should know that so long as Eve isn't welcome in your home, Brooke and Sawyer won't be coming there, either."

"How dare you threaten me! Go! Get out of my sight."

Connor rose and left.

Chapter 25

EVE SHOWED UP at the bedroom door, Molly's diary in hand, her face bleached of blood. "She knew."

Connor dropped the book he was reading as he lay in bed. "Knew what?"

"About us."

He sat up. "Impossible."

Eve sank onto the bed, opened the diary, and began reading.

> I know Eve likes Connor but I like him more. He's so dreamy!!! His eyes are bluer than blue and I want to brush back that lock of hair that falls on his forehead so bad!!! Eve's so beautiful and amazing she can have any boy she wants. But not Connor. He's mine!!! It's a good thing his name is Flynn or I'd have no chance, because I can tell Connor likes Eve, too. He's always watching her with this goofy look on his face. She has no clue, thank goodness!!!

Eve met Connor's gaze. His face was flushed, probably because of that "goofy look" comment. "Did you watch me in high school?"

He nodded. "I told you I liked you."

"This sounds like more than that."

"What do you want me to say?"

Eve turned to another bookmarked page in the diary and began reading again.

Connor is taking ME to the Sadie Hawkins dance!!! It was sort of a nasty trick to get Eve to ask for me. I bet Connor thought she was going to ask him to go with her. Too bad!!! This is my chance to show him how nice I am, and I plan to make the most of it. Connor Flynn won't know what hit him. I love him!!! Soon he'll be mine forever. Sorry, Eve, but you had your chances. Your fault if you didn't take them.

"This doesn't sound like the woman I knew," Connor said, shaking his head. "Molly was never a conniving person. She was always generous and giving."

"Absolutely," Eve agreed. "Except, obviously, where you were concerned."

She turned to a third marked passage. "This was written years later. She was cleaning out boxes and apparently found her diary and wrote a final entry."

I can see why I was so worried about Eve loving Connor—and Connor loving Eve—when they were teenagers. All these years later, the sparks still fly whenever they're in the same room together. I trust them both implicitly. Neither of them would ever betray me. But I feel guilty knowing that I may be the reason they aren't spending their lives together as a couple. Maybe they would never have gotten past the feud between their families, but they manage to coexist just fine in my home. Which leads me to believe that if I hadn't been in the way, true love might have won out. I'm so sorry, Eve, for stealing the man you loved. I know that's why you're still single. You're so careful to hide your feelings whenever Connor's around. That's how I know they still exist.

And Connor, my dearest love, I know you love me, but I wonder if you would have married me if you weren't afraid you might die before you had a son or daughter to leave behind. I took advantage of the love you both had for me to take what I wanted—and needed—from each of you, which meant your own desperate desires remained unrequited.

I hope someday both of you can forgive me. I'm so sorry I came between you. If the day ever comes when I'm no longer here, I hope you find your way to each other.

Eve's throat was so swollen with emotion that she barely managed to finish reading the last sentence. She looked up to find Connor's eyes glistening with tears. When he blinked, one slid down his cheek.

"She never said a word," he said. "I had no idea she knew I had feelings for you."

"Or that I felt that way about you." Eve set the diary on the end table and crawled across the bed toward Connor.

He opened his arms and the two of them lay together, holding one another close.

Eve swallowed over the knot of guilt in her throat. "She hoped *we* could forgive *her*."

She heard Connor struggle to swallow back more tears before he said, "Yeah."

"How could she stand it?" Eve wondered.

"She loved us both. And she knew we loved her."

Eve was silent for a long while, remembering all the times she'd visited her friend when Connor was home on leave. All the times she'd coveted him while her best friend had stood by and watched. And *known*. The sorrow she felt was unbearable.

"Do you suppose we were fated to be together?" Connor asked.

Eve shrugged. "The fates can't want us together very badly or they wouldn't be doing such a great job of shoving us apart."

"It does look like the odds are stacked against us," Connor agreed.

"I don't want to take the job in Nevada," Eve said, her face hidden against Connor's throat. "I just don't think I have any other choice."

She put her fingertips against Connor's lips to still his protest. "I called the editor today and told her I'd take the job."

She felt Connor's arms tighten around her, as though he could keep her close, when they both knew that in thirty days she'd be gone. For a couple of weeks. Or maybe a couple of months. And maybe again and again and again.

Eve's heart hurt. "I don't want to go," she said, her throat aching.

"And I don't want you to go."

The lovemaking that followed began with tender

kisses and soft, reverent touches. But the knowledge that, just when the truth of their longtime love had been revealed, it might be the beginning of the end of their lives together, turned their caresses into desperate touches and transformed soft forays into demanding explorations. Until they were both clutching at naked flesh as though to hold on forever to the final moment of exultation.

Eve was still gasping for breath when she rolled away from Connor into a tight ball of misery. He slung his arm possessively across her body, pulling her close.

"We still have a month to come up with some way to keep you here," he said fiercely.

"You never told me the result of your talk with your father. Is there any hope—"

"He's revoking the trust," Connor said flatly.

"Then all hope is lost."

He leaned up on his elbow and shifted her onto her back so he could look into her eyes. "That doesn't sound like the indomitable woman I know. And love."

Eve's heart skipped a beat. They might have felt love for each other all their lives, but the words had never been spoken. Until now.

She searched his beautiful blue eyes for the truth. "Do you love me?"

"More than . . ." He didn't finish the sentence. He cleared his throat and said, "More than I ever imagined it was possible to love someone."

Eve was glad he hadn't said he loved her more than Molly. A comparison wasn't possible. They were two completely different women, both of whom had loved him. And both of whom he'd loved back.

"What are we going to do, Connor?"

He turned out the light, then lay back down, easing her head onto his chest so she could hear the strong beat of his heart. "We'll figure out something."

Eve was almost asleep when she realized she hadn't returned the gift he'd given her. She leaned close to his ear and whispered, "I love you, too."

She heard a gurgle as he swallowed hard, but he said nothing. Eve hoped she had the chance to repeat those words many times in the years to come. Right now, their problems seemed insurmountable. She had to leave. And he might lose his ranch. And there seemed no way to avoid the separation that would result.

Eve slid her arm across Connor's chest and snuggled close. She would put her mind to work overnight. Maybe it would come up with a solution by morning.

Chapter 26

"WHERE THE HELL is my daughter?"

Eve stared through the screen door at the madman standing on the back porch. His eyes were bloodshot, black stubble shadowed his cheeks, and his face looked haggard. She shoved the door open and said, "Pippa's missing?"

"You know damn well she is!" Matt retorted. "She told me she was going shopping in town, but she never came home last night."

Eve arched a brow. "And from that you concluded that I had something to do with her disappearance?"

"You know goddamn well you and those bratty sisters of yours—"

"That's quite enough swearing for one conversation," Eve said as she joined him on the back porch, letting the screen door slam behind her. "I've got two impressionable kids sitting in the kitchen eating breakfast."

"Where's Connor?" Matt said, looking beyond her shoulder.

"He left early for town, which is where you should be if you're looking for Pippa."

His eyes narrowed. "What do you know?"

"What you just told me! If Pippa went to town, that's probably where she is."

"I've been all over Jackson. Twice. She isn't there," Connor said. "Those sisters of yours swore up and down they had nothing to do with her being gone, but I don't believe them for one minute."

Eve could see Matt was crazy with worry.

He pulled his Stetson off and ran an agitated hand through his hair, then put the hat back on and tugged it low on his forehead. "You're my last resort."

Eve hesitated, then said, "Do you think Pippa might have taken off because you want her to give up her baby?"

Matt's jaw dropped. "How the hell—"

Eve opened her mouth to cut him off, but he'd already cut himself off. "I accidentally overheard the two of you talking," she admitted. "Your daughter seemed as determined to keep her baby as you were that she should give it up."

"The choice is hers. But raising a baby isn't kid stuff. It's hard work. I should know, I—" He cut himself off again.

That was the second time Matt had let Eve catch a glimpse of his life. It was hard to imagine him as a teenager raising a little girl on his own. What had happened to Pippa's mother? He still hadn't said a word about why he'd gone so far away or stayed gone for so long.

"Why do you think my sisters or I had something to do with the fact that Pippa's missing?" Eve asked.

"How about Taylor's threat to make me sorry I ever came here?" Matt said. "I should have thrown the twins out on their fannies last week when they let

King's Tennessee Walker stallion into the pasture with my quarter horse brood mares."

"They did *what*?" Eve said, aghast.

"Not that they admitted to it. God knows how many mares that stud covered before I got him out of there. That means I'll be waiting a year for some very expensive quarter horse mares to deliver their mixed-breed foals before they're any use to me. Not only that, I have to wait to see how many mares are pregnant before I can breed the rest of them. I gave those two hellions a good piece of my mind and a warning that if they tried another stunt like that they wouldn't have to wait a year to find themselves without a roof over their heads."

"So you think they've graduated to kidnapping?" Eve said doubtfully.

Matt met her gaze with bleak eyes. "I think they resent me enough to do anything."

Eve shook her head. "They wouldn't hurt Pippa."

"No. But they might help her run away again. Did they know she was pregnant?"

"I didn't tell them."

"A paragon," he muttered.

"Look, I'll be glad to ask Taylor and Vick if they know anything. But I think you're barking up the wrong tree."

"What did I do that was so bad?" he murmured. "Why would she run away?"

Matt was asking questions to the air, but Eve took the opportunity to answer them. "Maybe Pippa wants some time on her own to think. When she's ready to come home, she will." Eve hesitated, then added, "Unless you believe there's a chance of foul play."

A couple of young girls had gone missing in the past around Jackson and been found murdered, but that villain had been caught. Still, that didn't mean there weren't other crazy people out there. When she saw the sudden dread in Matt's eyes, Eve was sorry she'd mentioned the possibility that someone had taken his daughter against her will. Most likely Pippa was all right, but Matt would likely suffer the torment of the damned until he knew for sure.

"The sheriff's office won't do anything because she's considered an adult," Matt said.

"Maybe Pippa will call you once she's settled, wherever that turns out to be."

"Maybe. Maybe not."

"Why wouldn't she?"

"Because she knows I'll come get her and bring her home," Matt said through tight jaws. "Like I did the last time."

"From what I overheard, the circumstances then were vastly different from what they are now," Eve said.

Matt rubbed a hand across his nape. "How much did you hear?"

"That she ran off with a man who lied to her about the fact that he was married."

"A lot of ringers—that's an Australian cowboy—leave their families behind in the city, and that's what this lowlife did. He pretended to be free and single—and in love with Pippa—and she was innocent enough to fall for him.

"I should have sent her off to boarding school in Brisbane or Sydney so she wouldn't have been so lonely, but I . . ."

He turned his back to her, and Eve saw him surreptitiously swipe at his eyes.

Eve had filled in the rest of his sentence. *Would have missed her too much.* Clearly Matt had gone through a great deal to keep his daughter and raise her, and he'd wanted to extend her childhood as long as possible. But like so many choices parents had to make, this one had backfired.

Eve didn't want to feel sorry for Matt, not after the ruthless way he'd shoved her horses off the ranch. But he was clearly a man at the end of his rope. "When was the last time you had something to eat?"

He turned back around and said, "I need to keep looking."

"At least stop long enough to have a cup of coffee," she urged.

He pulled his hat off and turned it in his hands while he considered what to do next. At last he said, "All right."

Eve was surprised he'd accepted her offer, but he was so antsy she pulled open the screen door and held it for him to enter before he could change his mind.

When the screen door squeaked, Brooke turned to look and yelled, "It's Uncle Matt!"

"Hi, Uncle Matt!" Sawyer called out.

Eve turned to Matt, her brow raised, and said, "When did you meet Connor's kids?"

"I stopped by the Lucky 7 when they were visiting there and Aiden introduced me." He ruffled Sawyer's hair and pulled one of Brooke's pigtails. "Hi, kiddos."

"We're not kiddos," Sawyer said. "We're kids."

"I stand corrected," Matt said as he turned around

a kitchen chair on the opposite side of the table and straddled it.

Eve hurried to pour him a cup of coffee. "Cream? Sugar?"

"Black is fine."

Eve set the coffee in front of him, then collected her cup of tea and sat at the end of the table.

"Did you come to see Daddy?" Brooke asked.

"I'm looking for my daughter, Pippa."

"She's not here," Brooke said. "Uncle Brian said she was going to live with Uncle Devon."

Matt bolted out of his seat. "What?"

Brooke took one look at Matt's ferocious expression and shot an anxious glance at Eve, who'd also come out of her chair. "Did I say something wrong?" the little girl asked.

Eve crossed to lay a reassuring hand on Brooke's shoulder. "No, sweetie. It's fine."

"Where did you hear that?" Matt asked.

"When we were leaving church last week. Uncle Aiden said Uncle Devon should keep his nose out of other people's business, but Uncle Brian said Uncle Devon could do whatever he wants, 'cause he's a big boy."

Eve was astonished at how much Brooke had remembered of a conversation she'd apparently overheard in passing. The Flynn brothers obviously hadn't taken account of the fact that little pitchers have very big ears.

Eve glanced at Matt and said, "It looks like you're accusing the wrong relatives of absconding with your daughter."

Matt was shaking his head, his brow furrowed. "Why sneak around? Why not say something to me?"

"Maybe because Pippa doesn't want to be yanked back home?" Eve suggested.

Matt made a face, conceding the truth of what she'd said.

"What are you going to do?" she asked.

Matt's shoulders slumped and he sighed. "I don't know."

He headed for the door, too self-absorbed even to say goodbye to the kids, and Eve followed him.

She turned back before she stepped outside to say, "When you're finished, put your dishes in the sink and go play. I'll be back in a minute."

Outside in the sunlight, Matt's face looked even more ravaged at this new betrayal. "Where the hell does Devon live?"

Eve shook her head. "I'm not sure. He's got a place in the mountains, I think. You have to believe that Devon only offered Pippa a place to stay out of the goodness of his heart. Of all the Flynns, he's the one who's gotten into the least trouble. She'll be safe there. Maybe you should leave well enough alone."

"She's my daughter."

"She's twenty. That's plenty old enough to know her own mind."

"I didn't ask for your advice."

"You're going to get it anyway. Let her be. You know where she is. You know she's safe. Give her time and space. Let her decide if she wants to come back home."

"How do I know she's really there?"

"I'll ask Connor to find out and let you know."

"You'd do that for me?"

"I'd do that for her."

"Good enough. Make it soon."

She nodded. "As soon as Connor gets back I'll have him find out what he can."

"Thank you. If there's ever anything I can do for you, let me know."

Eve couldn't keep the bitterness from her voice. "You've done quite enough. I don't think—" She interrupted herself and stared at him speculatively. "As a matter of fact, there is something you can do."

"What?"

"I'd like to hold an event at Kingdom Come."

Matt arched a brow. "I'm listening."

Ever since Angus had issued his ultimatum to Connor, and Connor had refused to have their marriage annulled, Eve had been thinking about ways Safe Haven could be funded. She would have her earnings from the *National Geographic* shoot, of course, to throw into the pot, but in order to do the most good, Connor was going to need a lot more money.

She was very aware that they lived in one of the wealthiest counties in the country. Seasonal folks wouldn't be back until the summer, but there were plenty of ranchers and businessmen who lived here year-round who might be willing to donate money to help maintain a ranch dedicated to providing R&R for veterans.

"I'm not sure if you're aware, but Connor lost his funding for Safe Haven."

"I heard Angus threatened to cut off his trust fund. I didn't know he'd actually done it."

"He did," Eve said curtly. "In order for this ranch to continue to provide free services to veterans, we're going to need to raise a lot of money. I want to hold an old-fashioned barbecue at Kingdom Come and invite as many folks as possible to come and make a contribution."

Matt looked skeptical. "You think that will do the job?"

"Leah's setting up a Safe Haven website where people across the country can make donations, and I've gotten an agreement from *National Geographic* to mention that vets are working with a herd of wild mustangs at Safe Haven, along with the website URL where people can contribute. We'll probably need another function, maybe a picnic, later in the summer when more of the out-of-town folks are here. But I'd like to hold that event here, so people can meet a few veterans and see Safe Haven in operation."

"Why didn't Connor say something to me about all this?"

Eve flushed. "Connor doesn't know I've set all this up."

Matt raised a brow. "I see. An event is going to tie up operations at Kingdom Come for at least a day, maybe more."

"I guess it will."

He eyed her speculatively. "But it's for a good cause."

"So you wouldn't do it for me, but you'll do it for the vets?"

"I'm doing it for both."

Eve was surprised Matt was willing to help now, when he wasn't before. But maybe he was learning that she wasn't who he'd thought in the beginning, just as she was learning the same about him.

"Goodbye, Matt. Connor will be in touch."

He put a finger to the brim of his Stetson, then turned and walked wearily away, as though the weight of the world lay on his shoulders.

As he reached his pickup Eve called after him, "Be sure to apologize to my sisters."

He held up his middle finger and said, "When hell freezes over!"

Chapter 27

CONNOR HADN'T BEEN entirely honest with Eve. He did have supplies to buy in town, but he also intended to make a stop at the café where King Grayhawk met up with his friends on Friday mornings for breakfast—not to be confused with the restaurant where his own father met up with his cronies. He had an idea how Eve could do the assignment for *National Geographic* closer to home, but he needed her father's help to make it happen.

He'd gotten in touch with her editor at the magazine to confirm what Eve had already told him. It was possible to change the location of the wild herd Eve photographed, so long as it was a bona fide herd of *wild* mustangs, including a stallion and pregnant mares. And the mares had to be delivering their foals in May. The May birth dates weren't as much of a problem as the editor seemed to think, since Connor had learned from Eve that most mustangs delivered in May or June.

"But to my knowledge, no such herd exists near Jackson," Eve's editor said.

"Not at the current time," Connor agreed. "That may change shortly."

"Someone you know have a little pull with the BLM?" the editor asked.

"Could be, ma'am," Connor replied. "Eve will be in touch to let you know whether the project will be done in Wyoming."

"I'll look forward to hearing from her, Mr. Flynn. One way or the other."

Now all Connor had to do was convince King Grayhawk to use his political influence to get the BLM to move a herd of wild mustangs to Safe Haven.

Connor had one ace in the hole. While he'd *purchased* a thousand acres of land, the dude ranch had *leased* another four thousand acres for ninety-nine years. That lease had another twenty-nine years to run. Many of Eve's current herd of mustangs were being broken to the saddle and would soon have new owners. There was plenty of water and grass to support a herd of thirty-five to forty animals—in the summer. He'd gone to Aiden to ask for help with hay over the winter.

"You're out of your mind," Aiden had said. "Just let Eve go to Nevada."

"I'd let her go, if I didn't know it will break her heart to leave. She loves the children, Aiden. And she loves me."

Aiden had looked skeptical at that final admission. "That happened pretty damn quick."

"We've always loved each other," Connor said. "We just never did anything about it because of all the stuff going on between our families. You can help us stay together if you'll agree to pay the price of hay for the herd over the winter. I'll plant my own, so you won't actually need to buy the hay. But it's not planted yet, and I'm pretty sure I'm going to need to prove to the BLM that I can feed the herd if necessary, so I need a guarantee from you. Will you do it?"

"Is this going to help you keep Safe Haven up and running?"

"Eve's earnings will support us until I can figure out a better solution. She has to take the job. The only question is whether she leaves us behind to do it, or is able to do it and still tuck the kids into bed at night."

Aiden shook his head. "If you can get a herd moved to Safe Haven, I'll provide a guarantee that you'll have the winter hay you need."

Connor's throat contricted with gratitude toward his brother. He swallowed past the ache and said, "Thank you."

"You realize that when you ask King to help he's going to tell you to take a short hike off a tall cliff," Aiden said in a gruff voice. "I hate like hell for you to bow down to that son of a bitch."

"I'd walk through fire for Eve. Bowing down to King Grayhawk is child's play."

Connor had been plenty brave in front of his brother. Facing the man himself was another matter. He took a deep breath and opened the door to the café. His heart was beating hard in his chest, and he licked at the sweat above his lip. Kowtowing to King Grayhawk might seem like child's play, but confronting one of the great monsters in your life was not.

He was immediately assaulted by the smells of bacon, biscuits, and coffee, the clatter of cutlery and dishes, and the murmur of dozens of voices. The man he was seeking sat with three others at a booth in the back corner. Connor strode into the café as though he belonged there. The sudden hush was testimony to the fact that he was a Flynn in Grayhawk territory.

Like a cop who needs to watch for the bad guy, even when he eats, King Grayhawk was seated on the aisle with his back to the wall. When he looked out into the restaurant to discover the cause of the quiet, he couldn't help but see Connor's approach.

Connor watched King stiffen, saw his shoulders brace and his chin come up a notch, ready for what he surely expected was some sort of confrontation. Connor had decided to speak with Eve's father in a public place, in front of his friends, for the same reason Eve had arranged for him to meet his father in church—the hope that King would be forced to speak civilly to him.

On the other hand, having his friends close by might also preclude any sort of compromise on King's part. Connor realized he was going to need to separate King from his cronies in order to discuss the favor he needed.

When he reached the booth he said, "I need to speak with you privately."

"I'm having breakfast," King replied.

"It's important." When that got no response he added, "It's about Eve."

The wedding of a Grayhawk and a Flynn had provided plenty of juicy gossip in a small town like Jackson, and it was clear from the frown on King's face that he didn't want this possible conflict between the couple to become more grist for the mill.

King pulled the napkin from his lap and set it on the table, then rose and said, "Follow me." He headed for the back of the restaurant, pausing at the service counter long enough to say to the man behind it, "Bubba, I need your office."

"Sure, King."

Connor realized from the ease with which King asked and Bubba answered that Eve's father must have done this a number of times when he needed privacy to conduct business.

Compared with the restaurant, which was decorated with Conestoga wagon wheels and sported a western print on the cloth cushions in the booths, the office was definitely a part of the twenty-first century. King took a seat in a high-backed black leather swivel chair behind a glass-topped desk, leaving a shorter-backed black leather chair on wheels in front of the desk for Connor. He hesitated, then settled into the chair.

Having arranged the situation so he was in the position of power in the room, King asked, "Why are you here? Is Eve all right?"

Connor's pulse began to pound as he realized how much was at stake. If he didn't approach King in the right way, Eve was going to be forced to leave to pursue this assignment. She would receive other offers in the future, he was sure, to travel to do her work, but by then he hoped the kids would realize she was going to be a part of their lives for good and always, and he and Eve would have cemented their lives together as a couple. He just wanted a little time together at the beginning of their marriage to show her how much he cherished her. How much he valued her. How important she was to his happiness and the happiness of their children. So this was a very important conversation.

Connor began, "I don't know if you were aware of it, but Eve received an offer from *National Geographic* to photograph a herd of wild mustangs in Nevada."

From the way King's brows rose, he hadn't known about the offer. "This is what you called me away from breakfast to discuss? I know the girl can take pictures. What's the problem?"

"My kids need her." Connor hesitated, then added, "And I need her."

"So tell her to stay home."

"I don't want her giving up her dreams for mine."

King snorted. "Sounds like you have a problem."

"It's one you can solve," Connor said, continuing doggedly in the face of King's snarly response. "Again, I don't know how much you know about my ranch, but—"

"I know everything. Including the fact that Angus has pulled the plug on your trust, and you're about to be flat broke."

Connor flushed. "Then you know how important it is for Eve to take this assignment. We need the cash. I've figured out a way she can stick around Safe Haven and still do the job for the magazine."

"I'm listening."

"I need you to convince the BLM to settle a herd of wild mustangs on the four thousand acres of leased land I have at Safe Haven. And I need it done before the mares in the herd drop their foals this spring."

King guffawed. "Oh, is *that* all I have to do?"

"After two terms as governor of Wyoming, are

you suggesting you don't have enough friends in high places to make it happen?"

"The BLM is run by the federal government," King pointed out.

Connor lifted a brow. "So? You don't have any friends in Washington?"

King templed his hands before him. "Why should I do this?"

"I love your daughter and I want her to be happy. I believe being able to do her work and still be home to care for the children is important to her. And it's little enough, don't you think, after that trick you pulled on her and her sisters."

King scowled. "Don't be judging what you don't understand."

"I understand Eve came to me because you threw her out. I thank you for that, because without your callousness we never would have found each other. If you can't do this, tell me now and you'll never hear another word out of me. But if you can, I'm asking you to make it happen."

King stared out the window into the alley behind the restaurant, so it wasn't the view he was considering.

Connor waited him out, forcing himself to stay silent.

"I can't guarantee anything, but I might know someone with enough clout to get this done," King said at last.

"Thanks," Connor said.

"I haven't done anything yet."

Connor stood. "You're willing to try. That says a lot."

"Take care of her."

"It's the reason I wake up in the morning," Connor answered simply.

"I'll be in touch when I have an answer. Now get the hell out of here and let me go finish my breakfast."

Connor didn't walk out of the restaurant, he floated out on a wave of euphoria. King was going to help. Eve would be able to take her amazing photographs without needing to travel to another state. If the BLM cooperated. If they could find a herd of horses with pregnant mares to move. And if they could get them moved in time.

Connor had a lot of faith in King Grayhawk to make it all happen. Like Connor's own father, he was a man able to move mountains. Connor's only fear had been that King wouldn't care enough about Eve to help. He was glad he'd been wrong.

Now he just had to wait and hope for the magic to happen.

Chapter 28

"MOMMY, MOMMY! COME quick!"

Eve came running, her heart in her throat, when she heard Brooke's cry for help. She still wasn't used to being called "Mommy," and her heart nearly stopped when she heard it yelled at the top of her daughter's lungs. She shoved open the screen door and bolted onto the back porch, expecting blood and tears. Instead, she found Brooke pointing at a tractor-trailer that had pulled up behind the house.

Eve heard horses neighing and realized the truck was full of them. "What in the world?"

The driver opened the door to the cab and stepped down. "Hope I'm in the right spot, ma'am. I was told to deliver these mustangs to Safe Haven."

"This is Safe Haven."

"Is Connor Flynn around?"

"What is this?" Eve asked, gesturing toward the truck full of horses.

"His herd of wild mustangs."

"*His* herd?" Eve put a hand to her forehead to keep the sun out of her eyes as she took a closer look at the horses, which had no numbers branded on their necks, as they would have if they'd been adopted after a BLM roundup. "Where did these wild mustangs come from?"

"Idaho," the driver said. "Got an order from the BLM to relocate them to Safe Haven." He opened the order and read, "One stallion, sixteen mares—four of which are pregnant—four two-year-old colts, three yearling colts, three two-year-old fillies, and three yearling fillies. Thirty mustangs in all. I need Flynn to sign off that he got them."

"I don't know exactly where—"

"Daddy!" Brooke called. "Look what we got!"

Eve whirled and saw Connor loping toward them from the Main Lodge, a wide smile on his face.

"They're here!" he said jubilantly.

"You were expecting this?" Eve said.

Connor nodded. "Not this soon, and not for sure."

"How did this happen?" Eve asked, her pulse thrumming with excitement.

"I'll tell you everything as soon as I sign for them." He signed the manifest and gave the driver instructions where to offload the herd.

Eve turned to Connor, her mouth filled with laughter, her eyes filled with tears. "What did you do?" she asked. "How did this happen?"

Connor grabbed her under the arms and swung her in a circle, woo-hooing the whole time.

"Do me, Daddy," Brooke yelled.

"Do me, Daddy," Sawyer begged.

He set Eve down, then picked up one kid under each arm, and buzzed the porch like an airplane, finally dropping them on their feet.

As Eve helped to steady the two dizzy children, Connor threw his head back, shoved his arms into the air, and shouted, "We have wild mustangs! Mommy doesn't have to go to Nevada!"

"Yay!" Brooke said, clapping her hands and jumping up and down.

Sawyer clapped his hands, but Eve wasn't sure he understood why they were celebrating. Brooke did. Eve had sat down on the bed next to her stepdaughter the previous evening and explained that she was going to have to leave in a few days to go take photographs of wild horses in Nevada.

"I don't want you to go," Brooke said emphatically.

"I don't want to go. I have to go. It's my job."

Brooke had flung herself against Eve and sobbed, "Please don't leave, Mommy."

Through a blur of tears, Eve had seen Connor standing in the doorway, his hip canted, his face grim.

It was the first time Brooke had ever called her "Mommy." Eve's stomach was so tightly knotted that she thought she might vomit. But there was no escape from the trap in which she was caught. Brooke wanted her mother. And Eve had to leave.

Nothing Eve had said to Brooke, no promises of Skyping or phoning or texting or returning soon, had been able to console the little girl. Eve had spent the night crying in Connor's embrace as he tried to comfort her. Throughout it all, he hadn't said a word about arranging for a herd of wild horses to be brought to Safe Haven.

"Can me and Sawyer go down to the corral and watch them let the horses out of the truck?" Brooke asked.

"Sure. But hold your brother's hand and wait at

the stable for us," Connor replied. "We'll be right there and walk you down to the corral."

Eve watched as the kids trotted away, then turned to Connor and asked, "Why didn't you tell me about this last night?"

"I didn't want to offer false hope. I didn't find out for sure it was going to happen until early this morning, when the mustangs were already on their way."

"I need to call my editor. I need to—"

"Yes, you do," Connor interrupted. "But don't be surprised when she isn't surprised."

Eve's jaw dropped. "You contacted my editor?"

"Just to be sure this would be all right with her, if I could get it worked out. She's expecting your call. That is, if you're okay with taking your photographs here, rather than Nevada."

"Am I okay with it? Are you nuts?" Eve's grin spread across her face. She couldn't stop it. "I'm over the moon with it! How did you manage to talk the BLM into letting you host a band of mustangs?"

"King made it happen."

"My father arranged this?" Eve felt a rush of love for someone who'd lately been a villain in her life. "All on his own?"

"I might have pointed him in the right direction. But he was the one who talked to all the right people."

Eve threw her arms around Connor's neck and kissed him.

He enthusiastically returned the favor. "What was that for?" he murmured against her lips.

"Because I love you. And because I have a confession as well."

He kissed her again. "This sounds serious."

She lowered her gaze and said, "I've arranged a fund-raiser." She looked up into his eyes and continued earnestly, "Matt agreed to let me use the facilities at Kingdom Come—mostly to thank you for checking with Devon to confirm that Pippa *is* living with your brother on his ranch in the mountains—and Leah helped me arrange everything so it could be held the last Saturday before I left."

"This is happening *tomorrow*?" Connor asked incredulously.

Eve nodded. "Uh-huh. I couldn't decide whether to tell you or not. I decided to make it a surprise."

Connor's eyes narrowed. "What, exactly, are you raising funds for?"

She took a deep breath and admitted, "Safe Haven."

Connor let her go and took a step back, his excitement dimming as though a sudden thundercloud had covered the sun. "I don't need charity."

She reached out to hook her arm through his and started walking toward the corral, dragging on his arm until he fell into step with her. "It isn't charity, Connor. It's fund-raising. There's a big difference. You're not the one benefiting from these donations— it's the veterans who stay at Safe Haven. And the more money we have in our war chest, the more soldiers we can help. Right?"

Connor nodded.

"So I scheduled a barbecue at Kingdom Come and invited all the locals to attend and make a contribution for a good—a noble—cause: to help the men who've fought to keep them free."

"Matt gave you permission to do this at Kingdom Come?"

Eve nodded. "Leah helped me set up a website for donations, and every one of your brothers RSVP'd that they'll be there." She shot him an anxious look and said, "Angus is coming, too. Oh, and all my sisters will be there. And King, of course."

Connor stared at her in awe. Or consternation. Or disbelief. Or maybe all three.

"Say something. Are you okay with what I've arranged? Have I made a mistake?"

Connor kissed her quick and hard. "I think the idea is brilliant." He patted Eve's hand and chuckled as they started walking again. "Everybody in town will likely show up just to see what happens when all those Grayhawks cross paths with all those Flynns." He shot her a cheeky grin. "That alone should be worth the price of admission."

Eve caught her lower lip in her teeth, suddenly realizing that she'd set the scene for a knock-down, drag-out fight between two powerful families. What had she done?

Chapter 29

"How do you think it's going?" Eve asked Leah as she surveyed the three hundred or so people who'd shown up for the First Annual Safe Haven Barbecue and Dance. She had to speak loudly because the country band was playing the Cotton-Eyed Joe, and everyone on the dance floor set up on the lawn was yelling "Bullshit!" at intervals during the song.

Leah finished clearing one of the many tables covered with a red-checked cloth, adjusted a chair in the grass, and perused the bustle on the immense front lawn at Kingdom Come, where an entire spitted beef was being turned over a fire. "Good music. Good food. Good drinks. Open wallets. What's not to like?"

"The glares shooting between Grayhawks and Flynns," Eve said as she glanced from the table where her father had set up camp with Matt and his son, to the table where Connor's father was surrounded by his sons and Matt's daughter. "Why on earth would the Flynns show up at an event being held at Daddy's ranch?"

"That's Aiden's doing," Leah said. "I have it straight from the horse's mouth—excuse the expression—that 'Connor is doing important work that needs to be supported.' Aiden made sure that everyone from Angus on down showed up today and made a significant financial contribution."

"I'm glad Devon showed up with Pippa, so Matt can see that she's all right," Eve said.

"On the other hand, Pippa hasn't spoken to her father. There's more going on there than meets the eye," Leah said speculatively.

"You might be right," Eve said. Leah was definitely right, but as far as Eve was concerned, Pippa's secret was hers to keep for as long as she could.

Leah crossed to a convenient trash can, but before she could dump the paper plates and beer bottles she'd collected a waitress took them from her, smiled, and said, "I'll take care of those for you, ma'am."

Eve's attention was distracted by the sight of Matt headed for the table where Pippa sat beside Devon. Eve dropped all the paper plates and beer bottles she'd collected into the appropriate cans and moved swiftly toward the confrontation she was afraid was about to happen. Matt wouldn't dare create a scene. Not in front of all the benefactors they'd managed to get here today. But even as she approached the table where Devon and Pippa were seated, Matt's voice got louder and harsher.

"You have no right to keep Pippa at some remote ranch in the mountains, especially with that wolf you keep for a pet in the house at night," Matt said. "She needs—"

He cut himself off, and Eve realized that he'd almost blurted that Pippa needed to be making regular visits to her obstetrician.

Pippa's face had bleached white, and she'd instinctively put a protective hand over her belly, where her baby was growing. Eve wondered if anyone except her knew what the gesture meant.

"Please, Daddy," she said as she looked up at him. "I'm where I want to be."

Matt lowered his voice, but his tone was even more stringent. "Come home, Pippa. You need to be with your family."

"She is with family," Devon said in a quiet voice. "Sit down and stop making an ass of yourself. Pippa's old enough to decide what she wants to do with her life."

Eve was astonished at Devon's defiant response. She watched Matt's eyes narrow as Devon laid a protective hand on Pippa's shoulder.

"Get your hands off of her," Matt snarled.

Devon's hand fell away as he rose to face Matt. "I only—"

Matt took a swing before Devon could finish his protest. To Eve's amazement, Devon dodged sideways, and Matt's fist never touched him. Matt was gathering himself for another swing when King arrived at the table and said, "That's enough."

Matt turned to King, his eyes tortured, his voice rough as gravel, and said, "Butt out, old man! You've done enough damage to my life, don't you think? This is none of your business."

Eve searched for Connor, who'd been having a beer with several of the veterans from Safe Haven. As though she'd summoned him, he suddenly appeared at her side.

"What seems to be the problem, Matt?" Connor asked.

"Nothing that concerns you," Matt snapped, his

eyes darting from Connor to King to Devon and back again like a baited bear.

"You're disturbing my guests," Connor replied in an even voice. "Folks are here to enjoy some barbecue and beer, so let's skip the fracas. You can settle this another time."

"Please, Daddy," Pippa said.

It was Pippa's heartbreaking plea that made the difference. Eve watched Matt pull in his claws and saw his neck hairs unhackle, like a wildcat when the danger is past.

"Fine," Matt said through clenched jaws. He turned to Devon and added, "But if I find out you've touched so much as a hair on my daughter's head—"

"They're related, for Christ's sake!" Connor said.

Matt looked straight at Connor and said, "No. They're not."

Brian was out of his seat. "What the hell are you talking about?"

Angus kept his eyes on his hands, which were picking at the label on his ice-cold beer.

"Figure it out for yourselves," Matt said. Then he turned and stalked away, King following after him.

"Dad?" Devon said. "What is he talking about?"

"He's making trouble where it doesn't exist," Angus replied. But he never raised his gaze from his bottle of beer.

Eve was spellbound by what Matt had suggested. Devon wasn't related to the rest of his family? She remembered how she'd noticed he was the only one of the Flynn boys who looked the least bit different from the others. Was that because another man besides Angus was his father?

Eve had another thought. Maybe the reason Angus Flynn had never remarried wasn't because he could never love another woman as much as he'd loved Connor's mother, but because he'd been betrayed by the woman he loved most, who then died bearing another man's child.

The shock of Matt's announcement still hadn't left Devon's face, or that of his brothers, when Leah arrived at Eve's side and said, "It's time you stopped playing peacemaker and started enjoying the party."

She took the beer out of Connor's hand, set Eve's hand in its place, and said, "Dance with your wife."

Connor seemed willing to comply, but he paused long enough to say to Devon, "We'll talk about this later."

"No," Devon said. "We won't. As far as I'm concerned the subject is closed. Would you like some more barbecue, Pippa?"

"Yes, I would," she said in a surprisingly calm voice. "But I can get it myself."

Connor opened his mouth to continue the conversation, but Eve tugged on his hand and said, "I'd love to dance."

Connor shot one last glance at Devon, whose face revealed nothing of the turmoil he must be feeling, then smiled at Eve and said, "Come with me, Mrs. Flynn."

Eve mouthed "Thank you!" over her shoulder at Leah, then followed Connor onto the dance floor. He set his arm around her waist and took her hand as they danced to the "Tennessee Waltz."

"I can't believe we've been married for six weeks, and we're just now having our first dance," Eve said. "You're pretty good, by the way."

"Molly always said . . ." He paused, then looked into her eyes without apology and finished, "I was light on my feet."

"She mentioned that to me," Eve said, acknowledging that memories of Molly would arise from time to time and would always be a part of their lives. "I have to agree," she added with a laugh as he twirled her under his arm.

When the song ended, Eve realized that Leah and Aiden were standing together at the microphone in the center of the stage where the band was set up.

"Ladies and gents," Aiden said. "I want to introduce my brother, Connor Flynn, who started Safe Haven, which is the reason we're here today. Connor, come on up here."

Over the applause from the gathered guests, Eve said, "Did you know he was going to ask you to speak?"

Connor nodded. He took her hand and helped her onto the stage, which was a step up from the dance floor.

"My wife and I want to thank all of you for coming here and supporting the veterans who find refuge at Safe Haven," Connor said, sliding his arm around her waist and pulling her close. "Now have a good time. Drink, dance, and eat lots of barbecue!"

The guests clapped and shouted their support.

Leah took the microphone from Connor and said, "You might have heard that my sister and Aiden's brother recently married. They haven't been properly feted, so this barbecue has just become a wedding reception for Mr. and Mrs. Connor Flynn."

"Eve, welcome to the family," Aiden said, kissing her cheek.

"Connor, welcome to the family," Leah said, kissing his cheek.

Eve was struck dumb. Dozens of colorful balloons were suddenly released into the air. Frank showed up at the edge of the stage with Brooke and Sawyer in tow. Brooke was wearing a frilly party dress and Sawyer had on a tiny western suit. Taylor and Victoria pushed a cart onto the dance floor that held a three-tiered wedding cake.

"Did you have any idea they were going to do this?" Eve asked Connor.

He shook his head. He turned to Aiden and asked, "What's going on?"

"Exactly what Leah said: a wedding reception. You may have noticed that I managed to get Dad here. Leah made sure King showed up when it looked like he might skip the whole thing. Against all odds, we got both families together in the same place." Aiden shot him a crooked grin. "Of course, with the exception of Leah and myself, none of them are speaking to each other, but you can't have everything."

Connor laughed. Then he turned and gave Eve a hard hug. "What do you say, sweetheart? Shall we go cut the cake?"

Eve took his hand as they left the stage and joined her sisters on the dance floor, where the cake had ended up.

Taylor handed Eve a knife and said, "Go to it!" while Victoria grinned and said, "Let them eat cake!"

To Eve's surprise a photographer showed up and said, "I'm ready whenever you are." Eve felt tears of gratitude fill her eyes as she met Leah's gaze. Her simple wedding had been lovely, but it would be equally lovely to have pictures of today's events to savor in the days to come.

She waited for Connor to place his hand over hers as they cut the cake. Then she took a large chunk of the vanilla cake with lemon crème frosting—trust Leah to make it her favorite—and stuffed it into Connor's mouth. It ended up being smeared around his face, and Eve was happy to kiss the sweet stuff away, all of the fun captured by photographs they could enjoy forever after.

Eve watched their two fathers, hoping that they would come over to congratulate them, but neither man moved. As Connor's brothers approached, Eve's sisters left, as though by some prearranged agreement to avoid conflict between them, and Connor's brothers were suddenly slapping him on the back.

As Eve watched her sisters disappear back into the crowd, she felt a welling of gratitude for what Leah and Aiden had been able to accomplish. For this day, at least, both families had come together in a common cause, and despite the nasty scene between Matt and Devon—and Matt's astonishing revelation—had stayed to celebrate a marriage between Grayhawk and Flynn. Separately, it was true. And neither parent had offered congratulations and best wishes. But it was a first step. A baby step. And who knew what the future might bring?

"Happy?" Connor whispered in her ear.

"Deliriously."

He turned her in his arms and said, "I love you, Eve."

Two small bodies slammed into Eve's and Connor's legs.

"Mommy! Daddy! Can we have some cake?" Brooke asked.

Eve tipped Brooke's chin up. "You look beautiful, young lady."

Brooke beamed.

"Do I look beautiful?" Sawyer asked.

"You look as handsome as your father," Eve said.

"Can I have cake, too?" Sawyer asked.

Eve laughed. "Yes, to both of you."

As they raced off to rejoin Leah, who was cutting pieces of cake for everyone, Eve turned her gaze back to Connor and said, "In case you were in any doubt, I love you, too."

Connor smiled. "Glad to know we're both equally crazy."

"What do you mean?"

"Only two fools in love could believe that a marriage between a Grayhawk and a Flynn would ever work."

Eve laughed. She threaded her fingers with his. "As one crazy fool to another, I'm glad to be in love with you."

Connor kissed her hand, then pulled her into his arms. His voice was low and fierce as he said, "Now that I've got you, no matter how many flare-ups and fights there are between our two families, I'm never letting you go."

Eve slid her arms around his waist and laid her head against his beating heart. "Someday, somehow, peace will come. Until it does, I'm yours, today, tomorrow, and always."

Eve turned her face up and kissed her husband.

Letter to Readers

Dear Faithful Reader,

I hope you enjoyed *Sinful,* the first in my King's Brats series of Bitter Creek novels. Watch for *Shameless,* Pippa and Devon's story, coming soon, followed by *Surrender.*

If you would like to learn more about veterans working with wild mustangs, check out the Mustang Mentor Program, which works through the Mustang Heritage Foundation. Veterans choose a Bureau of Land Management wild horse, untouched by humans, and transform it into a gentle, adoptable animal in only one hundred days (www.mustang heritagefoundation.org).

To learn more about how to protect America's wild mustangs, check out Protect Mustangs.org (http://protectmustangs.org); Return to Freedom, American Wild Horse Preservation and Sanctuary (www .returntofreedom.org), and Wild Horse Education (http://wildhorseeducation.org). You might also enjoy the inspiring documentary movie *The American Mustang: The Movie.*

More than forty of my novels are now available as eBooks. Those of you waiting for *Blackthorne's Bride,* the final book in my Mail-Order Bride series, can stay updated by joining my website mailing list at www.joanjohnston.com, liking me at Facebook.com/joanjohnstonauthor, or tweeting me at www.twitter .com/joanjohnston.

Joan Johnston

If you thought Eve and Connor's story was *Sinful*,
Pippa and Devon's love is downright

Shameless

Don't miss the next installment in Joan Johnston's
King's Brats series

Coming soon from Dell

Keep reading for an exclusive sneak peek!

THE INSTANT EVE and Connor walked away to dance, Pippa jumped up from her seat at the picnic table and fled. Why did her father treat her as though she were still a child? She felt furious. And frustrated. And frightened. She was unwed and pregnant with a child whose father she loathed as much as she'd once loved him. But she wanted this baby with all her being, and she was determined to raise it on her own, no matter how many obstacles her father, however kindhearted his intentions, put in her way.

A strong hand caught her arm and dragged her to a stop. "Pippa. Wait!"

She whirled and snarled at Devon, "I'm not going back to live with my father. Not today. Not ever. If I can't stay with you, then I'll—"

"I was going to ask if you're ready to go home. With me."

Pippa huffed out a breath. "Yes. I am." She met Devon's gaze and realized she'd been so focused on her own troubles that she'd forgotten about his. "Are you all right?"

His voice was low and hoarse as he asked, "Where did your father get the idea that I'm not Angus's son?"

"I have no idea. I wouldn't be surprised if he made it up as an excuse to get me to come back home."

"I noticed my father didn't deny it."

"He shouldn't have to," Pippa said. "Why would you believe such a thing?"

Devon met her gaze and said, "Because I'm not like the rest of them."

"What?"

"I don't look the same. I don't want the same things. And Angus doesn't treat me the same way." He shrugged and said simply, "I've never felt like I belong."

"Maybe it's because you're the youngest."

"Maybe it's because I had a different father. And because I killed my mother when I was born."

Pippa didn't know what to say or how to comfort him. She merely took Devon's hand in hers and said, "Let's go home. Beowulf will be hungry."

Devon's gray wolf, which he'd raised from a pup, was always hungry. He was huge and he wasn't fully grown yet.

Devon sighed. "I suppose I'm not likely to get any answers from Angus today. I'm not sure I want to know the truth."

As they walked back to Devon's pickup, Pippa tried to imagine what he must be feeling. How awful to discover that your mother had cheated on your father—if, in fact, that was what had happened. If Devon had a different father, what had happened to him? If he was out there somewhere, did he know about Devon?

Pippa realized that her life at Devon's remote mountain ranch had just gotten infinitely more complicated, because the "relative" she'd been staying with might no longer be related to her. She eyed Devon askance. He might not have the same black hair, blue eyes, and over-six-foot height as his brothers, but to her, his lithe build, gray-green eyes, and dark brown hair were even more attractive. She was tall, but he stood tall enough to make her feel protected within his embrace, which he'd offered strictly as solace the day she'd come to him seeking a place to stay.

Pippa hadn't felt shy running around in a robe with Devon in his pajama bottoms because they were second cousins. She hoped this revelation wouldn't interfere with the ease they'd found together. Even if they weren't related, there was no chance of anything romantic happening between them. She wasn't interested in getting involved with anyone after what she'd just been through.

Not to mention the fact that she was pregnant. She hadn't told Devon about the baby because she only planned to stay with him until she could figure out what to do with the rest of her life.

As Devon helped her into the cab of his pickup, a courtesy he never failed to offer, Pippa realized that she admired his kindness and affinity to animals even more than his looks. Beowulf wasn't the only wild animal he'd rescued, but she'd learned that he usually nursed them back to health and then released them into the wild again. However, Beowulf would have been in danger because he no longer feared humans, so Devon had kept him.

"I hope you're going to hang around for a little while," Devon said. "Despite what your dad said about me."

"I don't have anywhere I have to be. If you're willing for me to stay, I'm willing to stay."

"Good," Devon said. "I've been living alone a long time. It's nice to have company."

Pippa wondered what Devon would think when he found out who it was he'd really welcomed into his home. That she'd run away with a married man and was pregnant with his child. That the small town in Australia where she'd lived had found her behavior so shameful that her father had agreed to return to a place he'd sworn he would never visit again in his lifetime. And that she'd come with him because she'd wanted to escape the label of adulteress that would have branded her forever after.

But she didn't have to tell him today. He had enough to deal with today, and maybe for a while yet. Her pregnancy didn't show. So long as she could hide it, she would.

And when you can't? What is Devon going to think when he realizes you've been lying to him all along?

Maybe she'd be gone from his ranch before that happened.

And go where? With what money? Your only skill is whispering wild horses. Can you really do that when you're the size of a hippo? You have to tell him.

Pippa sighed.

"Are you all right?"

"I wish . . ." She let the words hang in the air. She wished she'd done a lot of things differently.

"Yeah," Devon said. "So do I."

Pippa smiled and reached out to brush his forearm in a gesture of friendship. "Thanks, Devon."

"For what?"

"For understanding."

He shrugged. "I've been where you are, Pippa. Believe it or not, I had to run away from home, too."

"Really?"

He smiled. "Angus had a fit when he found out I'd bought this ranch in the mountains. Told me I was crazy to live so isolated from other people. Told me I was just like—" He paused, and looked at her with a shocked expression. "Angus cut himself off. He never said who I was just like." Devon's mouth flattened. "It must be him I'm like. My biological father."

"Maybe you should try to find him."

"What point would that serve? He's nothing to me."

"Except it seems you're a great deal like him."

"How did we get on this subject?" Devon said irritably.

"We were wishing things could be different."

The silence between them grew oppressive. Finally, Pippa could stand it no longer. "Is it true that Angus has figured out a way to ruin King?"

Devon laughed. "You really know how to change the subject."

Pippa grinned. "I thought that was what you wanted."

"The answer to your question is yes. It's not a sure thing yet, but your dad might have come all this way for nothing. He might end up losing Kingdom Come to Angus."

Pippa's grin disappeared. "You're kidding, right?"

Devon shook his head. "Angus has been pretty closemouthed about when the ax will fall, but he's been gloating that the day is coming when he'll finally have his revenge for my aunt's death."

"Is there anything King can do, or my father, to stop him?"

Devon shrugged. "Who knows? By the time King figures out what Angus has been plotting, it may be too late."

"What about my dad? He left everything behind to come here. What's he supposed to do?"

"I don't have an answer for that."

Pippa turned to face Devon. "Is there any way we can find out what Angus intends?"

"What would you do with the information?"

"Tell my father, of course."

"You've run away from your dad, but you still want to help him?"

"He's my father. I love him." *And he has good reasons for wanting to protect me.*

Devon shoved a hand through his hair. "I don't know, Pippa. I don't agree with what Angus is doing. But he's my father and—" His lips pressed flat and a muscle worked in his jaw as he cut himself off.

Because Angus might not be his father, Pippa realized. And he'd apparently treated Devon differently than his other sons.

"All right," Devon said. "Let's do it. I've never supported Angus's desire for revenge. I'll see what I can find out."